MORE THAN
YOU KNOW

Also By Melissa Malouf

It Had to Be You: The Joan and Ernest Story

No Guarantees

MORE THAN YOU KNOW

MELISSA MALOUF

DALKEY ARCHIVE PRESS
Champaign / London / Dublin

First edition, 2014

Library of Congress Cataloging-in-Publication Data
Malouf, Melissa.
More Than You Know / Melissa Malouf. -- First edition.
pages cm
ISBN 978-1-62897-044-9 (pbk. : acid-free paper)
1. Self-realization in women--Fiction. I. Title.
PS3563.A4332M67 2014
813'.54--dc23
2014001100

This publication was partially supported by the Illinois Arts Council, a state agency, and the University of Illinois (Urbana-Champaign).

www.dalkeyarchive.com

Cover: design and composition by Mikhail Iliatov
Printed on permanent/durable and acid-free paper

For my beloved co-pilot

ONE

Almost a year ago now: that first day out on the road in the early morning, mid-July. Out of that house I'd been holed up in for too long, out toward the rest of my life, more or less out of my mind.

I was finally going to Vermont, to the Jensens, to Hannah and her husband. Going going gone. I had no idea what else to do with myself but ask them face-to-aging-face what they did thirty years ago to make my three friends die. To ask them why my own entanglement didn't kill me too.

After all, I was out to pasture. Early retirement. No more sullenly mohawked students to preoccupy me, no more sometimes-enviable tattoos, no more heartbreaking thank-you notes for the C+. My years would no longer begin in September. I had no more excuses, no commitments. No family. It was just me and them: the smiling Hannah Jensen and her husband. And them: the three dead young men with whom I went to graduate school—Eric Langland, Richard Stone, and Darrell Farnsworth. "Untimely deaths" is a phrase one could use to make a tidy story of it. If one had never met the Jensens.

So there I was—*me*, Alice Clark of all people!—driving across the country, headed for Vermont, on my way from Riverside to my first stop: Las Vegas. A place so off my beaten track, so unlikely a spot for yours truly to visit under any circumstances, that it seemed all too appropriate for my mad undertaking.

As it turned out, my night in Las Vegas didn't stay in Las Vegas—it eventually ended up here with me in Vermont, in the shape of Barbara Dulaney (she wouldn't mind that word, *shape*). I'll get to that.

There might have been no night in Las Vegas. Outside of Barstow, I ran out of gas. Outside of Barstow: which is to say, on that stretch of highway that takes you into the Mojave Desert. Not a good place to be reminded that you're alone, and that driving over the speed limit with a rock 'n roll station blaring from the radio doesn't make you any younger, and that the maps and guidebooks, the bottled water and the chilled green apples there in the front seat do not mean that you are adequately prepared to drive long distances, do not mean that you can relax now and let your mind do what it most likes to do—remember, imagine, fret, remember, fret some more, accuse, excuse, accuse some more.

The late morning sun got hotter as I sat there conducting a pointless, prideful struggle—because I didn't want to walk back, westward toward where I'd started from. But up ahead, only miles of desert, was out of the question. So. Damn.

What an old-lady image of ineptness and defeat.

We'll see about that, I told myself as I locked the car, took to the shoulder of the highway, and became, I thought, statuesque. So that if anyone passed by, what they'd see would be a "distinguished" woman in a khaki cotton dress, red canvas shoes, wearing dark, blind-man's sunglasses, carrying an over-stuffed handbag, and holding her head up as if she'd planned this walk all along.

A trucker honked as he sped past me, as the false wind he created blew up a real dust. And I wondered: does such honking always mean you're "lookin' good"? Or can it just as well be derisive?

I was pondering this matter, bucking myself up, when a car stopped, a big old fin-tipped gas-eater of some American kind, and reversed until it caught up with me. The engine sputtered off, a car door opened. I kept walking.

"Hey, lady!" A man's voice yelled at me. "Do you need a lift?"

I turned. The man draped one arm over the open door of his car, the other rested on the roof. Tap, tap, tap went his fingers on that roof.

"No thanks."

"You run out of gas?" He was shouting, as though the distance between us were the size of a canyon instead of several yards. Perhaps he assumed, given my age, that I was hard of hearing.

I turned again, ready to offer a scolding. But he looked to be the sort of man on whom a scolding fries to a crisp—then he'd pop the tasty tidbit into his remorseless mouth and grin.

He was wearing a saggy pair of gray pants—they might once have been part of a business suit—and a light pink golfer's t-shirt whose turned-up collar and unbuttoned buttons were supposed to look sharp but were stubbornly failing. A darkly tanned man of desert places, with thin black hair that needed a washing—he seemed to be neither young nor old. I couldn't see his eyes (he, too, was wearing sunglasses) but I supposed they were not unlike his spooky lips, which resembled thick rubber bands that have lost their elasticity.

"Yes," I told him. "But you go on. I'm fine. I know the way back. And it's only a mile or so."

He stepped away from his car, shut the door. Here's what I was thinking: I'm bigger than you are, mister. You don't want me to be knocking you in the head with this purse, believe me. Besides, this road isn't deserted, somebody drives by now and then. They'll wonder whether you're bothering me. So don't. Just watch your step, fella.

In other words, I was afraid of him.

"I'd getcha there and back in ten, fifteen minutes. By foot, it could take you an hour just to get there." He walked up to me then, just as another car went by without any sign of slowing down to find out if I were all right. I guess there are times when a gal can be *too* statuesque.

"The walk will do me good." I smiled. "Thanks anyway. Bye now." Good manners: what you resort to when you wish you had a handy can of mace in your purse, or a bodyguard at your side.

"It ain't right, ma'am."

"I'll be just fine. Really."

"The whole world ain't right. I mean, isn't right."

A crazy, I thought. One who corrects his own grammar: does that make him more crazy than most?

I fumbled out an "oh don't worry," managed an embarrassed—for both of us—little wave, and then did an about-face. But that didn't stop him. He spoke, loudly, to my walking-away back:

"It isn't right that everything's so wrong these days that a lady in distress can't accept the aid and assistance of a goodly and well-meaning citizen of these United States—you hear me, ma'am?"

"I'm not in distress." I turned to say this, but we were not having a conversation.

"These days the good Samaritan could turn out to be a so-called man dressed up as a woman, which used to be a phenom I scorned just as much as I did any other, but I have been forced to conclude that the man who dresses in a woman's clothes aims to disassociate himself from the same fact of the male condition that I have witnessed: and that is, the chivalrous man, the man of honor, has been outmoded, outvoted, and un-damn-done by men rich and poor alike, all colors and creeds of 'em, all ages, who inflict mistreatment upon each other and most especially upon the women they were once upon a time supposed to protect and provide for with all manner of courtesy and ceremony. And you can tell me 'til the cows come home that a woman can protect herself and provide for herself, but that doesn't change the fundamental truth that it would be better for everybody if the mistreating men hadn't turned the pitiful, old-fashioned rest of us into darksome strangers that no good woman, no woman with any sense worth talking about, would trust any further than she could throw an anvil into a swamp. You hear me?"

I heard all of it. Then I heard his car door slam, the motor roar up. I was thinking: he's crazy, all right. A Miniver Cheevy gone over the edge.

Soon it was clear that he hadn't kept going into the desert, that he'd made a U-turn, and I told myself that he wasn't, no he wasn't, he couldn't be crazy enough to run me down.

I was right. He wasn't. He raced by me, flooring it, spewing fumes as he picked up speed. I walked back to my car. I needed to sit down, I needed some of that bottled water. Was I a wreck? No question. But it wasn't only that encounter: it was that the whole thing, the whole coast-to-coast pursuit, felt like a mistake, an utter miscalculation of my abilities. I may as well have donned a spacesuit that morning, instead of a comfortable dress, and declared myself an astronaut.

I was still in the car, working myself up for the task at hand—which had become not simply walking back to one of the service stations at the edge of Barstow, but fighting off the you'll-never-make-it boogeyman—when the same big gas-eater pulled up behind me. I made sure, with my elbow, that the door was locked.

In the rearview mirror, I saw the man lug a five-gallon gas can from the back seat of his car. He saw me watching, signaled for me to pull the lever, to open the lid of the gas tank. He was all business, no loosely grinning lips. I got a ten-dollar bill out of my purse, rolled down the window half-way, and waited.

Eventually, I heard the gas tank lid snap shut. Then he was there, at the window. "It ain't and it is not right," he said.

"But you are."

"Not very. And not often," he told me. "Put your money away, ma'am."

"I can't let you—"

"Yes you can. This one's on me."

"I can't tell you how much I appreciate—"

"No, you can't." He had his hands on his hips, and he was moving, rocking ever so slightly, ball-to-heel, ball-to-heel, back and forth.

"Then I guess I'll be on my way. Are you sure?" I still had the ten-dollar bill in my hand.

"I'm sure."

"You are a genuine Galahad, sir."

"Keep that tank full. And get yourself a car phone."

"Many thanks."

"Yeah."

I pulled out onto the highway and looked back. My knight in shining armor was standing next to the empty gas can in the shoulder of the road, with his legs spread apart like a gunslinger. His right arm was raised above his head—and there was his fist, and his stout middle finger pointing skyward, and then the redundant shout: "Fuck you, lady! You hear?"

If I may second, or third, the motion: Fuck you, Alice.

For putting yourself on hold for decades. Not the body parts, of course, the hereditary and inevitable arthritis, the starting to go gray, the wrinkles in the forehead, the things that tell you years in fact happen. But for the routines and the reticence that kept you in place and out of the picture—the moving picture, the kind that means plot and change and surprise. For the far too few times you have ever said "fuck" anything. For doing nothing more important than lasting, far easier to do because you've been for so long too much on your own, nobody watching over you, listening, noting your nightmares. You came rather quickly—wasn't it decades ago?—to believe it when you say "I'm fine."

The changes that have happened to me in the last year have come in all sizes. I've found ways—and they have no doubt found me—to keep myself too busy to sit down with the changes, to look them in the eye and listen to their litany of potential hazards, let them talk me into getting under the covers for days at a time, tell me that I will of course fail to be someone other than the Alice I have always been.

If you turned out in your adulthood, as I did, to be a baker of brownies, a fussy decorator of the Christmas tree, someone who always has on hand fresh batteries for the flashlight and Band-Aids in all sizes, decks of cards, a big box of crayons, and two extra leaves for the dining room table, then living alone is a curious business.

You cannot avoid seeing that you are prepared for an onslaught of relatives or friends: on the lookout, so to speak. Garnished for grandmahood, poised for a partner. The life you are not leading sits on your shelves and in your cupboards, an unwound clock.

Perhaps you pretend to be not only "fine, thank you" but relieved: you remind yourself that your nights, your music, your Band-Aids are, as they say, your own. You are likely to be the envy of your harried, husbanded co-workers. You can eat, or not, when you please. You can take your sherry in a paper cup or, if your mood requires, your best piece of crystal. You can talk out loud to whatever needs a talking to: you can ridicule your appliances, plead with the roof to last another year, curse your hair. You can wear the same old clothes all weekend, sleep in them, if you like.

There are times, now and then, when the relief seems not in the least feigned. When you regard yourself as not so different, after all, from those solitary grown-ups who quite deliberately choose to live in uncluttered apartments. Take their meals at restaurants. Go to the beach at Christmastime and keep well out of range of anything reminiscent of chestnuts roasting on an open fire.

There are those other times, however, when you note the dust on your serving dishes and champagne flutes. The party-time row of ever-unlit candles on the sideboard. The tablecloths in their original wrappings.

What I was telling myself a year ago was that it would be a good thing to get rid of most of this stuff, to let Hannah and her husband reel me in at last, land me on their doorstep in Vermont out of breath and plump with my misgivings, my keepsakes, my secrets and theirs. It was time to go after the bad guys. Me, I thought, included.

Childless women in my profession suspect all along, I'll bet, that when the time comes, they won't be entitled to empty nest syndrome. They know that their years of giving attention, of trying to give comfort and hope as well as instruction, at best supplement nests already built, however well or badly. We know this all along. I told myself that what we build, instead of nests, are dreamboats, schooners of possibility. Bon voyage! we call out as our students leave the place of our ardent professional regard, without a backward glance.

Hannah Jensen with children: that I could picture, but it was not a welcome sight. There was music, there was Hannah playing a flute or a clarinet, something like that. Whatever it was, she was playing it like a pro, the music was splendid, lyrical. Each note was an enticing confection, a sticky come-on. The happy mouths of the freckle-faced children were rainbow-colored with popsicle juice. They jostled and poked one another as they skipped behind their ponytailed, pied-piper mother. Her husband waved as they passed, smiling his peculiar, flirtatious, and impatient smile.

I wish that it were impossible for me to see myself as one of those children: giggly and gooey, skipping behind her, fascinated and enamored, not in the least concerned about looking where I was going. But there I am all right, even now, among those at the head of the pack. Eric is there too, and Richard, and Darrell, skipping toward the ledge.

Here's an old black and white photograph of the four of us that tells me something different each time I look at it, which is not often.

Sometimes the photograph says almost nothing. It takes on the tight-lipped airs of a forced acquaintance. Or it presents itself as a mere document, a record. More than thirty years old, black and white, eight by ten, just the facts, ma'am. That's how it is sometimes. There is nothing quiet right now about this picture.

There we are: full of our particular versions of overworked good fellowship. In need of a good night's sleep, in a good bed, with somebody close by who wants nothing more than to do some tucking in, serve a cup of tea or a milky nightcap, say a prayer. The four of us were graduate students then, in varying stages of finishing our doctorates in English and American literature: Eric Langland, Richard Stone, Darrell Farnsworth, Alice Clark. We wanted to be professors of literature when we grew up.

The young people in this photograph have in common not only the bags under their eyes, but also the rumpled appearance of the distinctly unwealthy. Two of them wear glasses held together with tape or paperclips, and, except for Darrell, each is in need of a haircut. Darrell is taller than he looks, about five eight. His reddish brown hair is short, his body round and wide—a bourbon drinker's body—

as is his smile. He keeps a case filled with pens and pencils in his shirt pocket, like a math teacher. His other pockets are full of scraps of paper containing the titles of books he means to read before he begins his ever-delayed dissertation on Coleridge. At thirty-five, he is the oldest. You wouldn't be surprised, on the basis of this photograph, to learn that Darrell eventually gave up on the dissertation, married his childhood sweetheart, had at least four children, voted Republican, and became the most sought-after teacher in one of the local high schools—though none of this happened.

Richard's pockets are empty (he is noted for asking, "Do you have any change?"), but his head is full of literary quotations, which you wouldn't know unless you took a class with him. In ordinary conversation, he is careful to remain a "man of the people." Richard is working on becoming a sage, and to that end his bushy brown hair is wild, his body is gaunt, and his forearms are tattooed with symbols whose meaning he refuses to reveal. In the photograph his arms are around the shoulders of Darrell and Eric, and you can see that he loves them. And you could imagine that Richard would turn out to be an adoring husband, more than once, maybe more than twice, and an unruly professor—a dabbler in Buddhism and dissident politics whose work on Walt Whitman would finally earn him tenure at someplace like UC Santa Cruz.

Eric is looking at the camera, but it is clear that he would rather not be, that this is against his will, that the weight of Richard's friendly hand on his shoulder is welcome only insofar as it is momentary. Eric's glasses are thick and black, his long-sleeved shirt is black, his lanky hair is black. But his dark eyes let you know that he is not cultivating an appearance, not doing a Hamlet. No, he would just as soon disappear. He doesn't know what he is wearing. What he knows is that his studies have been interrupted, that he'd be better off, perhaps, in a monastery. He looks as though, if left alone, he would provide us with a handful of well-wrought, meticulously-researched works of scholarship that will keep on being read. But can we leave him alone? Apparently not.

The young woman in the photograph is standing next to Eric, but she is not part of the hug. Her hands are tucked into the pockets of her loose jeans. She is as tall as Eric, almost as tall as the six-foot Richard. Her light brown hair is fixed in a bun; her glasses dangle from her neck on a hand-me-down chain. She looks like the assistant headmistress of a snooty girls' school. The photograph does not suggest a future for her that is different from the one that happened. Who would want to spend a lifetime with that person?

These days my hands keep wanting to curl into fists, my toes are knotted and inflamed. They look like grubs. They look like the ugly sound of that word, "grubs." I sometimes fear that I will at last give birth and that my offspring will be a hump between my sorry shoulders. An unsuckling and silent papoose.

I wish like hell that I'd been part of that hug.

The four of us had been officemates for about three years when Hannah came onto the scene. Act Five, I'm tempted to say. Enter Hannah Jensen. Before long, curtain closes on a stage strewn with bodies.

But no—it wasn't that simple. For one thing, it was a gleeful Hannah who took our photograph that day. We posed for her, we might even have stood on our heads if she'd asked. For another, all of our names appear in Mr. Jensen's diary. He was in on it from the start, helping Hannah weave her seductive web. Even now, having seen them after all this time, having been given more than glimpses into how they operate, I remind myself that the Jensens' sex life is none of my business.

Did Hannah Jensen pick me, or did I pick her? This is another part of the story I'm still working on.

I met Hannah in 1965 at the University of California campus back in Riverside, where she had transferred in as a junior (at twenty-five, an unusual undergraduate, but not unheard of). I was a graduate teaching assistant by that time, and she was new in town. She asked me for directions to the library. I spoke them. I pointed. Then I accompanied her across campus, right to the door, walked her inside, introduced her to my favorite reference librarian.

Me: instant guide, instant mentor, as if I had nothing better to do. No friends, no officemates, no classes to prepare, no research to get on with. There is this: I was recently divorced and de-stepmothered. No doubt I needed someone to take care of.

That's not the whole of it. Look at her, Alice. Remember.

She was blond and lightly freckled, shapely in an athletic way, boyishly hour-glassed. She wore her thick hair in two puffy ponytails that bounced against her neck. She was not a kid but she seemed like one. And she was little, not much more than five feet tall (this keeps coming back to me, as if I wanted it, her littleness, to be the wand with which she performed her spells). She wore expensive, tasteful sweaters and slacks. No blue jeans, nothing untucked that ought to be tucked.

As soon as she spoke, you knew that she was not a native. You found out that she was from Austria. "Salzburg," she told you, and she said it the way it's supposed to be said. Her accent was endearing, quaint. You wished you had such an accent, such hair, such colorful clothes. You immediately befriended her because she was new to this country and because she was adorable.

Now look at yourself, Alice. No joy there. Hannah was all of the you that you weren't. She had come to America with her American husband, Mr. Jensen, who worked for IBM. She said the name of the company as if she were telling a dirty joke, a silly pre-adolescent joke that was charming coming from the cutie-pie lips of that small grown-up foreign woman.

I was also a grown-up woman, and did not feel the least bit threatened by those lips, by her silly joke. I was already thinking of Hannah as a younger sister, guileless and lovable. No stealer of boyfriends, if I'd had one. Certainly not a liar. Definitely not a killer.

For the year that Hannah was in my vicinity, I was devoted to her. She frightened me sometimes, especially toward the end. But I took that, and take it, as part of her appeal. She was "little" but never small.

Too fearless to be genuinely cute, but never un-cute. Too married to be the ingénue her ponytails announced her as, but always, to some extent, the "innocent abroad." Playful and savvy. Cunning? I didn't mind. I didn't put my mind to that possibility until after Eric was dead. And then I banished, tried to banish the thought.

"I am becoming American, thanks to Mr. Jensen!" She clapped. I'm not sure why I didn't.

"You will help me, Alice."

At the time, when we met, when we became friends, I thought of myself as "taking her up." And paid little if any attention to the ways she was doing the same with me.

I was asked at my retirement party to say something impromptu about my more than thirty years as a professor at the city college in Riverside, where only the football games might be something to write home about. And maybe the air-conditioned classrooms we finally got in the 1980s.

How long ago that already seems.

I ended up telling a forgettable joke about a blackboard that would not be erased, and everyone sort of laughed. Not at the joke, seems to me, but at their very own funny old broad: their tennis-shoed recluse with the foggy spectacles and the long hair that she still wore in a fifties French roll. Treasured her electric pencil sharpener, had no computer, no VCR, no answering machine, no cable TV. My almost new-millennium colleagues young and old always presumed that Alice Clark was a frump, and I always let them.

They were not, after all, entirely wrong.

Opera glasses, of all things, mother-of-pearl with shiny brass fittings: that's what they gave me. I have never been to the opera, but I do use them for bird-watching now and then.

I did not tell my smug colleagues that my job has for the most part served me well as a lengthy detour, a long postponement, which would have been longer still had my whining bones not said, loud and clear, No more. You're through, lady. Kaput.

Though I lived nearly all my life underneath the San Bernardino mountains—or so it seemed on certain clear days—I had been to Palm Springs only once, with Hannah. And with my mother, long ago, I took the boat to Catalina. (I threw up on the way there, she threw up on the way back.) I'd been up to the local mountain-lake resorts, Arrowhead, Big Bear, many times. I used to go to the beach in the off-season, but later, with the traffic, it took hours to get there. I hadn't been farther north than Santa Barbara, hadn't crossed any borders since I was five—and that was in a plane, New York to California. As unbudging as Riverside's old navel orange tree, there sat Alice Clark, a monument to untested staying power. What a sight.

The Jensens seem to have known all along that I would do this, seek them out eventually, on my own, not wait for a coincidental "crossing of paths" but place myself all-too-flatfootedly in theirs. They didn't have to invite me, as they invited Eric.

The day after that retirement party, I started packing and sorting, even discarding a thing or two, one drawer at a time. (What a stasher and hoarder I became! Worse than my mother—I'd hoarded her hoard.) I took my time, but it was not that I was reluctant. It was that it dawned on me, no light in that dawning, that going to them now, after all these years, had to signal an ending, a leaving, a kind of death. I couldn't see myself making a weekend visit to them and then flying home, where there would be no stack of papers to grade, no requests for recommendations to fulfill, no meetings to attend, no lover on the phone (that ended too many years ago). They were it, the Jensens, never far from my thoughts though I hadn't seen them in decades.

Making up for cowardice: is that possible?

In any case, I told myself that I needn't rush, there was no deadline to speak of. I could take it slow, give myself a last look at everything. Besides, these awful hands of mine could manage just so much without a long pause, a plunge into hot water, a creamy massage. They've become ugly prima donnas, and me, I'm their doting servant.

The statistics say that at not much over sixty I should be too young for all this gnarling. Be that as it may. I did a lot of pausing those last few days in Southern California. Pausing, remembering, letting bits and pieces look me straight in the eye and speak my need to go at last to Hannah and her husband, to ask them why my friends so incongruously died, to tell me what I didn't do to save them, to tell me why, why *me*? Why am I still alive?

TWO

Here on the kitchen table in what I want to think of as my "safe house" in Vermont, though this safety has too much to do with my dark angels being down the road a piece, is the board game called *Clue.* One of several such relics from my brief period as a step-mother—my only period as any kind of mother, until now, thanks to Bunny and her father.

It was Hannah Jensen who pointed out to me that there is no card in this game that represents the victim.

"We have only suspects, Alice. Where are the victims?" she asked me, her face all a-dimple. Smart as they come. That moment still wows me. Those intelligent eyes. Blinking blue lights.

Now Hannah is nearly as old as I am. And she has grown plump—heavy-chested and big-bottomed. Her teeth, like many of mine, have been provided by a good dentist. She was, in her mid-twenties, when I knew her, an undaunted and always-unchubby eater of chocolates and creams and caramels. Valentine sweets, she called them, year-round, no matter what sort of box they came in, no matter who gave them. To Hannah Jensen, if there were chocolates in her vicinity, there was an aura of courtship, a love poem in the making. She would offer to share her sweets as if she were divulging amorous secrets. And my officemates and I were all ears.

Whatever the condition of her teeth, or her bottom, there is still that tip-toed bounciness: her ever-discombobulating way of announcing her immigrant's "Americanness." That never-refused flag-waving sparkle in her eye. The girl-wonder smile, which tells you that she is capable of everything—and still, to this day, makes you imagine what that's like, makes you wish you were that way too, at least on an experimental basis. I don't believe she spends any time hunched over a heap of regrets, her face creased with impossible needs. Like the need to revise the story of her life, to know then what she knows now. I can't picture her estranged from her aging body, or from any too dangerous world, such as ours has become—victims all over the place.

I can't picture it, even now. But I know this middle-aged Hannah is no more real than the college-aged one. An advertisement for herself.

I had known her for only a week or two when she called one evening and told me to put on a scarf, she was coming to pick me up and take me to Palm Springs for an ice cream sundae, to thank me for being her new friend. I thought: This is nuts. Driving over an hour into the desert for a sundae? This is all out of proportion, foolhardy, and marvelous. Yes, I told her, why not?

She drove a British sports car, and she drove it as anyone would, fast and with the top down. We did some shouting at each other—"Perfect night for this!" "Terrific car!" and so forth—since real talking was out of the question. And I don't recall any conversation of note as we wolfed down our ice cream sundaes at the Baskin-Robbins in Palm Springs (which looked no different from the one in Riverside). We ate quickly, like bandits, because, just after we placed our order, Hannah told me that she had to be back in an hour, had to be there before Mr. Jensen arrived home from a late night at the office.

She dropped me off at my house about fifty minutes later. I must have been more frightened than I knew—my legs were like overcooked lo-mein as I stepped out of that rich-girl's car and waved a limp good-bye. But what I remember most about the harrowing drive back that night was the urgent maternal voice in my head reminding me, too late, not to take candy from strangers.

It was hugged-in-spite-of-himself Eric who for years staked out the biggest claim on my dream-life. Monastic Eric—or so I thought.

There was more than one dream, but there was almost always, to start with, a narrow path, a warm and watery peacefulness. I am moving into it, following it, following Eric. He is there, in front of me, and he knows that I am with him. Close but not too close. We are comfortable that way, with a short distance between us. The autumn leaves are doing their seasonal finale, the big colorful kick-dance before they fall away and make room for next year's line-up. Always, in the dream, I keep going, keep believing that, this time, before long, he will turn and we will look at each other. He will take a step or two in my direction. I will take a step or two in his. Our friendship will turn into a love story. So I keep going, following him and hoping, but once again he is gone. Again and again he is over a cliff. Or into a hole. Or caught in a trap that swallows him up and swings him into the highest branches of the trees, where he wafts like a broken blackbird. I had been following close but not close enough. There is always, in the dream, that moment when I might have saved him.

I have fruitcake tins filled with rubber bands and masking tape, paper clips and staples, and four different kinds of glue. I have a lovely Tanzanian basket full of thread and needles. Safety pins in a pickle jar. I have a yardstick, a ruler, and two tape measures, one cloth, one steel. In a sturdy pink shoebox I keep spools of string, lightweight and heavy duty, a plastic tray that contains nails and screws in all sizes, a small jar of tacks. I have an old hammer and a nearly new set of screwdrivers, an electric drill, two dull but adequate saws, a caulking gun. There are extension cords in various sizes, and washers for the sinks and hoses. I had these things then and I have them now. Many books I left behind, but not my toolbox.

Here is a storybook tale. One about a world where these things could have helped me to mend the gaps that kept me close to Eric, but not close enough. It's a busy little world, abuzz with patchings-up and re-assemblings and timely rescues. With tinkerings that don't manage to stop either the clock or the sickle but do their noisy best to stave them off. Everyone in that world is equipped with a tool-belt, with pincushions and extra light bulbs and life jackets and aloe vera. They almost never sleep, but they don't seem to mind. There isn't, in that busy place, a bit of time for dreaming.

I want to end up in such a place, to live out my days there, mending, not dreaming.

Let's say you are not overgrown in the first place. Say you are petite, as Hannah Jensen was, proportioned to fit gracefully into a life that will some time or other require hunkering down. Is it easier to grow up? Is it easier to sidestep, without an awkward stumble, the inevitable accumulation of mistakes and losses? Is it easier, if you are a featherweight, to negotiate the narrow spaces that keep you close to and apart from those you love? Probably not. But I have not forgotten what it was like in high school, when the civil defense alarm went off and we were supposed to get under our desks, prepare ourselves for a nuclear attack. I was already my full height, five-foot-nine. Which is to say, I had to choose which part or parts of me would go unprotected as I tried to scrunch myself beneath that little wooden desk.

Maybe that kind of choosing is what we mean by growing up. A sorry plan on somebody's part.

When I was doing that sorting and packing, that relinquishing, I came across Mr. Jensen's diary.

I knew it was there somewhere. But it was a long time ago when I put it away. I thought that if it were out of sight I could better ignore the blanks it kept on asking me to fill in, what I couldn't help thinking of as "the plot." But I was wrong: its banishment from the desk, the bedside table, the kitchen counters, spoke for a long time just the way the banished have always spoken—pleading and relentless and homesick.

I found the diary buried in a box of old clothes—a sheer hot-pink caftan, summer scarves and ribbons, youthful sandals, a young woman's things. I must have thought that no one else would ever look for it there, among frivolities this big body rarely put to good use.

The diary, dare I say, is stolen property.

From the first moment I looked at its pages, there was no question of my returning it any time soon. It wanted to be studied, deciphered.

So I told myself. Once I'd presented Mr. Jensen with the flat-out lie that I knew nothing about it, I couldn't give it back—so I told myself.

Mr. Jensen, I've since found out, knew all along—not only who "borrowed" it, but also who kept it.

I shouldn't call it a diary at all, though the word is embossed on the red cover. There is no discursive writing inside, no revelations or reflections, no detailed memories, no stories per se. There are only our names—Alice, Eric, Darrell, Richard, Hannah—in various couplings and combinations.

Darrell Farnsworth was the one who found it, as he was browsing through the Jensens' cookbooks. He was proud, *proud*, he said, in his usual some-words-bear-repeating way, to hand it over to me for safe-keeping, as if it were an unearthed treasure. "Between *The Joy of Cooking* and the *I Hate to Cook* book. No kidding," he said. "I kid you not."

But he looked more ashamed than proud. Bloated and ashamed. Not ashamed about the theft—we were all, at the time, after what Hannah had been through, looking out for her, looking for clues. Darrell was ashamed about his having been to their house again, accepting another invitation to drop by for a drink. He hoped that I would understand why he had ignored my warning. "It's as though I never, *ever* heard of the word 'resist,'" he told me. He didn't go on to explain, and he didn't have to. I knew what he was getting at. Hannah Jensen was irresistible.

I had never heard Hannah refer to her husband as anyone but "my husband," or sometimes, with a quick trill of a laugh, as "Mr. Jensen." Nothing else. His name also appears in these meticulously calligraphied pages. Bradley. Brad.

Mr. Jensen was then and is now narrow, as bony as a maple in February. Cheekbones, nose, mouth, fingers—all elegant in an edgy sort of way. As if they were secretly itching to be thick and vulgar.

He used a cigarette holder, a short one, some shiny wood, mahogany maybe. Not ostentatious, but you would take note of it. You would have to remind yourself that he was not a foreigner.

Legs crossed, one dangling and beautifully-shod foot would point upward and stay that way, unmoving, like an origami wing. A piece of work, that Mr. Jensen.

There was a time when the sound of his whispering voice seemed entwined forever within the curls around my ear. I would not have felt much pity had some good witch cast a miserable old-age spell upon him, given him bones full of air, as light as bubbles, as fragile as crystal, so that the merest breeze would sting. I have a bit more pity now, but only a bit.

There was never a time when I wished such a fate upon Hannah. Not even now—which surprises me.

The first page of the diary is blank. The next one has my name on it: a calligraphied ALICE, pure black, right in the middle of the page, two lines below another name, HANNAH. Her first H and my A are the largest, most medievally ornamented letters—so that when you turn to the page, your eye is first drawn to a vertical, virtually audible *HA*!

Darrell Farnsworth was the only one of us who was born in Riverside, eldest son of one of the major growers until he had a dire late-teenage falling out that left him definitively disinherited. "The best thing, the *best* that ever happened to me," Darrell often said. Almost as often as he said that the Korean War was the best thing that ever, ever happened to him: "They put me in Intelligence. I've had a mind ever since."

On the basis of this training, Darrell thought that he could decode Mr. Jensen's diary. He would come over now and then, after putting in too many hours browsing at the library, not writing his dissertation, and he would drink and study the diary.

He was not troubled by the way his own name appears a diminished thing, an afterthought, in my view, always smaller than the other names that appear on the same page.

Darrell the Barrel, as he invited us to call him (we didn't accept that invitation), becomes, in the pages of the diary, a lacey hem, marginal décor placed artfully in relation to a big bold BRADLEY and to HANNAH. His name is always with theirs. The two of them, and then him.

He said, "That brilliant son of a bitch has made me pretty, Alice, *pretty*."

Less than a year after Hannah came into my life, she and her husband moved away. Darrell was buried in Riverside. Richard was among the dead in Vietnam. Eric Langland was with the Jensens in Vermont. And then two months later he was dead. Here is the newspaper clipping. It was sent to the secretary in the English department across town, at UC Riverside, where I was still in graduate school at the time. There was no personal note included. The clipping was sent simply in order to inform what would have been Eric's alma mater, had he not gone off with the Jensens. We received no other word of Eric's death. The astute secretary presumed that I would want to have it:

> A man in his late twenties, not a native to this community, was found in the Chittenden Reservoir yesterday afternoon, an apparent suicide. The police have reported that he was wearing heavy boots, jeans, and a hunting jacket. The pockets were weighted down with stones and books. There was an empty bottle of whiskey near the shore and no sign of injury to the body. He has been identified as one Eric Langland by his landlords, Mr. and Mrs. B. W. Jensen. His body will be sent to his adoptive parents in Seattle.

When I found this among my keepsakes as I was packing up and sorting, I sent a telepathic message to Eric Langland's former so-called landlords: I am on my way. My uppity memory defies my sorry bones. I can do this. The long postponement is over. I am piecing the story together, and I'm armed. End of message.

A second message, to Hannah: I'm on my way. I'm ready to know who we are. And were. You and me.

I took out the map and the phone book, determined the area

code, and called the operator, Vermont Information. She repeated the name—"J-e-n-s-e-n?"—and said the phone number. I talked her into giving me the address.

Were I the "landlord" in the story of Eric's death, I'd have flown the coop in the middle of the night in some sort of hooded cloak. Taken myself to a faraway and rock-ridden place where water is hard to come by and people know how to keen. But they haven't budged. They are still here, the Jensens, in a small town in Vermont that is not far from the Chittenden Reservoir. And now I am too.

Eric became, in a gossipy small-town newspaper, the very thing I believed he could most do without—a body. The thing you weren't supposed to notice, one way or the other. You wouldn't have said about Eric that he carried his body in such and such a way. It carried him, with as little fanfare as possible. If you gave it a second thought, wondered what the flesh beneath his buttoned up and buttoned down clothes looked like, felt like, smelled like, you would blush with shame and tell yourself to stop it. You were not to give his body any second thoughts. In another country or time, he might have covered everything but his eyes, like a Muslim woman.

So I assumed. So I made him out to be. Drew a circle around him and turned him into a totem of dedicated scholarliness, the ideal, disembodied partner, deadened to intimacy. I did that to him. I see that now. I still don't see what I was afraid of. Why I insisted, when he was alive, whenever I was in his company, whenever he was in my thoughts, on my version of him.

Small, dark eyes. And a face that was angular but undramatic, pale and unblemished, severely boyish, if that makes any sense. You wouldn't have called him movie-star handsome, but he was attractive. He would have attracted your attention, left you curious, left you thinking of front doors not just shut but locked, of fists tight all night long and fondnesses subdued. You would have thought he needed a friend. Perhaps you would secretly have adored him.

You meaning me.

THREE

Keep your eyes peeled: a gruesome piece of advice, when you think about it. But I'll admit to saying it more than a few times to my young neighbor back in Riverside, now a roommate, a ten-year-old good fairy of a girl whose given name is Constance but who calls herself Bunny because, she says, it rhymes with sunny and honey and money and funny. "Maybe I'll have a better chance of being happy when I grow up?" And maybe, I thought but didn't utter, there is something to be said for grasping at straws.

Bunny's mother was not a happy person. A neighbor who was not a friend. You engage in small talk if you happen to run into one another. "How's that clever daughter of yours?" Things like that. You try not to run into one another if, on one such occasion, one of you has said, "I hate my life." I didn't say that. She did.

Bunny lived three doors down with her father (her mother "went off somewhere" when Bunny was eight) and the round of girlfriends who moved in glossy and hopeful, moved out uncombed and door-slamming.

Bunny's father is a good-looking carpenter with more business than he can handle. He seems a decent sort—apparently as fickle as they come with grown-up females but devoted, if not entirely to his daughter, then at least to his fatherhood, and there's something (or other) to be said for that.

Bunny told me that the girlfriends always left things behind, just in case. One left an antique wing-backed chair and matching ottoman. Another bequeathed European kitchen utensils, a new coffee pot, vases to be filled with fresh-cut flowers. The last one left behind a big orange cat.

"When I grow up," Bunny told me, "I'm going to have a blue and silver pick-up truck that can carry all my pots and pans and cats while I search for a regular husband."

She guessed one of the things I was about to ask, and added, "I won't start the search until after I graduate from college."

"Good plan," I said. "Where will you look?"

"High and low."

"Stick with high."

"The whole time?"

"Trust me."

Bunny tried for a month last year to talk me into taking her with me. She wanted a summer in Vermont. She wanted a summer anywhere but Riverside. "The dang heat keeps getting hotter," she said. "It's even too hot to *think*, Alice." She'd been studying a map and reading up on the place. She knew more about Vermont than I do even now. The names of the lakes and the ski resorts and the maple syrup factories. The schedule for the ferry that crosses Lake Champlain. What I knew is that Robert Frost used to live here, and that Hannah Jensen and her husband do now.

Robert Frost: those of us who grew up in the forties and fifties grew up thinking of him as a rumpled old rhymer, a wise and mildly wise-acre tiller of the soil. His rhymes were often sweet enough, simple enough, to teach to children. We didn't hear the snarls in his poems, didn't know, until later, the frightful domestic details—Mr. Frost as son-of-a-bitch.

Sometimes becoming enlightened is the same as becoming uneasy. It sometimes has so little to do with light.

When I was quite young—Bunny's age—I often daydreamed the lives of the families who occupied those big houses on the hill across the street: the sorts of things an only child who lived in a two-bedroom apartment with her widowed mother would imagine. An only child with only a cupful of imagination, filled mainly by her mother's nighttime talk of the way things might have been. The way they were every day in Never-Never Land.

I gave those hilltop families aproned mothers who didn't have to go to work in the mornings. Fathers who, on the weekends, cheerfully supervised chores and organized outings. I gave them all sit-down dinners on fashionable plates. Interesting tales to tell about the things they had accomplished, the people they had observed, the books they had read.

I gave them light everywhere, coming in through the grand windows. As if each house were a theater, as if each family member were a star whose daily life was thrilling and meant to be seen.

I don't believe that I longed to live in such a spot-lit place. A glimpse inside was all I wanted.

For a short time, I became friends with a girl named Ruth who lived in one of those houses on the hill. She had an older brother in high school and a father who was a doctor. She had a housekeeper and a swimming pool and a mother who stayed home during the day—planning good meals, I assumed.

I didn't understand why, after school, Ruth always wanted to come to my "house," as she called it. So I hammered away at her, the way girls then learned to do—with elaborate pleases, followed by wounded looks and long silences. She finally relented.

Inside her big house with the bay windows, the curtains were all drawn. Ruth said, "It's cooler that way, I guess."

We tiptoed through the living room, where her mother was asleep on the couch. Ruth's mother was wearing slacks and shoes and a short terry-cloth bathrobe. She seemed to have begun the day but changed her mind.

Ruth said, "She's always like that. Sean told me our dad gives her pills. To calm her down."

I wanted to meet her brother, Sean, but he was in his room with the door locked. He yelled at us in pig latin: "Uckfay offay!" Posted on his door was a drawing in colored pencils of a screaming boy. Ruth said, "That's Sean. He calls it Self-Portrait on Tuesday."

The housekeeper was in the kitchen, ironing. She didn't remove the cigarette from the corner of her mouth when she told us to keep quiet or go someplace else. Ruth turned to me and said, "Satisfied?"

Bunny, God love her, wants a truck, not a bay window. She once asked me, "Why didn't you ever look for a new husband?"

"Because I've never owned a truck?"

"You could get one. A green one, everything green, even the what-d-ya-call-it."

"Upholstery?"

"Yeah. And a license plate with your name on it."

"I'm too old now, honey bun."

"You're just saying that because you're a scaredy cat, aren't you, Alice?"

"Sometimes. Maybe mostly."

"I'm not scared of anything," she told me.

"We're both asking for trouble, aren't we?"

"Yep, I guess we are."

I gave Bunny a bicycle only after she promised with all manner of crossing her heart that she would never forget to wear a helmet. She tried mine on, one of the first of its kind, bulbous and heavy, and we both burst out laughing. I proposed to buy her a new one, sleek and up-to-date. It took well over an hour at the sporting goods store for her to pick one out—it's purple, with black and white wings above the ears. I told her she looks like Mercury in that helmet. She told me she looks like a poisonous mushroom. And she does—but she wears it nonetheless.

For all the right reasons I didn't mention to Bunny that I've never worn mine, though I've had it for years. I never could get used to the damn thing. Not because it's clunky—which it surely is—but because, from the beginning, when I had my first real bike, I too much enjoyed the look of my shadow, my wild hair lifted and whipping like a horse's tail. Down deserted dirt roads and in the school playground I would go as fast as I could, then faster, racing the shadow-girl with the flying hair, who didn't seem to be afraid of anything.

Several years and bikes later, when going for a ride became a matter of exercise, of fighting off the middle-age spread, I would head out in the early morning, early enough to witness the good aim of the seasoned paperboys, the flower-mangling misfires of the newcomers. I stayed away from the main drags for the most part, even though at that hour they were empty and hushed. In low gear, for the benefit of my legs, I toured the better neighborhoods up near the Victoria Club golf course. I could hear the nighttime sprinklers cease, one by one. I saw front porch lights blink off, smelled the sweetly nutty magnolia trees, and bacon frying. The dog-walkers would give me a wave or a nod, as if to say yes, me too, it's a blessing to be out at this awakening time of day. I went just fast enough to make a breeze that would eventually unloosen from the bobby-pins a few long strands of hair, faint echoes of that galloping shadow-girl.

I once saw a pretty woman in a pink negligee run after her dressed-for-work husband as he headed for his car. She hit him in the back with the yellow pages. Twice. She didn't say a word, just walloped him as hard as she could. He ignored her, got in his car, and drove away. Another time I saw a teenage girl climbing from the wide branch of a pearly sycamore tree into an upstairs window. And once I saw a balding, heavy-set man at the bottom of his driveway, fetching the newspaper. As I passed, he opened his bathrobe and showed me his genitals. He gave them a little underneath fluffing, but that didn't do anything to banish the image of a half-collapsed apple-shaped pin cushion, with its stem drooping to one side.

I had to stop cycling a couple of years ago, when my back began to beg for mercy. On one of my last mornings out, I rode through downtown and then circled the lake at Fairmont Park as fast as I could go, blew my tidy French roll into a mess of remembered pleasure.

Before I left Riverside, I took Bunny shopping for some red cowboy boots. To cheer us up.

I ought to have been an expert at partings by that point, the way some people, after years of practice, know exactly how to host a dinner for two or for twenty guests. They're so good at it, their friends encourage them to write a book on the subject, and they do. And the book is filled with useful advice, as well as pretty photographs or "down-home" illustrations.

In my case, despite all the practice, all the leave-takings, despite all the "Bye," "Love you," "See you later, Alice," "Vaya con Dios," "Take good care," I couldn't write one useful sentence on the matter, except maybe this one: You don't get used to it. Period. Closure is for suckers.

When Bunny was only seven or so, I told her the story of how, back in the days when I required tucking in, my mother would often say a goodnight in the voice of a movie actress—Lauren Bacall, Katharine Hepburn, Marlene Dietrich, and others, all stylish and low-pitched. "Dahling," she'd say, "Ah'll wake you at seven. We set sail for R-r-rio at nine. Sweet dreams." Then she would turn off the light and for a while I would practice (sans talent) my imitation of her imitation, and I would imagine setting sail for the place she called R-r-rio, or boarding a train she called the Orient Express, or greeting the uniformed driver of the "cahr coming 'round" in the morning to whisk us off to someplace other than the same old school, the same old department store. My mother, I told Bunny, almost never forgot to sprinkle the close of our hum-drum days with stardust.

At the time, all Bunny had to say was, "Marlene is a really neat name." Later, though, she discovered mimicry. And, like my mother, she put it to good use. During the week before my departure, she would speak to me only "in character," as it were, and she wanted me to do the same. At the saddlery, where we bought the boots, there was Bunny saying, "Zank 'eaven zey 'ave zeez boots in my size!" The character was Maurice Chevalier as seen in *Gigi* (we'd watched the video together one night at her house, when I volunteered to babysit, though it turned out that her father was home long before he said he would be). "From now on, Aleez, vee speak zis vay and no uhzer." Bunny didn't say so and neither did I, but the goal of this game seemed to be to write the imminent fact of our parting out of the script. We were not ourselves, after all. We were Maurice. We went by the book. Bunny's book.

Her Maurice was much better, much funnier than mine—she zanked 'eaven for everything under zee sun—but she didn't seem to notice my lapses. She was earnest about keeping up the game right to the end. The day before I left, at her request, I made Crêpes Suzette for our afternoon snack, and a mess of her father's kitchen. She clumped around in her red cowboy boots and talked almost non-stop about "zee classamates zat are driving me knots." And for this, as you can imagine, I was grateful. Bunny kept us laughing.

I remember that we ate far too much, but did manage to save one crêpe for her father. Then we cleaned the place up—there was flour everywhere, and sticky splashes of Grand Marnier on the countertops. When it was time for me to go, we hugged each other but not for long. Bunny pulled back so that we could be "French" about it, kiss each other on both cheeks. Then she said, "Donut zay anyzing now, Aleez, egzept bone swear."

FOUR

I SENT BUNNY A POSTCARD from Las Vegas: a photograph of long-legged female dancers adorned in glitter and hot pink ostrich feathers. With an eyebrow pencil, I drew an arrow and wrote "moi" next to one of the dancers. On the other side I did not say much more than "I made it. So far, so good. Much love." I didn't write a word about running out of gas or about what happened after I checked into the Sahara hotel and went down to the casino to play some blackjack by way of adhering to the revised Plan A.

The original Plan A went like this: You will get some sleep and then have a brief vacation in some appropriate place. Death Valley, say.

So I had a nap and a long bath. Then I put on new nylons and one of the two good dresses (not new, but classic enough to last for a few seasons) that were in my biggest suitcase. I did my hair up in the usual twist, but used a pair of shiny black barrettes. I got out the pearl earrings. In other words, I was doing battle against the sundry attractions of retreat, against the Alice who was telling me to quit this driving to Vermont nonsense and head on back. To hell with all versions of Plan A.

I put on my heels and told that Alice to keep her views on the matter to herself.

Perhaps that's why I was already in a bit of a fighting mood when I sat down at one of the blackjack tables with fifty dollars in chips and a glass of white wine.

Or maybe it was standing in a sluggish line to purchase those chips, or the cost of the glass of wine, or the three separate people who said, "This is your first time, isn't it, lady?"

It was about five in the afternoon. The movie-set chandeliers, the glamorous indoor palms, the smartly-outfitted waiters and waitresses—none of this set the tone of the casino. None of it could compete with the sense that, for the most part, urgent business was going on there: the players were not partying, they were concentrating, they were praying, they were figuring the odds, they were counting or even more diligently not counting their losses. For all this concentration, the place was manic with sound: coins clanging their hopeful way into row after row of flashy slot machines; baritone croupiers calling for bets to be placed; roulette wheels spinning; cards being shuffled and betters cheering, moaning, whistling for more drinks. There was music, too, piped in and almost audible—a man's voice, singing. Sinatra, I think. But whoever the singer was, no one seemed to be listening.

I heard myself say—not for the last time on this trip—Give it up. You don't belong here.

Then I said, Speak for yourself.

I found a seat at an out-of-the-way blackjack table. There was one other person there, a middle-aged woman, maybe a little younger, so leathered by the sun and indebted to Revlon that it was hard to tell. Her blond hair was both short and "big," fifties cocktail waitress style. And she was wearing a mauve-colored sundress sort of thing. Whatever it was, its purpose was to display her large and well-tanned breasts.

When I sat down, one barstool apart from her, she said, "What are you looking at?"

You wouldn't have mistaken this for a friendly question.

True, I could have responded with a "Pardon me?" or a "Nothing," or even a "That good-looking man over there in the gray suit." But no.

I said, "I'm looking at what you apparently want me, and everyone else, to look at."

The dealer laughed and said, "Darn tootin'!"

I glanced around—guilty smart-mouth that I was at the moment—to see if anyone else had registered this exchange. You know what I mean: you expect someone to be standing right there, just within earshot, shaking her head at you, or stroking her left index finger with her right one, giving you the "naughty, naughty" sign. I guess it's the well-mannered version of yourself you're squeamishly looking for, hoping she's not paying attention.

The woman got up and stood next to me. "Take a good look, missy." She cupped her hands beneath her breasts and lifted them. "An eyeful, aren't they?"

The dealer said, "Man oh man."

Poof! Bye-bye guilt. Whether she meant to or not, the woman had let me off the hook. Was anyone besides the dealer watching this aggressive display of her eyeful? I didn't want to know.

I said, "I think you've made your point," and then turned to the dealer, a tall, bench-pressed man with dark curly hair, who seemed to be more interested in my reaction than he was in her extravagant twins.

"Have I made mine?" She of the twins would not be ignored.

The dealer shrugged. He looked as if he spent no more time in the casino than the job required. What I mean is, he looked exceptionally healthy. He looked like a vegetarian, a practitioner of meditation, a guy who belongs to two gyms and no political parties.

"Can we begin?" I asked him.

The woman released her breasts, let them settle back—still a couple of show-offs—into the push-up bodice of her dress. She continued to stand next to me. "You and me," she said, "we're not done yet."

"What is it that you want?" Did I sound like a schoolmarm? No doubt about it.

"An apology."

"Evidently, I embarrassed you. A miscalculation for which I do indeed apologize."

The woman said to the dealer, "She's jealous, isn't she?"

Again he shrugged. "Beats me."

She turned her back on him and leaned in closer to me. "You're jealous, aren't you?" Then she placed a hand on one of my breasts.

Before she could say "Not bad for an old woman," my forearm knocked up against hers, got her off of me. Then she said it: "Not bad for an old woman," and laughed, patting me on the back as she took the seat next to mine. "Let's play some cards."

We anteed up, the dealer shuffled and dealt, I sipped the wine, she lit a cigarette. We were getting down to business as if no scene had occurred—which yours truly couldn't let last for long.

"What was all that about?"

Instead of answering my question, she said, "My name's Barbara." She pronounced this, like a child, "bra-bra." Apparently, I was supposed to laugh.

"That's a joke," she told me. "Most people get it right away, you know?"

"It's just that, frankly, it's not funny."

"What's your name?"

"Alice."

"Frankly, Alice, I think you're stuck up. You've been giving me a hard-ass time from the get-go. Dainty pearl earrings, la-dee-da. They're real, aren't they? Thought so. Oldish though you are—sixty-something, right?—you remind me of some of the girls I went to college with. Yep, I went to college, Alice, would you believe it? Fresno State, B.A. in psychology, 1975. I'm here for a twentieth class reunion. And, like, as you can see, I'm having a fine old time reconnecting with the friends of my youth—that guy over there in the Bermuda shorts, for instance. Do you see him? Mr. L.L. Bean? That's Elliott, originator of the joke on my name. Almost good-looking, isn't he? So you're probably wondering, did I do it with him?"

"I'm not—"

"No. Did he ever cop a feel? Yes. More than once, and from every girl who had even the newest little set of protrusions under her sweater. Big score-keeper, that Billy. You ever been with one of those? Didn't think so. Now he's a Wall Street something-or-other. But I had him figured for unchanged on a thing or two. These two. Thelma and Louise, I call them these days. Louise is just a tad bigger, and a tad the worse for wear, since she's the tit of choice. Anyway, sure enough. 'Bra-Bra!' Elliot yells when we run into each other at the luncheon this afternoon. Big hug, blah blah blah. I was wearing this same dress, and I told him, right up front, 'Thought I'd make it easy for you this time, El.' He took a good look but then he said, 'No thanks.' *No thanks.* Do you believe it, Alice? So you're about to ask: Is he married?"

"I was about to—"

"The answer is no. Going steady (as if that ever stopped him)? The answer is no. Gay? The answer is—give or take anything's possible—no. Are the stuck-up girls who have become stuck-up middle-aged women giving us the evil eye? The answer is, of course they are! So who's the bastard here, Alice? Him or them? The answer is: the whole damn bunch. That's Teresa Bonaventura he's talking to now. Right after college she married into vineyard money. Check out the earrings—bigger than yours, but the same aren't-I-a-nice-lady message. Now guess what?"

I said, "She's not a nice lady."

"Rightaroni, woman! How can you tell?"

"I'm not sure."

"Look. Think. Come on, Alice. For chrissakes, this is important. A gal your age ought to know by now, in an instant, who the people are who can do you some harm."

"I've never been good at that," I told her. Images from Richard Stone's "going away" party started to came into focus. I pushed the "off button," so to speak. "You're not one of them, are you?"

"You wouldn't ask me that if you thought I was."

"Fair enough. But what with all the mistakes along the way—"

She reapplied her lipstick. "I'm not one of them, Alice. And you know it." What was it about the way she said this? I remember hearing encouragement, as in "Alice, you're a better judge of character than you think," but there was something else, some note of defeat or failure—on her part? On mine? I think she heard it, too. She was blushing.

"Yes, I know it," I told her.

Barbara laughed too loudly, the way you do when it's time to change the subject, when you're cornered, or when you're about to speak words you don't want spoken. "Listen to us!" she said. "Oh so serioso!" Still laughing, as if she were having the time of her life, she looked over at Elliott and waved her fingers. He waved back. Teresa Bonaventura glanced at us, but didn't wave.

"Your friend Teresa has mean eyes. Ungiving, as dead as those gray kind of marbles, the ones they call 'steelies.'"

Barbara applauded. "I'm buying you a drink, woman." She called for a waiter and ordered two Manhattans on the rocks.

The dealer said, "You two better start paying attention. You're losing your shirts."

Barbara swiveled her bare shoulders at him, offered him another look at her extravagances. "You'd like that, wouldn't you?"

He dealt the cards and said, "You're overall a nice lady, miss. I don't understand why you have to act like a tart."

"A tart?" Barbara looked at me for a translation.

"A loose woman."

"You don't understand," she said to the dealer.

"No."

"What are you, some kind of Buddhist? Do you live in a cave? Have you by any chance experienced the twentieth century? It's *1995* for chrissakes! 'I don't understand,' the man says. Is he for real, Alice, or what?"

Barbara was bringing me into it without taking her eyes off the dealer. They were staring each other down, like tomcats who'd found themselves in the same backyard for the first time.

"I think you two should see a marriage counselor."

Of course they heard me, but they seemed not to. They didn't take their hostile eyes off each other. Just kept on staring, half-closing their eyes for meanness' sake. Then the dealer rubbed his chin. Was he backing off? I think so, yes.

"I don't understand," he said, "why you have to act like a tart *in public.*"

Barbara smiled, but not as though she had won hands down. Not yet. "So your life in the cave, in private, is not without some of the old-fashioned, simple pleasures?"

The look they were giving each other was still aggressive, but it had changed, as if it had been run through a sieve, a filmy piece of cheesecloth.

"The private pleasures," he told her, "they're not always simple, and they're rarely old-fashioned."

"All the better."

"It's a shame to waste even a hint of them on strangers and no-account classmates from the bygone days."

Barbara's smile wasn't that of a victor, but it was winning. She gave it to him, then to me, then to him again.

A man of principle, one had reason to assume, he kept his eyes off the prize.

At that point, I was of course more than ready to announce myself a definitive odd man out, offer good nights all 'round, and suggest that the two of them meet later for this, that, and the other thing.

But Barbara said to me, once more, "Let's play some cards."

And we did, until nearly one o'clock in the morning. At around ten, I think, they brought us a snack right there at the blackjack table. Turned out the dealer ordered it, manipulated the protocol, apparently didn't want us (meaning Barbara) to go elsewhere for non-liquid sustenance. We were good card players, good company, hilarious betters. But I should add that, when the three of us eventually shook hands and went our two separate ways, in no precise sense had either Barbara or myself lost our shirts. I was twenty dollars to the good. Barbara was fifty, and still as dressed as her dress would allow her to be.

She called me the following day, just before I checked out. It was about eleven o'clock, and I'd had a sandwich and some orange juice delivered to the room—far too bleary to handle the downstairs hubbub, the constant clinking of the slot machines.

Barbara said, "Hey, party girl!"

"I think you've got the wrong number."

"Now don't be getting all pearl earrings and la-dee-dah on me. How's about a poolside margarita before you go?"

"You'll be the death of me, young lady." She made me laugh, that woman, I have to say, so that I almost took her up on her offer for a poolside drink. But I said, "No, I take that back, you won't. I intend to live a while longer. And I'm getting ready to check out. I want to make a little headway while it's still daytime."

"Vermont, right?"

"Eventually."

"Whatever lifts your skirt up. I've never been near the place. So you're saying that this is, like, it? Nice meeting you? Sayonara, baby?"

I told Barbara that I hoped it wasn't "it," and that if she ever needed to reach me she could do so by contacting Constance Harris in Riverside, California. She calls herself Bunny. She'll know where I am when I get there, I explained as I gave her Bunny's address and phone number.

"What is this Bunny? A stripper, or what? Does she work at Disneyland?"

"No. She's just a ten-year-old."

"Your contact person is a ten-year-old?"

"You'd like her."

"I'll take your word for it, Alice."

"Are you and the dealer—?"

"Yep. We're an item. The only eensy little drawback so far is that he's way too male, y'know? In the sense of rough around the edges, and comes equipped with lots of edges. But who am I to be Miss Nitpicky?"

"Don't sell yourself short."

"That goes for you, too, Alice. Keep your antennae well oiled, okay? And promise not to forget me."

An easy promise to keep, that one.

The dealer, Phil Barnett was his name, ended up, a few months later, losing his new girlfriend. Not, as far as I know, because of the rough edges. Not even because—though, according to Barbara, there was nothing eensy about this drawback—he was in fact a vegetarian. She left him when she found out that he was a sleight-of-hand-man from way back—a double dealer, a professional cheat. Barbara put it this way: "I've washed that man right out of my everything."

I know this part of the story because Barbara Dulaney has since given away all of her sundresses, introduced Thelma and Louise to cardigan and turtleneck sweaters, and moved back east, to this place of mine that Bunny has dubbed "The Ranch." As much as I was moved by the way Barbara and I were both, and so differently, sorry excuses for women, I don't think I would have welcomed her—I think I'm right about this, but I'm no expert in matters of roommates—if a few other things hadn't happened on my long way to Vermont.

FIVE

I WAS THE SORT OF GRADUATE STUDENT who memorized poetry beneath an appropriately leafy tree—preferably a jacaranda, a swoon of lavender blossoms. I was in love with my love of the profession, sappy and studious and, at twenty-eight, already married and divorced. Party girl? Ever? Not even close.

Divorced, of all things. And not just divorced but *left*. As in: Thanks a million, but too-da-loo, lady, we're outta here.

It ended after four years, when Ted and my stepson Danny (who was nine then, mopey and lovable and wanting to be called Daniel) decided to reunite with the rehabilitated first wife, the real mother. They went, as they called it, home. I prefer to put it this way: before Ted and I hung up a virtual "Going Out of Business" sign, there was another one on the front door that welcomed all impediments. So much for love that's the marriage of true minds, Will Shakespeare (but I think you knew this was, not to put too fine a point on it, always bullshit).

I used to dwell on the faces of my husband and my stepson at that moment when the three of us were standing on the yellowing lawn in front of that house of mine where we had tried to make a life—a good house, small and in need of repainting then, but good. As for the life, well, not good enough. There was the rented truck at the curb-side—a replica of the one they'd used when they'd moved in with me—packed with their things, and the two of them were trying not to show me how anxious they were to get going. So of course they showed me.

We all knew that I knew, and we pretended not to know. We weren't good at that. We said "I love you" and "I love you, too" and "Bye."

That was that.

I was no longer a stepmother. Stepping in, then out. I haven't seen either of them since the day they put their belongings into that truck and went "home" to Pasadena. But I have heard Ted's voice: he became a radio newscaster. I don't know what he's doing now. He's been off the air for years. Perhaps he, too, is retired, planning a next move that will be different from all the others, that will have far more to do with endings than beginnings.

After we divorced, I used to listen now and then, at the top of the hour, to his station. Tuning in seemed a friendly thing to do. He'd always wanted to get out of sales, to land such a job, to be free from direct and therefore arduous contact with what he called "the fucking public." I was, you could say, glad for him.

I was considerably less glad on that frost-bitten December morning some thirty years ago when I heard his voice briefly mention on the radio what had "supposedly" happened at the UC Riverside campus, to "a twenty-six-year-old coed." He did not say her name, but I was angry nonetheless, filled with a vague sense of violation and a desire to tell him that he was talking, far too matter-of-factly, about *my* Hannah.

I was as wrong about her as I was about *my* Eric.

From the moment we became officemates, he kept me in a state of wonder, though he made no special effort to be mysterious. He just wasn't talking—not about himself, not to me. And I let my imagination tell me that he had taken a vow, or virtually taken the Fifth, that his reticence issued from a need to focus only on his studies, to protect his brilliant mind from the invasions of mere talk.

News bulletin, woman: You were behaving, Barbara Dulaney might say, like a fucking English major! Too true.

There would be the occasional opening and I'd take a step or two forward—

"You've been to London, haven't you?"

"Only in books."

"You know the place as if you'd been there."

"I read a lot, Alice."

"I know you read. But what else do you do?"

"I write papers, teach freshman comp. Same as you. At the moment, though, I'm trying to read—" but I wouldn't get anywhere. I didn't know where he was from until after he was dead. I didn't know that he'd been adopted. I did know—I suppose his silences taught me to know—that these things didn't much matter. Not in the short run. What mattered, at least until Hannah Jensen took over, were the old poets.

> Shape nothing, lips; be lovely dumb.
>
> . . .
>
> Be shellèd, eyes, with double dark.

Did I ever get anywhere with Eric Langland? Maybe. At least, at the time, one afternoon on Mount Rubidoux, it didn't seem to be nowhere.

Mount Rubidoux, in West Riverside, with its cross at the top—more a good-size mound than a mount—is a hands-on site. A place for Easter morning services, and for sweethearts on Saturday nights. A good place for star-gazing and for underage drinking. A monument to whatever you did there, or hoped to do, or prayed for. To costs of living that have nothing to do with dollars. I knew the place well, but hadn't been up there since I was a teenager, when hilltop brooding was part of the weekly routine.

Was it for brooding that I found myself, one late afternoon in May, no teenager by far, heading for the old haunt? That's probably true.

Eric was there that day. He was sitting near the top, reading, with his back to the sun. And there, above him, was the big weather-beaten cross that had been placed on the summit back in the hopeful first decade of the twentieth century.

I was telling myself that Eric needed a friend who would love him, who would never pry, who was comfortable with silences, who would share his literary interests and tastes, who might occasionally tease him but who would never aggressively flirt, never wheedle. He needed somebody safe. Someone acquainted with the night, but not its servant. He needed Alice Clark.

I'd like to think that, if he hadn't gone off with the Jensens, if he'd stayed here and stayed alive, I would have dropped all that garbage and written him a love letter.

I remember that I didn't step forward, didn't want to bother him. It was enough to look for a while. At Eric bent over his book. At the boulders initialed in spray paint. At what little there was left of the Santa Ana River. It made sense to me that somebody would want to leave a mark there, a graffitied signature. Why had I never done so?

After a few minutes, Eric looked up. He didn't seem surprised to see me. It was as if we had arranged to meet, to share the sunset. He seemed—yes, I wanted him to seem—to have been waiting for me. "You're here," he said.

"I've been here for a while."

"I know," he said.

"I didn't want to disturb you—"

"Nor I you, Alice," he said.

I took this—his knowledge of my presence, his letting me alone, his saying my name as if it mattered—as a special act of kindness, an offering. And maybe, in fact, it was. Maybe he wasn't just being polite when he invited me to join him up among the boulders, in the shadow of that old cross. Maybe he didn't look at me when he ventured that invitation because he had already offered too much. Maybe he said so little as we sat together and watched the sun go down because he didn't want words to spoil it.

We knew no Hannah Jensen then, no Mr. Jensen. They wouldn't enter our lives until the coming fall term. The silence between us was not yet filled with the sorts of thoughts I never thought I'd think.

I managed, for a while, to follow Eric's lead. There we were, doing something together, quietly, in a good place, side by side, close but not too close. Between us, keeping our legs from touching, was the book he'd been reading. I don't remember how long we stayed that way, letting the landscape do all the talking. But at some point I had to speak.

"I haven't been up here in years."

At the sound of my voice, Eric looked my way. There was a pause as he brought himself back from wherever he had been—someplace where small-talk is unheard of.

He gave me a smile and said, "I figured as much."

"You did?"

"Your shoes. They're not meant for walking up hills, among rocks."

I had on a slick new pair of loafers. He had noticed such a detail, paid me that kind of attention, the very kind I paid to him. We're in sync, all right, I thought.

I was wishing that I had worn a nicer sweater, had put on a little more make-up. In no time at all I was imagining our arms around each other, a tentative first kiss, and then another. The fresh, boyish smell of his face.

"You're right," I laughed. "I'm definitely ill-equipped."

He waited for a moment—was he waiting for that smile of mine to shut up?—before he asked, "Who isn't, Alice? Ill-equipped is unfortunately the name of the game."

He looked away from me, seemed to be headed back to where it was quiet, but he spoke a last thing along the way. "What I meant was that the Boy Scout motto makes sense if one is on one's own, if basic survival is the issue. But no one, not one of us, can really 'be prepared,' as the saying goes, when it comes to other people."

"True," I said.

If one could, I thought, one wouldn't be able to fall in love.

End of conversation. We watched in silence as the smog-encircled sun settled itself upon a nest of peach-colored clouds, and began its westward disappearance. Then Eric stood and held out a hand to help me to my feet. I reached out for his other hand as well—did I have only balance in mind? But then we were standing just inches apart in a gracious twilight, hands clasped, face-to-face. In some other story we would have kissed the kisses I had fantasized. We would have done what the moment expected of us, what our hands as spokesmen for our bodies were telling us to do. At the time I was more than ready to follow the formulaic script. But then he let go of one of my hands—sooner, not later. He did keep hold of the other one as he led me down among the boulders.

One-fifth giddy girl, four-fifths cautious divorcée approaching thirty, or vice versa: that was me when I was around him. Beside myself whenever I was beside him.

Not long after that encounter on Mount Rubidoux, we ended up sitting together, Eric and I, shoulder to shoulder at his desk in the TA's office we shared with Richard and Darrell. It was early evening and I was about to call it a day, go home and make myself a drink, have a bath, read more Henry James. Eric, the true scholar among us, would work a few more hours. He was writing a paper on Burton's *Anatomy of Melancholy*.

"What's so funny?" I asked him.

"Was I laughing?"

"Almost."

"Look at this."

I pulled up a chair. Eric indicated the passage that had made him smile out loud, almost laugh. He was inviting me to read it, our shoulders were touching. He smelled like wool, like a thick old blanket. We were almost cheek to cheek. I could feel his breath close to my ear. Burton's prose is too erudite for my modest wit-level, but I got the gist of the passage: among the many causes of melancholy he studiously describes in his *Anatomy*, there is the failure (on behalf of celibacy or avoidance of sin or simply bad luck) to engage in sexual intercourse. "Omission of venery," Burton calls it.

"As in a failure to make love," I said, as if I were merely analyzing the text at hand.

"His use of the term 'venery' doesn't exactly—"

"I get it. He's talking about semen build-up."

"As long as you're using 'semen' loosely," he told me, pointing to the text.

"Burton includes women."

"That makes sense."

It made unnerving sense to me that the studious Eric Langland would use a peculiar seventeenth-century book as mediator, as vehicle by which he might indirectly express an interest in Alice Clark.

We looked at each other. I still, now and then, dream the feeling of that look: a safe, serene, uncomplicated, wrapped-in-a-blanket feeling. I believe it when I hear myself say that if Eric had lived, if he had returned from his time with the Jensens here in Vermont, I'd have turned that blanket into a love nest. I'd have taken all the risks, broken the rules, said the words, shared my hide-out.

One exhale later, and the look was over.

Eric began whistling the first couple of bars of "Melancholy Baby" as he turned the page to resume his studies.

He gave me a smile. A parting gift. "See you tomorrow, Alice."

SIX

SOON INTO OUR FRIENDSHIP—was it really within days?—I found that I'd told Hannah about my long-dead father, my ailing mother, my failed marriage. That wasn't like me, which I took to be a good sign. I didn't take it as a good sign that Hannah subsequently included Mr. Jensen in what I thought was a private girlfriend-to-girlfriend conversation.

We were meeting again for lunch in the student union. Her tray seemed to be as full as her book bag. How I envied that young woman's ability to *eat*! There were more than a few times during those first weeks of our friendship when I secretly thought that Hannah personified the petite blonde who was trapped inside my big brunette body. My physical self merely a temporary cocoon or shell. So that if I were only patient enough, undisturbed, and in just the right location, I'd eventually feel a fissure, then a splitting open and out she'd come, the real me! First thing I'd do is let her eat a large piece of chocolate cake.

The little blonde version of my wished-for self bit into her roast beef sandwich and announced: "My husband says you think you must be by yourself because of your father."

I moved some lettuce toward the dollop of salad dressing. "Hannah."

"What?"

"I wish you wouldn't tell your husband what I've told you about myself. He doesn't know me. We've never met."

"Do I know you, Alice? Mr. Jensen is good at this American knowing. He is helping me to know you better. He says, because of your father, you do not want any more accidents, ever."

"I can't stop them."

"My husband is right, then?"

"No. He's wrong. And I don't like this."

"You do not like what?"

"I don't like that we're talking about somebody I've never met, who happens to be talking about me behind my back. Offering diagnoses. I don't know. It's too—"

"Husbands and wives talk about everything, Alice. Are you going to marry Richard?"

"No."

"Eric?"

"Cut it out, Hannah."

"I love the way you talk. With these expressions. 'Cut it out.' You mean: Don't say this. Delete that sentence, am I right?"

"Delete all of the above."

Hannah laughed out loud, her momentarily taut, grown-up mouth glossy with mayonnaise.

A few weeks later she came to our teaching assistants' office. Eric and I were the only ones there, at our desks, reading, his hunched back facing mine, his uncut black hair forming an awning around his face. I didn't interrupt him for introductions.

Hannah was tearful and pouting. I think it crossed my mind that, though she was twenty-six, she looked as if she had just been excluded from a game of jacks or four-square.

She was not doing well in her courses, she told me. Her work, according to the advisor responsible for midterm reports, was disappointing. Not at all what he expected, given her transfer records and recommendations. Eric did not look up when Hannah almost shouted that she might be kicked out of school.

I said things like: Your advisor is jumping the gun. Perhaps all you need is more tutoring in the English language. No? You already have a tutor? Well, how about some extra practice. We won't call it tutoring.

We'll call it talk, girl-talk. I'd be glad to help. *Gratis.* You'll be fine. We won't let them kick you out. Don't worry, kiddo. It's going to be all right. You'll see.

We arranged that she would come to my house a couple of times a week, from five to seven or so. We would talk, read out loud, tell stories, play some cards, gossip. It would be casual, fun, and so what if I didn't know beans about calculus, in which she'd received her worst grade? Surely I could help.

I was too busy saving the day to wonder why the upset Hannah seemed to vanish in an instant. And why, as soon as I had guaranteed my help, she turned her attention to Eric. But I wondered since.

Right after I'd set up our "deal," Hannah gave me the hush sign with one small finger to her bow-tie lips, and then crept up behind him, drew his hair back, and whispered something in his ear. Whatever it was, Eric turned and looked at her, and then at me. He was smiling, sort of—but he looked as if he had just taken a bite of the very food that always made him sick.

"Eric Langland," I said. "Meet Hannah Jensen." No doubt I too looked sick.

Eric just shook his head and returned to whatever he had been reading.

Hannah turned back to me and said, "We have said our names to each other a long time ago, Alice. I know all of your friends here."

"What? How?" (As if that office were my private property, I confess. And as if those guys were mine, too.)

"You do not put your life here every minute of the day. I have already greeted these smart men here who share your office."

Then Hannah winked at me—me, the frumpy graduate student, but somehow, nevertheless, the delightful Hannah's lady-in-waiting, her bosom-buddy, her accomplice.

When she came to my house for what we weren't calling tutoring, she spotted the board games that were then stacked on top of one of the bookshelves. She asked me to teach her how to play *Clue.* The

Scrabble game might have been more appropriate to the task at hand, but I liked her idea. I liked her playfulness. I liked listening to her talk. I remember thinking that her advisor must have confused her with someone else—that Hannah was in fact exceptionally bright. So bright that, after our first round, she turned *Clue* into a game that would include the faces of the victims by letting the suspect cards count either way.

We worked out new rules. Not one, but two of the suspect cards would be slipped unseen into the special envelope, along with cards that designated a weapon and a scene of the crime. The process of elimination would be the same, but the player who eventually deduced the correct contents of the envelope would not be the automatic winner. She would be a mere police officer, a collector of data. Once the facts and the faces were revealed, each player, the shrewd detectives, would "tell" the crime, turn the elements into story. The sleuth with the best story would be declared the winner.

I was not clever, not at all modern. My stories were half-baked and boring. Mr. Green is killed by Mrs. White for the life insurance money, or to clear a space for an illicit romance, and the like. Hannah's stories sounded like dreams, the kind a ladylike lady is not supposed to have, or at least never tell out loud. This was especially the case after she decided that we would expand the possibilities, add more potential killers and victims to the envelope, sometimes more weapons.

I can see her here, sitting across from me at this table. She looks right at me as she tells her stories. She is having fun. On one occasion her story went something like this:

"Mrs. Peacock has a pretty name, but she is an ugly woman. She wears the hat of a man and the ring of a queen. Nobody wants her at all. But this is not very true. The people who are in the envelope with her want her, kind of. One of them wants her cane, the other one wants her hat. They are Mr. Green and Professor Plum. Mr. Green is almost an insanity case, who has wanted Mrs. Peacock to hurt him with her cane and to choke him with her ascot and to smother him with the big breasts that he knows are hidden underneath her blue jacket. Professor Plum has wanted to be wearing her hat. He cannot buy one for himself because he is only a poor professor, the way you will be, Alice.

"Both of these men do the killing of Mrs. Peacock in the billiards room, where she has won many games of billiards against them. They are thinking 'fucking bitch!' because they have to stand with their billiard sticks hanging down, doing nothing, while she puts the balls where they must go. Bang, bang, bang, she wins all the time. So they kill her with the rope and with the revolver. Then Professor Plum puts on her hat, while Mr. Green beats his own shoulders with her cane—"

Hannah would look at me, smile, and win.

In those days, I carried a palm-sized anthology of nineteenth-century love poetry in the pocket of my jacket, immersed in Rossetti's regrets.

> Better by far you should forget and smile
> Than that you should remember and be sad.

It was a gray denim jacket, cheap but tailored to look as if it were part of a suit. For several months, I wore it every day. Meager means supplied me with the perfect excuse to give in to my childhood envy of the Catholic girls who got to wear uniforms to school. The jacket, a black turtleneck sweater or t-shirt, loose jeans, tennis shoes: my uniform. No more worrying about fashion, about trying to be pretty.

I grabbed that same jacket off the hat rack by the front door on the night that I gave Hannah a ride home, the night she was raped. I remember removing the little book of poems, draping the jacket over her shoulders, and asking again whether I shouldn't take her straight to the hospital. "He'll take me," she said. Meaning Mr. Jensen. I still have the book of poems, but I never saw that jacket again.

Hannah bought me a new one: navy blue suede, luxurious. She bought things for all of us.

Alice: suede jacket, Appalachian loveseat for the backyard, a green parakeet, a fine leather edition of *Portrait of a Lady*, and an elegant little derringer.

Richard: new tortoise shell glasses, meal coupons from the university cafeteria, (good for three meals a day for a year), a beautiful leather belt, and a bowie knife.

Darrell: a blue cardigan sweater (cashmere), five cases of Wild Turkey, and a Korean saber.

Eric: the *Oxford English Dictionary*, four flannel shirts (Pendletons), a haircut, new glasses (wire-rimmed bifocals that made his eyes too big), a rope, a revolver, a candlestick, and a wrench—joke presents, she called the last of these. And we all laughed as if we got the joke.

This bounty, this booty, came later, after we'd rallied round her rape case and seemed to be in no position to refuse her gratitude. And, though none of us ever said so out loud, we liked having a rich and generous and frivolous friend. True, Eric did not appear to like it—in his colorful new shirts he was as reticent and awkward as ever. But he wore them. I remember wanting him not to wear them, to refuse, to be more principled than the rest of us. By which I meant that I wanted him not to be beholden to her. If to anyone, then to me.

But it must have been magical for him—Hannah's attentions, her sexy girlishness, the gifts, the Jensens' big house with the bay windows that looked out upon a lovely half-acre of front yard, a majestic stand of eucalyptus trees, a small pond, a fountain, an enchanting statue of Hermes. Even had I tried, I couldn't possibly compete with all that. Eric must have gone away with Hannah and her husband too charmed, too spellbound to remember the difference between a dream and a nightmare, or to remember that, among his many other responsibilities, Hermes conducted the souls of the dead to Hades.

Another visit from Hannah to our office. One that told me something. I'm not equipped to say what. She was colorfully be-sweatered on a mild November morning, twirling among the heavy desks, passing out copies of a one-act play she'd written, flushed and bedazzling.

"I have a project in the drama class and all of you are going to be in it. Richard, you must play the part of the wounded soldier, and I want you to wear no shirt so that everyone can see the tattoos. Darrell is going to be the old father but not a wise man, okay, Darrell? Darrell is going to wear Bermuda shorts. Alice, you are the army nurse who calls all the soldiers 'my son' but they are not your sons because you are a barren woman. Your white uniform will be bloody but not once a mess. Eric is going to play a crazy soldier who wears the straight-jacket. Everybody memorize your parts. Tomorrow at lunchtime you must meet me in the theater and do all of your lines, okay?"

Then she was gone.

Richard said, "I like the 'my son' part."

Eric said, "Me too, Alice."

Richard said, "The pathos of it suits you."

I said, "Go to hell."

Darrell said, "We're actually going to do this, aren't we?"

I said, "I think we're going to do whatever she wants us to do."

Alice as Army Nurse, Spinster Lady. I don't suppose I need to mention that, though I'm no actress, I played my role quite well. We all did. You could say the roles were made to order.

I would like to believe that I am not alone in having entered my twenties as if I owned the place. Chin up. Shoulders capable and comfortably squared. No more adolescent anguish, no ominous middle-aged aches. For a few wondrous years, the world is your oyster, as they used to say. You are poised and deliberate, a high-diving, decision-making grown-up who keeps a sharpened pencil tucked over her ear and who does not hesitate to make eye contact with important people. You express smart views on several topics. It may be that you don't laugh much, or not loudly, but you know what you're doing, where you're going, and why.

But chances are good that it's during precisely this time that you make some lasting mistakes.

More than once, before there was a Hannah, I daydreamed a marriage between Alice Clark and Eric Langland.

In the evenings, after dinner, they would sit in soft reclining chairs—across from each other, no heads in laps, no stockinged feet entwined—and read the books they had to read for the classes they were teaching, for the articles they were writing. This would be a shared pleasure, this dedication, this scholarly quiet. They would speak lovingly to each other but would let the words on the pages of their books lead the passionate, the turmoiled lives. They would not hear any urgent needs in the sounds they emitted when they made love, which would not be often, but often enough. They wouldn't get mad at each other, not even a little. On Sunday mornings, before breakfast, they would have their coffee and oranges in the sunny garden. There would be order and serenity, a sense of relief, no clutter, no hastily-prepared meals, no children to pick up from piano lessons. When they had saved enough money to take a trip to London, they would arrange to go with a college tour group—no chance, that way, of getting lost.

Once there was a Hannah in our midst, there was haste, risk, turmoil, and getting lost all over the place. Imagine it: me doing cartwheels, at night, on the private golf course, trespassing. I didn't do them very well, but I tried. I must have looked like one of those young mothers who "relate" to their children by being as silly as they are.

There was no gap, as far as I knew, until she filled it. There was no desire to be petite and perky, to slide in dewy grass at night, to wiggle my bottom and horse around, to break the law. To be, that is, someone whose daydream of a marriage to Eric Langland might have included chairs moved out of the way, books awry, clothing in small heaps in the kitchen, the living room, the den, maybe fifteen minutes of slow-dancing naked in front of the fire before we'd have to go into the bedroom, and the next morning the first thing I would hear would be Eric in the kitchen, frying bacon, singing "Down by the Salley Gardens," badly, loudly.

One of my former students, who worked for the campus newspaper, took this photograph: Eric, Hannah, and I are the subjects. We are sitting on a bench—this would have been on the walkway in front of the building where our cramped office was located. And it would have been unusual for Eric to be there, outside, pausing in the sun, not reading at his desk. But Hannah asked him to sit with us for a minute, and he did.

Eric is between us, leaning forward, resting his forearms against his thighs, looking at the ground. I am in profile, looking away from him, looking into the wind, out of the picture. Hannah's face is tilted upward, her eyes are closed, her mouth is open. She seems to be saying something, or singing, to no one in particular.

Though our hands do not make the message explicit, we reminded the photographer of those monkeys who warn children against consorting with the devil. Hence the title he wrote on the back: See No Evil, Hear No Evil, Speak No Evil.

When he gave me this photo, which he pronounced "hilarious," I mentioned that children acquainted with the drawing of the three monkeys figure out pretty quickly that the monkey called See No Evil is not prevented from hearing it, speaking it. Same goes for the other two.

"Cool," he said.

These photographs I've mentioned were taken thirty-some years ago, in 1965. That's not an excuse or an explanation. But at the moment I think it matters.

True, things were about to get a lot worse. But for a while, in 1965, it seemed that we were going to be all right. We would, after all, recuperate from the assassination of the president. Nothing like that would ever happen again, not here, not to us. The signs were good, and we took note of them.

We took note, in 1965, when Sandy Koufax pitched a perfect game. And we couldn't seem to get enough of *The Red Skelton Hour* and *Bonanza* on the television. Uncomplicated laughs, undemanding heroics, that sort of thing. Michael Landon on his pinto, and those sideburns of his. America seemed to have everything to do with the

West and its wide-open promises. It was hard not to notice that the good guys were coming out ahead all over the place. Things were going to be all right.

People of all ages, as I recall, were unusually tuneful. The hills, the department stores, the playgrounds, the living rooms and dens—everyplace was alive with *The Sound of Music.* Many were innocent enough to adopt as a kind of anthem the words to Barbra Streisand's "People." On the radio, Dusty Springfield was singing "what the world needs now is love, sweet love." Sweet love, that's all we needed. That and loose, filmy clothes and more than a little pot. Ginsberg gave us flower power. Peace of mind was presumed to be there for the taking, if you were young enough, free enough, careless enough, and of course white.

A major sticking point. It was in 1965 that Martin Luther King and the freedom marchers were attacked in Alabama, and there were deadly riots in Watts. Malcolm X was murdered. And they started to send the troops to Vietnam, to give us the body count. But we were going to be all right. One government official—wasn't it Rostow?—assured us that the Vietcong would collapse within weeks. Of course they would. We knew what to do. The perfect game was possible. We believed in things, in dreaming the impossible dream, in almost everything, at least out loud.

Back in 1965, Riverside, California was still an agricultural town, a place of fortune-making orange groves, semi-Spanish architecture, and conservative politics. Our black, white, and Mexican neighborhoods were for the most part tidily segregated, and no one was making any audible noise about it. The university my friends and I attended was not a hotbed of anything. We paid some attention to what was happening in Haight-Ashbury, in Selma, in Watts—but not much. The guys, my friends, would not be drafted—grad school deferment for Richard, "four-eyes" status for Eric, too-old for Darrell (besides, he'd already served, and apparently not so brilliantly that the army was dying to have him re-enlist).

Our lives back then, like those of our neighbors and most of our classmates, were mainly small, domestic, secretive, and polite. We would talk, discreetly, among ourselves, but there was no notion that talk per se was valuable. There were no daytime confessional talk-shows, no cantankerous talk-radio. No one went to therapists—and certainly didn't talk about it if they did. Self-help was not a word anyone used. There was no rape crisis center, no shelter for battered women, no mention of abuse. No one was keeping track of victims of violent crime. No one was going public.

In 1965, in Riverside, we smoked serious cigarettes and drank hard liquor and didn't ask many questions. There were probably plenty of bad marriages, but people got sunburned more often than they got divorced. We were proud of our bomb shelters and our sexy starlets. Those of us who were too old for flower power, like myself, were inclined to believe in old-fashioned fire power—and that the enemy was identifiable, beatable, and, as they say these days, *other*. There, then, it was virtually unthinkable that the enemy could have your eyes, speak your language, smoke your brand, wear your boots.

In my next life I will raise a pasture full of sheep. There will be sheep-dogs everywhere. My puppies will be numerous. My hair will be short. My boots will be well-used. My lovers will love me. They will give me a baby or two. I will call myself Sheila.

I'm getting beyond myself. Thinking about the sixties, and about Sheila Kaplan.

She was already on the faculty at the community college when I got a job there—probably thanks to her, since she was the only member of the hiring committee who seemed to have read my work on Rossetti. And it didn't hurt that I had a Ph.D.—only two of us had one, I heard, of the twenty or so who applied for the job. My life might have been significantly different had I applied for a university position somewhere else, put myself on the "fast track," as they call it. There were good jobs then, all over the place. But I was in no frame of mind to leave Riverside. It was hard enough in those days for me to get out of bed, and I didn't want to angle for a position at the UC campus, my alma mater, where too many things had ended badly. But in the fall of 1967, there was an opening at the community college, and there was the fabulous Sheila in my corner.

She was a teacher of women writers long before it was the thing to do. A Jewish cowgirl who spoke Spanish with ease (much better than I do) and a minister of some sixties sort who presided at her students' weddings with a garland of orchids in her curly dark hair and a pack of Marlboros in the pocket of her long white robe. Sheila managed to get her two children grown and still smiling. She got her ex-husband smilingly remarried, if not grown. She's long gone now, went into the Peace Corps and never came back.

Did Hannah Jensen somehow prepare me for Sheila Kaplan? I'd prefer not to think so. Sheila's daring was all style and compassion. Hannah's was something else—unpredictable, hungry, kid-like. The common denominator here, it seems, is me. Would that I knew what to make of that.

Ah, there it is: Sheila prepared me for David. For Barbara. For Bunny. For Utah and Cheyenne and Omaha. For Vermont.

She will hoot with surprise when she learns what I've been up to. The Alice Clark she knew tended to spend her vacation time in her office, tutoring the football players and the unfortunate young women who doted on them, inventing serious obligations, always coming up with some reason not to accompany Sheila on any of her "head-clearing" sojourns. I think I was afraid that I'd wind up with her atop some too peaceful, too multicolored plateau, smoking marijuana or biting into peyote, clearing my head and then letting the knot in my throat unravel and unravel.

It's too late to tell that good woman everything now, in a letter. Especially since that "everything" is up in the air, like a meteorite waiting to be named, to have its trajectory calculated, its aim determined and—at least roughly—forecast. It will be surprise enough for Sheila to learn that I hit the road. And that, for a while, in my forties, had a lover.

Even I'm surprised that I haven't all this time been the chaste old-fangled lady behind whose back my students used to snicker. I have had some small measure of intimate companionship among the living. Nothing lurid. Nothing you could call bold or contemporary. Improper, definitely illicit, but decent, circumscribed. We kept the affair a delicious sliver, a small piece of the big pie that was his wife and family.

I met David MacLean at a lecture he delivered at the university campus in the fall of 1974. I was then on the brink of turning forty. He was well on the way to fifty. He was handsome in the same way that I suppose I am: which is to say, I'm no knock-out, though David once said that I reminded him of "the older" Ingrid Bergman. (Dream on, Alice.) I said that he reminded me of Santa Claus, a tall Saint Nick without the beard, without the belly, without the hat and the white hair and the red suit. He said, "Do I get to keep the 'ho, ho, ho?'" He would not have been David MacLean without it.

We were occasional lovers for a half dozen years. Passionate, dare I say, but never reckless. No public appearances together, and no back-breaking regrets. David was a godsend. He kept me in my body and out of my dreams, whenever he was around.

He lived then in San Francisco, a chaired professor of Renaissance poetry at Berkeley, much in demand, badly but thoroughly married, and considerably childrened. From the beginning we agreed—the choice was clear—not to fret over what was not to be, to enjoy the few times a year we had together, and to be indiscreet only behind the closed doors of my Riverside house. We talked little of the past, never about the future. We talked instead about our students, our colleagues, what books we were reading. We stayed in bed. We massaged and made love and took turns reading each other to sleep. I told him the thoughts my body had when we were apart, which was most of the time.

Eric's name came up once. Other than the one time, I managed to avoid all references to that particular chapter of my history. I must have known that I'd hear myself speaking about unfinished business, about dreams that turned desire into guilt, about suspicions that I had no words for. The very things I was doing my damnedest to keep stuffed away.

I'm reminded that, as a child, I was terrified by the jack-in-the-box. That first time, winding it up, not knowing that while the music played something else was happening, an ugly, worm-like clown was secretly uncoiling, getting ready to snap the lid open. *Pop!* I screamed and stuffed the thing back in its tin box and then wished that I hadn't touched it. For days I was certain that it would pop back out, all on its own. There was no question of giving it to somebody else: who would want such a thing? So finally I threw it away. And when I did, it snapped open. *Pop!* Even after all this time I can't find a smidgen of humor in that.

David: he could have.

He had big, beautiful feet, arched as if they could easily slip into a pair of huge high heels. But his toes told a different story. They were curled forward a bit at the knuckle. And the two smallest toes on each foot were folded in toward the middle one: imagine a poker hand, and you've snuggled your two deuces just behind your three nines, so that it might seem you were banking on only three cards. That's how David's toes were aligned. He was a child of the Dust Bowl, an Okie who, as a schoolboy, outgrew his only pair of shoes long before they could be replaced. A pitiful tale? Not to him. "I was too doggone prideful to go barefoot," he told me.

He took a new job years ago and moved to Atlanta. It didn't take long for our loving letters to become newsy, then chatty, then mere announcements—another daughter married, that sort of thing.

When I was a young girl, my mother took me once or twice to Knott's Berry Farm in Anaheim. I'd like to think it was merely a coincidence that my favorite activity there was panning for fool's gold. But probably not. I've kept it up, in one way or another, haven't I?

SEVEN

I LEFT LAS VEGAS cheered by Barbara's "blah-blah-blah," but not what you would call in good humor. The guidebooks convinced me, against their wishes, to make no side-trips, at least not yet. No tour of the Grand Canyon, whose "sheer immensity" I was in no mood to "feel." No afternoon in the "fairyland of red rocks," Sedona, where there are said to be "energy fields" which "humans with exactly the right attitude can tap into." Exactly the right attitude? Yipes. I wasn't up for finding one of those out of the blue. And, though it wasn't far from Las Vegas, I decided to skip the famous fifteen-mile gorge that takes you into the heart of Zion. The photos in the guidebooks, the descriptions, not to mention the plain-old lore told me I'd best not go there, best not listen to the ancient spirits that are said to reside in that part of the canyon, in those eerie, shouted-from-below bursts of rock, lest I hear them calling out everyone's name but mine. I suppose I was a little too attuned to my aloneness, hadn't had time yet to make the move from there to a comfortable solitude. Be that as it may, the voices of the ancients were out of the question.

As was the town of Beaver, Utah, which would have been an easy, en-route stop from Las Vegas. There is said to be an old courthouse in Beaver—now a museum—with a "must-see dungeon" of a jail and, in the park next to the courthouse, a statue of "the father of television." True, I was taken by this particular juxtaposition, but the father of television, Philo Farnsworth, shares Darrell's family name. I had no reason to assume that they were related, but I wasn't up for coming upon any ghostly resemblances.

So I set my sights on Piute County, and a B&B in the small town of Aurora, from where I could easily, next morning, get onto an interstate that would take me into Denver. I picked that B&B because I could get there in under five hours and there was nothing much to the listing in one of my guidebooks: four "modern" rooms, private baths, country breakfast, sixty-five dollars a night. A quiet place, I presumed—nothing there to attract child-laden families, a passel of jacuzzi-lovers, or a jeepful of new-age tourists.

Go ahead. Call me a grouch.

With more or less immunity, I think, you get to be grouchy when you become a person of a certain age. Which is to say, you get to grumble, fume, and fuss about things that you might have shrugged off a decade ago. It's a good idea to carry it off with at least an ounce of visible and audible grace, but in general, once you've reached a certain age, it seems quite all right if you slide into untempered curmudgeonliness now and then. You've earned it. You get to be grouchy, for instance, about the fact that cigarettes turned out to be poisonous. And that other people's hair doesn't thin out, even though they're twenty years older than you are—and you're *old*. When you become a person of a certain age, you discover that there are all sorts of things that have long since warranted cantankerousness. Like the food you get in restaurants that offer "all you can eat," and the watery drinks you're poured in bars during the "two-for-one happy hour"—not to mention hotels that advertise "children and pets welcome," and all sites or sights that are supposed to change your life, and about which you are expected to utter a drawn out Oh or Ah.

No thank you.

On the other hand (a phrase that doesn't always sit well with grouches, who want to be plain right, to see things one way, but I'm forced to use it time and again), that B&B in Aurora was a mistake. I'm tempted to call it a haunted house. The thing is, I wouldn't be able to swear that I had no part whatsoever in haunting it.

Yes, it was quiet all right. No children or pets in the vicinity. Indeed, when I arrived in the early evening, there was no one there—just a tidily handwritten note on the front screen door that read:

We do not accept credit cards.
If you intend to be a registered guest, enter.
If you do not intend to be a registered guest,
do not enter.

I reviewed my intentions. And while I was reviewing them, I got back into the car and drove a few blocks until I came to a small grocery store, where I found some white cheddar cheese, some surprisingly fresh French bread, three lovely plums, and a very good "black market" bottle of Merlot. Black market because I was in Utah, and I was at a store where they are not supposed to sell the stuff.

The lady at the counter, a woman my age or more (definitely more, I discovered) had the velvety face of a light pink rose, half open, at its most exquisite moment. The rest of her, I guessed, was all stem and thorns: her hands were skeletal, her elbows poked like kindling from beneath a glittery black shawl. Her white hair was pulled back into a tight bun. She looked at my bread and my cheese and took a drag from a thin brown cigarette, momentarily filling the space between us with a delicious-smelling smoke.

"I know you," she said. Her dark eyes, framed by artistically-rendered eyebrows that looked like the arched wings of a blackbird coming in for a landing, were as clear as they were weary.

"We've never met," I told her. "This is my first time in Utah. You must be mistaking me—"

"That's not what I mean." She took another drag and then she talked, as if she had no choice, as if her talking and my listening were expected of us, as if I'd come in not for groceries but for her story, for some small glimpse of my own. Now and then she paused on behalf of her elegant cigarette, but not for long.

"Before the war, the second one," she said, "I went to Provence. My father, Paul, he was rich that year, just that one year in his whole life. He rented a house for a month and took the whole family—me, my two younger sisters, Elaine and Sara, and our baby brother. PJ, we called him. For Paul Jr.

"Me, I was twelve then, more ripe than these plums. And there was my mother, of course. The whole thing was for her. Her name was Antoinette. She was French and she was beautiful, like her name. They used to say I have her eyes. But nothing else.

"We swam and fished, all of us, every day in a pond not far from the house. There were always flowers, wherever we looked. And there were shady trees in neat rows. You have not been there, I know that."

"Yes," I said. "That is, no, I haven't. I've never been there."

She went on as if I had not spoken.

"Nearby there was a boy I liked. He knew how to look at a girl and how to catch fish. We all ate so well there—bread, cheese, fruits, rabbits, ducks, sweets of all kinds, and the fish he caught. I liked the food almost as much as I liked the boy.

"The villagers, they rarely spoke to us, the children. But they seemed to adore him, my father. Cowboy, they called him. Monsieur Utah. They loved the smile he always smiled.

"My father was a happy man there every day, until the end. I was almost never happy, because I liked this boy. But later I found out that that was a kind of happiness, liking him so much. So much I didn't want to do anything else."

She was looking right at me, nodding her head to some slow rhythm, some music I couldn't hear. She waited for me to return the nod before she went on, as if we were in fact having a conversation, or were playing our separate but convergent parts in the same melancholy duet.

"My father, he changed at the end because she didn't come home with us. My mother, I mean. She refused, then disappeared. No more Antoinette. No more wife. No more mother. My father, he shrank after that. He got old in a week and walked with a cane. He told people here at home that he'd had an accident. I ran the business for him—boats for hire, out on Fish Lake.

"When I was seventeen I married a fisherman. He knew some French words. *Mon cher. Mon amour. Bouillabaisse.* He was from New Orleans. And he was a kind man. Like my father.

"Some women are glad for men who are kind to them, some are not. Me, after all this time, I still don't know which one of these I am. But more and more things begin to matter very little. Fresh flowers matter. Good cigarettes matter. Good bread, good cheese, good wine. They matter. But my customers in this village, they want soda pop and beef jerky. I stay only because I know how to. You understand what I am telling you."

"Yes."

"My two sisters and my brother left this place a long time ago. PJ, he worked in the stockyards in Chicago, then went to France to find our mother. But he never did. Instead, he took too much heroin and died. Elaine and Sara went to California as soon as they grew up and became pretty enough to live in such a place. They kept in touch with me for a while, then stopped. So that is all over. I have this store to run."

She put on a pair of reading glasses and began to ring up my purchases. Just like that, I was back to being a customer.

"I should tell you that the plums," she said, "I picked them out myself, yesterday, from the farmers' market in Provo. And I could sell you a good bottle of wine if you promise not to tell."

"Of course."

When she returned with the wine, I asked if I might try one of her cigarettes.

"They are sweet, like cigars," she warned me. "And strong." She moved the ashtray so that we could share it. "Where are you staying?" she asked as she wrapped up my things and set them into a paper bag as if each item were an egg.

"A place called Logan's B&B."

"Logan's?"

"Any reason why I shouldn't?"

"Did you hear of it from someone?"

"I picked it out of the guidebook."

"Some might say that Logan's picked *you.* But I am not saying that. Are you staying there for any length of time?"

"I'm on my way to Denver in the morning."

"May I ask whether you are in any particular distress that I do not already know about?"

"No. I don't think so." How else to answer such a question?

"You will be all right then," she told me.

"Is there something I ought to know before I lug my suitcase up the stairs?"

"Don't expect to see anyone. In the morning, he makes the breakfast. Bobby Logan, the son."

"Does he run the place?"

"In a manner of speaking." She bent down then and reached for something under the counter. Her shawl slipped to one side, and I could see that all the hard-to-reach buttons of her housedress were unbuttoned. Another woman on her own.

I was imagining that Bobby Logan was perhaps a late-century Boo Radley—recovered and public enough to be an innkeeper but nevertheless utterly private, as shy as they come, goodhearted but anxiety-producing, you know the story—when the lady at the counter handed me a business card.

"My husband had these made up. Last year, a few months before he finally died. He was proud of my store. But I say, I've known better. A long time ago. You know what I mean. My telephone number is on that card. Should you need anything." She then dropped into my paper bag, for free, a corkscrew I still use now and then.

Marie Nicole Lamarque, the card said. Proprietress of *Le Corner Store,* Aurora, Utah.

What I needed, as it happened, was not the kind of thing that you request of a stranger—even though in this case the stranger, Marie Lamarque, was somehow pre-acquainted with the likes of yours truly. I suspect that she knew what I'd find myself needing in the middle of the night at Logan's B&B: someone I would never see, never meet, who would help me to go on living.

As she predicted, I saw no one when I entered the large wooden house. But I heard the cello. An instrument I knew well: for classical music, the cello was one of my mother's favorites, especially as it heartbreaks its way through Rachmaninoff's concerto for cello and piano. What I was hearing—just barely at first, as if the source were tucked away in some remote corner of the house—was not a piece of music I recognized. So I paid attention, or thought I did, to other things.

There were elegant lights on here and there, and a pleasant scent, as if a woman going out for a gala evening had recently passed through the foyer. The furnishings were faux-antique, polished, made-in-America, perfectly situated. Not costly, but emphatically tasteful. And there were several paintings on the walls—a local artist's landscapes, I presumed—that depicted the immediate surroundings: woods and water, water and woods, all lightly awash, drenched in something that didn't seem to be fog. Right in front of me was a reception desk, an open registration book and plumed pen, a large vase filled with black-eyed Susans, and another note, in the same neat handwriting.

> Sign in. Choose one of the upstairs rooms.
> Number Two is already occupied.
> Breakfast is served at eight in the downstairs dining room.

I took my suitcase and my groceries straight to Number Four, at the end of the hallway. I was relieved to find as I went down the hall that the music was not coming from Number Two. Still, it was coming from somewhere, that relentless lament.

It was close to nine o'clock by the time I began unpacking my sorry nightclothes. What was called for in that room was satin—preferably white.

In room Number Four there was a ruffled white bedspread on the bed, and ruffled white pillows, no doubt stuffed with the feathers of white geese or swans. There was a white, satiny easy chair, and a glossy armoire whose handles and knobs were mother-of-pearl. On the small desk, near the window, there was a pewter vase filled with fragrant white peonies. Take my word for it: Room Number Four looked like the bedroom of a bride-to-be.

There was a shower but no tub, so I sat cross-legged on the yellow and white tiles and pretended that the hot shower was a waterfall. Even then, I could hear the cello. It seemed to be part of the waterfall, coming down all over and into me, and it remained there as I dressed for bed, ate a little, drank a glass of that good red wine, and tried to read one of the guidebooks. But I couldn't, and I couldn't turn on the small television.

I could do nothing but listen. It was as if there was no space, not an inch in my head for anything—no memories, no fretting, no images whatsoever—but the grieving of that music. Somewhere in that house, someone was playing that cello as if every note were about something lost, and a prophecy of all the losses yet to come, not just his or hers or mine, but everyone's. It put me into a state I do not wish to revisit, ever.

I'd been listening for an hour, maybe more, when, like a hypnotic, I got up from the four-poster bed and opened the door of my room. I had only one thought: I had to go there. I had to find the cellist and lie down next to the instrument, close enough to drown within that music, to fill myself up with it, to let go of everything else. For the first time, and with no second thoughts, no fear, no hesitation, nothing in my mind but going to wherever that music was, I wanted oblivion.

I was halfway down the hall when I heard the occupant of Number Two weeping. A weeping man, crying steadily—an intake of breath, then a sob, over and over. I listened outside his door long enough to know that his was no sudden burst of tears that would soon cease. It was as if he were as full as a bay at high tide, the sounds of his sorrow at the mercy of an unhurried moon.

It wouldn't be true to say that at his door I suddenly snapped out of it and came to my senses. But he stopped me, the weeping man in Number Two. What I remember is that it seemed to me dishonorable to ignore the living sadness he was unwittingly sharing. Though I was headed toward oblivion, he wouldn't let me in the meantime be oblivious.

I went back to my room but didn't weep, not until the cellist finally let that lament reach an inconclusive end. Everything that had been unbearable about the music, including the weeping man, was more unbearable when there was only silence, when I was myself again, but stuffed to bursting with regret. For all the times I told someone that I wasn't lonely. For all the choices that insured I would stay that way. For giving myself no abiding companion, no children. For letting myself believe that I trusted the Jensens with Eric. For acquiescing, shushing my suspicions, kowtowing to good manners, letting the years go by, letting them have him, take him away. I should have spoken up. I should have dropped everything and followed him. Period.

Sometime just before I woke up, I dreamed about us—but the "us" was not consistent. First it was David MacLean—who rarely appears in my dreams as so vividly himself, who is usually a fluorescent outline I recognize as David by his smell. In my dream that night he was photogenic and tall and delightful. We were in a flower-crowded hospital room, laughing. In the dream, he was talking like a cowboy, saying things like "yippee-ki-yay" and "hot-diggedy-dog." He was standing there next to the bed I was in, my hair all undone, a mess of almost-gray on the pillow. It seemed that I was having a baby. A girl baby he wanted to name Loretta. And that was fine with me.

David was still cutting up when the dream changed. I was connected to machines and lying on a gurney, not waving but drowning, and Eric was there, behind me, wearing those hateful new glasses that Hannah had bought for him, which made his eyes as big as walnuts. He was pushing the gurney as fast as he could, nightmare fast. He was telling me to live, but in the dream I couldn't breathe, I was in too deep. I seemed to be dying. He seemed to be already dead, so terribly pale and thin.

I heard the music, the mournful cello, that hypnotic dirge. I was sure that it was about to make me break apart in such a way that I would overhear the breaking, bone by bone, sinew by sinew. Turn off the music, I said in the dream, turn it off, put cotton in my ears, do something about that music. I asked him again and again, but he couldn't hear me.

Then I was moving over, making room, moving all those tubes and wires or whatever they were so that he could lie with me and hear my voice, but after he lay down he wasn't beside me anymore. Somebody else was. It was Mr. Jensen. I didn't see his face but it was certainly his whisper, no one else's, right there, whispering in my ear: "Alice is just fine, aren't you, Alice?" And then he said, "It's a girl."

Sheila told me once that all the people in my dreams are manifestations of me, anxious or hopeful images that emanate from the underbelly of my plain old self. At the time, I guffawed with gusto at her silliness, her psycho-babble. They're *them*, I insisted. That's the whole point. No, she said, the whole point is that everyone is you.

Sheila's take on the matter does not offer, it seems to me, any consolation or clarity.

At breakfast, I was alone in the Logans' airy, sunlit dining room. In heated serving dishes there were well-cooked sausages and bacon, scrambled eggs, crisp pancakes, fresh-baked rolls and cinnamon toast. There was orange juice and tomato juice in bright pitchers on the table, and another armload of fresh-cut black-eyed Susans. The coffee service was silver. Everything was perfect. And so all the more odd. There was enough food for at least half a dozen people, but the table was set for only one: me, apparently.

There was no sign of the man who had been weeping in Number Two. Could he have been Bobby Logan? I don't know. That would make him a very different Boo Radley from the one I'd imagined him to be.

I took a cup of coffee and one of the rolls to the place setting at the head of the table. There was a note leaning against the juice glass:

> The charge for one night is sixty-five dollars.
> Leave your payment under the paperweight on the front desk.
> If you do not intend to return for another night,
> draw a line through your name in the registration book.

After breakfast, while I was doing just that, leaving my payment and crossing myself off the list, I smelled it—the sweet, luxurious scent of one of those thin, brown cigarettes. No mistake about it.

EIGHT

If I'd had a real love affair before I met Hannah Jensen, would anything have been different? Would I have been able to see things, sense things, I didn't see, didn't sense? Would my imagination have been able to tell me something I should have known? Would I have been able to do something, to be close enough to intervene? Should I have? I don't know.

I do know that should-haves are my constant companions, as diligent as flies on old meat. What they do with the past, that sticky nibbling, is one thing—you get used to it, you tell yourself it happens to everyone after a while. What I'm not used to is the way the old should-haves make me edgy about the should-haves to come.

And now that I share guardianship with Bunny's father, now that he has sent her to me, the should-haves are more noisy than ever.

A couple of days ago, Bunny sat at the kitchen table after school while I rummaged for snacks. She sat without speaking, without fussing at her braids. Something was wrong. She was wearing one of those t-shirts whose slogan is "Just Do It." I put some crackers and some black olives on the table.

I should have suggested that we go shopping.

We were both quiet for a while. I was having a private and unfriendly conversation with the father or the father's girlfriend who mailed her that t-shirt. Bunny, as it turned out, was thinking not unrelated thoughts.

She finally spoke up. "Being a girl is hard, isn't it, Alice?"

I should have given her a simple yes.

Instead, I answered her question with a question—that typical, teacherly, evasive tactic. "It's not hard all the time, is it?"

"Almost," she told me. "Not right now."

"Only sometimes?"

"I said *almost* all the time."

"That you did." I should have been listening.

"I have to watch out all the time. Almost." She was sticking her fingertips into the pitted olives, absently, it seemed, more out of habit than mischief.

Should I have asked "watch out for what?" I suppose I didn't want to know how much she knew about how much there is to watch out for. I didn't want to frighten her by saying that I, for one, wanted her to watch out for everything, all the time, no complaining, just vigilance. So I took a step toward changing the subject.

I quoted Shakespeare: "'For some must watch, while some must sleep; Thus runs the world away.'"

Bunny drummed her olive-tipped fingers on the table. "If the dang bad guys would just go to sleep, then I wouldn't have to watch all the time."

"They don't go to sleep."

"That's what I've been trying to tell you!" She laughed then—happy with the reversal of roles, with being able to express exasperation. She began to eat those olives, one by one. And I let myself pray that I would last long enough to have another go at this talk, when she was older, habitually watchful, content with being a girl, and still safe.

The bad guys don't go to sleep.

I didn't think back then, when we were graduate students, to say that to Hannah Jensen. Nor did I always remember to have my car keys in hand when I walked through a nighttime parking lot, the way I do now.

Alice and Hannah: one beginning of our story occurred when I first met her, became her guide, her tutor, her big sister. Self-appointed president of the fan club. And she my passport to playfulness, to whimsy, to risk.

Another kind of beginning occurred after I had known her for about four months, and she brought herself to my house one night, just before the Christmas break.

It was close to ten o'clock, which I remember because I was meaning to watch the news, to catch a story about Timothy Leary.

I heard the pounding on the front door. Hannah pounding, not using the doorbell, calling me. Alice! Alice! Wake up! I must have called out something—I'm awake! I'm coming!—as I rushed to the door, fumbled with the chain lock, then took a look at her. That's how it went. There was no falling into my arms, no tearful collapse—none of the things the novels and the news had taught me to expect under such circumstances. She stood there and presented herself, as if to say, *Look*.

And so I looked. At the red bruise on her left cheek, close to her eye, and at the small blistery burn marks elsewhere on her face, three or four of them. I looked at her puffy lower lip, her unponytailed, matted hair, the dirt on her t-shirt, more burn marks on her arms, the soiled slacks, the busted zipper.

While I was looking, she laughed, a small quick laugh that told me she was in shock. I went to her, afraid to touch her for some reason, but touching her nevertheless, taking one elbow into my hand, leading her to the couch, saying things like: What happened? Who did this to you?

I remember that I went back to the door, re-locked it—locked us in, them out, whoever they were. I remember bringing her a glass of water, a steamy washcloth, ointment for the burns. I remember a stomachful of questions and dread. I remember everything.

"What happened?"

"I came to your house because it was near."

"Near to what? To where? The university?"

"Yes."

"How did this happen?"

"In the field there, for sports."

"Someone did all this to you in the football stadium?"

"I think so. I was at the library. Then I was leaving."

"Did you walk here?"

"Yes. Afterwards. I left my car—"

"After what? What happened?"

"He grabbed me."

"Did he take you to the football field?"

"He put me into his car and drove to the football field."

"What did he look like?"

"Look like?"

"You don't remember?"

"Like a cowboy, I think. There were boots and there was a bad smell."

"And he did all this to you?"

"He burned me with cigarettes. He slapped me here on my face. He bit my mouth. He raped me. Then he left."

"I'll call the police."

"No. Please. Will you take me home to my husband?"

"We have to report this. They'll find him and make him go to jail. That's how it works here."

"I want to smoke one of your cigarettes."

"Help yourself. You have to tell the police what happened."

"I don't know what happened."

"You just told me. You tell them everything. The whole story."

There are some things about my dear Riverside house that I miss. The well-shaded, concrete front porch that I'd kept painted a dark green. The small brick fireplace with its elaborate mantelpiece. The covered patio in the backyard, draped year-round with dark pink bougainvillea. The light that filtered through the flowers in the window box and lay like an heirloom tablecloth on the kitchen floor. The breakfast nook, a cushioned alcove, more cozy than this big kitchen/living room where I'm sitting now. Things stayed the same in that old house. The couch was where it had always been, the faded chairs, the bookcases, the pictures on the walls, the old Persian rugs. I miss the smell of the willowy pepper tree and the eucalyptus.

But that house became in some sense the scene of a crime. The kind that is a deed without a name—neither evil nor innocent. Greater than a mistake, less than a malfeasance. Not subject to civil or criminal law. And I'm the one who committed it.

I did not call the police that night. I called Eric Langland, brought him into it. My dear Eric. And he never got out.

"I'll drive you home," I said to Hannah.

"Call your friend Eric. He can drive us. He can bring you back here."

I didn't stop to think. I called him, asked him to come over. It was an emergency. "It has to do with Hannah." He was there in no time.

I met him outside on the front porch in order to explain, to give him a chance to take it in before he saw her, before his imagination began to work on those burns, the busted pants.

I thanked him for coming, for being the friend I could call. He didn't say a word through any of this: the explanation, the description of Hannah's condition, the repeated thank yous. He looked the way he does in the photograph that Hannah took: I'm here but I'm not here. I'm doing what you asked but I'm not comfortable. I'm your friend but I'm not my own.

Finally he asked me what I wanted him to do. I said that I was going to take her home, that I would like him to go with us, that I didn't know her husband. I did not want to go there by myself, or come back to this house alone. He offered to follow us in the car he had borrowed, then see me home.

But Eric was still there, at the Jensen house, when I left. I got Eric into it.

Richard Stone got into it all by himself—whatever the hell "it" was. I'm pleading not guilty on that score. At the same time, I'm hearing the words "on the other hand."

On the other hand, I'm the one who brought Hannah into the fold. I handed over the staff, let her be the chief Bo Peep, let her lose the sheep one by one by one. If the rape had not happened, would I have been more jealous, more protective of my little flock? More like a woman, dare I say, than like one of the guys?

I knew that Richard was ardent, poised to take my place as president of the fan club. I didn't know the rest until after the rape, when Richard couldn't stop ranting. I didn't know that the two of them had been meeting for lunch every Monday, Wednesday and Friday for two months or so. Or that Hannah would write down in her notebook his "wisdoms," as she apparently called them. I didn't know that he had revealed to her, and her alone, the meaning of his tattoos. That it had gotten to the point where he had to declare that their relationship was "strictly platonic."

I saw him the day after it happened. It was late. I'd been with Hannah all afternoon, then went by the office at the university in order to gather some papers. Richard was there, moving back and forth like a tiger in too small a cage. I didn't have to give him the news.

Richard Stone, son of missionaries, born on Easter Island, our guru, our lotus-eater, our hug-giving glue, our resident pacifist who had never uttered a curse in my presence, wanted to kill the guy ASAP, if not sooner.

"Boots? Cowboy boots? That's no goddamn help. Who doesn't wear boots in this town? But I'll find the bastard. Tell me the rest, Alice, tell me everything, not about her, about him. What does he look like? Is she all right? I need something to go on. Are the cops going to come up with a composite? I'll find the son of a whore and I'll kill him. Consider it done. Consider him dead and buried in a damp and shallow grave in the midst of hungry vultures. How is she? I'm telling you, Alice, somebody will fucking pay for this. He is going to eat those boots before he dies. One at a time, heel first. I will deliver him to the princess for the final blows. Is she all right?"

It was as if he'd been gathered into a dangerous weather system that had no intention of letting him drop easily to earth.

Richard's name appears in Mr. Jensen's diary several times, always linked with Hannah's. I don't mean merely linked, I mean wreathed. The letters form a poesy, a nosegay, two flowers intertwined, elaborated with petals and leaves. The names are sensuous, as extravagantly abloom as peonies in early summertime. On one page there is a round black bee atop Richard's R. On another a tiny winged sprite is swinging from the middle of Hannah's H.

The first time I looked at these pages, I was, for a moment, envious. Why hadn't my name inspired such lovely whimsy, such fragrant allusions to some of the poems of Robert Herrick? But the moment passed. On all of those pages there is a narrow-nosed man-in-the-moon in the upper right-hand corner, looking down at the flowering names and leering.

Cowboy boots. That was the only substantial clue we had to go on.

Standard Riverside wear, as common as jeans and Marlboros.

Darrell's boots were new, polished, a notable combination of black and cream-colored snakeskin. They added two inches to his height.

Eric's boots were worn but not worn out. They were black, etched with elegant steer horns across the middle, just below the pointed toes.

Richard's boots, worn out, almost heel-less, were an auburny brown, modestly etched at the ankles with crescent moons.

Mr. Jensen's boots were red and black, with silver-tipped toes. They were made in Italy. They probably cost more than we were paying for tuition.

My boots were old but in good shape. They were brown and rounded at the toe, not pointy. I didn't wear them often, because they made me even more too tall, but I wore them.

The detective's boots were also snakeskin, milky scales outlined in gray. His were authentic, stained with horse manure. They smelled like a ranch. I was with Hannah when he interviewed her on the afternoon following the rape. Hannah pointed to his boots and said, "They were just like that. Like yours." She smiled at the detective, as if their acquaintance had a history.

"*My* Hannah," according to me, did not lie to me. Not about Eric. Not about anything. Maybe only about the things she couldn't quite remember, like the story of what happened that night.

When I got to the Jensen house on the afternoon after the rape, Eric was not there. Hannah told me that they'd had a late breakfast together. Eric wouldn't look at her, she told me. And he ate too fast, "like a little boy late for school." I wasn't there to learn anything about Eric, I'm sure I told myself. I was there to take Hannah to the police department.

The police asked me questions while Hannah looked at mug shots and composite features. They wanted to know why I was there. Was I a witness? I did not tell them that I had seen Hannah laugh when I opened the door and looked at her battered little body. That momentary laughter was bothering me, but not enough to turn me into an insinuator. Nor did I tell them that as soon as we entered her house she said something to her husband in her native tongue. *Alles ist* something or other. While I answered their questions I also told myself: Mind your own business, Alice. Don't make something out of nothing. So I told the police that I was not a witness to anything, and I thought I was telling the truth.

The night of the rape, Mr. Jensen asked me to help him bring in the drinks. We were alone in the kitchen for a few minutes. I was too shaken to spend even a moment trying to size him up. I came away with only the haziest impression of him, and it was all about his eyes. But I remember clearly the sound of ice going into the glasses, peanuts poured into a small crystal bowl, the words that passed between us.

"Hannah ought to go to the hospital," I said.

"My thought exactly. I must say, I relish such moments of consanguinity. Especially between strangers. It bodes well."

"Consanguinity?"

"We agree."

"Then shouldn't we be—?"

"Taking her to the hospital was my exact thought until I saw that she requires no immediate medical attention."

"How can you be sure, Mr. Jensen?"

"You brought her straight home. I am putting my trust in your judgment."

"Hannah insisted. If I'd had my way—"

"You could have overruled her. You chose not to. Alice did have her way, by letting our Hannah have hers."

"I don't understand." I was putting it mildly, believe me.

He handed me the bowl of peanuts and one of the glasses and said, "Let me answer your next question, which you are now reluctant to ask."

"Yes, do."

"I will of course call the police."

"Good. Thank you."

"Shall we?"

Two days later, a detective showed up at the office on campus. He was polite and apologetic. He said that he wanted to save us the trouble of calling us in to the stationhouse. This wouldn't take long, he said, just a few minutes with each of us, privately. Not including Miss Clark, who'd already given her statement. Eric was first on his list.

Darrell, Richard, and I stepped into the hall.

"Why us?" Darrell said. "*Us* of all people."

"It can't be that they suspect you guys," I said. "None of you looks anything like the drawing."

"The hair is like my hair," said Richard. "'Bushy and unkempt,' according to the description."

"But reddish-brown, like mine," said Darrell.

"And he's got my mouth, right? Come on, you two," I told them, "you're *not* suspects. Have either of you taken a good look at the composite drawing Hannah came up with?"

"I couldn't," Richard said. "I read the description, and even that—"

Darrell put his arm around Richard's shoulders. "They'll find him," he said.

"One of us should have gone with her to the library," Richard said.

Richard looked at me then, reminding me without saying a word about the night, long before any of us knew Hannah, when I ran into him in the library stacks. He noted how late it was, offered to walk out with me when the time came. Later, before I stepped into my car, we kissed and then kept on kissing, long enough to know that that would be the end of it, we wouldn't do it again, we wanted things to stay the way they'd always been.

There in the hallway that day, Richard was looking at me, making me remember. Was he letting me know that nothing was ever going to be the way it had always been? That even our friendship was in question?

Then Eric opened the door and told us that Darrell was next. "It's *them* he's asking about," he said to Darrell. "No sweat."

Darrell went inside.

"The Jensens?" I asked.

Eric said, "He's got nothing."

We waited in silence for Richard's turn. Eric wandered off. He wasn't there, in the hallway, when Darrell came out and Richard went in. He wasn't there when Darrell reported that the detective asked him to look again at the composite drawing, asked him whether it brought anyone to mind. "Richard will have to look," Darrell said. "He's gonna make Richard look at the drawing, make him think about it."

I was sure that the detective was just toying with all of us. But why? I saw the bruises, the burns, Hannah's bloody lip. I know what I saw, for heaven's sake.

You won't be surprised that, despite what I think I know now about who did what to whom, I worry about Bunny. About what she's already learning about telling the truth, about being a girl, about what these have to do with each other should she get into trouble and need someone, some policeman, to believe her.

I've been hurt.

Are you sure?

It's *obvious*!

Not to us.

I'm telling the truth.

Prove it, young lady.

I'm telling the—

There, there. It's only natural for a girl to get confused now and then.

NINE

It was unusually cold on the night that Hannah and I made dinner together and played *Clue* for the last time. I remember her dainty fingers rolling pieces of lemon-juiced chicken in flour and bread crumbs. The diamond ring that would have looked garish even on my long fingers. The white angora sweater that was too big for her and hard not to pet.

This was perhaps three weeks after the rape. We were easy with each other, with our roles as the tall one and the little one, the supporting actress and the star whom everyone was making a fuss over.

Richard was to arrive later, for some dessert and talk and drinks. Hannah had to get home, but she wanted one round of the game first.

We were at the point where one of us had figured out that the special envelope contained cards for the wrench, the kitchen, Colonel Mustard, Miss Scarlet, and the gray-haired maid, Mrs. White, when Richard showed up. Eric was with him, not sullen, but clearly, it seemed to me, dragged along, talked into it. Darrell would have come too, Richard told us, but he'd promised his students an extra session (though the new term had only just begun—this was so like Darrell), and grinders from Delia's, one of the town's most beloved old hangouts.

The guys helped themselves to beer and the rest of the fried chicken. I filled them in on Hannah's clever reinvention of *Clue*. "At last we've got some identifiable victims in this game." Me: showing off a little.

I told a racy story that involved the tidy Mrs. White making a definitive pass at the Colonel. Said Colonel, an aging cad, had come into the kitchen, wrench in hand, muttering about the plumbing but in fact intending to discover what pink riches lay hidden beneath Mrs. White's crisp uniform. Does she put up a fuss? Not a whit. Without any ado, the dear old lady removes her glasses and unbuttons a button. So they are of one mind—delightful! However, the Colonel had only recently bedded Miss Scarlet, who is as pink, in all the right places, as they come. Alas, just as Mrs. White is about to be de-bloused, Miss Scarlet enters the scene, picks up the discarded wrench, and promptly dispatches the secretly sultry Mrs. White.

I wish that I were misremembering my old-fashioned diction. In any case, I thought I'd given Hannah a narrative run for her money. But her version went like this:

"Miss Scarlet looks like a loose one and Mrs. White looks like a tight one. But they are both not happy women. They are in the kitchen being sad together. Quiet and sad. They do not have any words to say what they are sad about. Or maybe they do not want to say those words. Then Colonel Mustard goes in through the door that is always closed so that the guests in the mansion will never see a mess in the kitchen. When he comes in, the women look at him and then they look at each other. They do not like his mustache or his monocle or his eyebrows. They do not like the way he smiles and stands with his chest out. But he does not know this. He says he wants some lunch. He wants a roast beef sandwich. He wants tomatoes, he says, and he does an up-and-down thing with his eyebrows. When sad Mrs. White reaches under the sink for the wrench, Colonel Mustard pats her bottom, and keeps on patting. Then Miss Scarlet says to Mrs. White, I'll hold him for you. Miss Scarlet flexes her muscles, which are big and tan and beautiful, like a young man's. She pins the Colonel's arms behind his back. The Colonel smiles and smiles. Holy smoke, he likes these girls. He doesn't care that Miss Scarlet is holding him—"

You can imagine the tortuous rest, which began with Mrs. White clasping the old man's mustache and lips in the wrench, then yanking.

Hannah looked at me the whole time, as if the others were not there, as if their attentive presence made no difference. I didn't want to play the game with her anymore. I didn't know what the game was anymore.

But at the time I laughed, made light of it. "You wicked little sicko. You win, as usual. How do you dream this stuff up?"

Eric and Richard admonished me that night after Hannah had gone, after they'd seen her to her car. Back and forth they went, all but wagging their fingers at me. Eric went first.

"You shouldn't have called her a sicko."

"She might think you meant it."

"A wicked sicko. Come on, Alice."

"Her story was about how sad she really is, don't you see that?"

"And women in general."

"You're forgetting what she's been through. A brutal rape, Alice."

"Besides, it was only a game."

"And she's just more inventive than you are."

"Less repressed than the rest of us."

"A sad but free spirit. That's our princess."

I said, "You guys can't be serious."

They shrugged. They shook their heads as if I were the one who didn't get it, who had somehow missed the point, and not just missed it but didn't have a clue what in hell it might be.

Sometimes you see something coming but you just stand there disbelieving and tongue-tied, afraid to make a move, so that an onlooker might take you for blind.

My three friends became Hannah's campus escorts, day or night. She didn't go to the library alone, or the bookstore, the cafeteria, the parking lot. If she wanted to do an errand off campus between classes, one of them went with her. They were dogged, dog-like: Darrell became her burly St. Bernard, always on call, bearing spirits. Richard was her bloodhound, alert and on the trail. Eric, it seems, was her devoted spaniel.

As for me, I was left to my own devices. Which were not numerous, and, truth be told, not inventive. But I was a loyal, if mongrel, member of the pack.

Hannah's rape gave yours truly a shove. I went to the chancellor and demanded better lighting in the parking lots. I got nowhere. He opened the drapes in his upper floor office and invited me to look at the view. "Miss Clark," he said, "this is not an urban campus. This is a peaceful place, where violent crime is infrequent, as you well know. It was an isolated incident."

An isolated incident. Bad things happen, but not to us. Bad things happen to people who are in the wrong place at the wrong time. Who "tempt fate." Lightning strikes the cow too full-bellied and sleepy to follow the herd to the barn. Stupid cow. Dumb blondes. An isolated incident. You feel some compassion, but in the end you shrug, you open the drapes and look at the view.

That isolated incident refused to leave us alone, or we didn't let it. It attached itself to us and we to it. With it, on behalf of it and in its light, we made a public spectacle of ourselves. We had never been less isolated.

I don't mean "we," exactly. I mean me.

Being on the lookout for the perpetrator, distributing the composite drawing, nagging the police, making demands of a deaf bureaucracy, turning Hannah into a kind of celebrity. Day after day was intense and fraught. It was, for a while, exhilarating.

I never asked Hannah for the details. It was up to her to tell me, if she chose to. And she did.

We were having a late lunch together in the commons. For me, the usual salad and iced tea, no sugar. For her, the usual meaty sandwich, potato chips, brownie. I was being optimistic, telling her that the composite we'd posted everywhere would surely get results. I was going on about it—high from the chase, high on my role in her story as the character-most-unlikely who would nevertheless make things turn out the way they were supposed to.

As if she hadn't been listening, as if we'd been in the midst of some other, intimate conversation—the one I was perhaps too pointedly not engaging in—Hannah said, "It was a strange thing, Alice."

"What was strange?"

"The way he did it," she said.

"You don't need to tell me—"

"I want you to know."

"All right." It wasn't all right.

"He did not do it with his penis. He did it inside me with something else."

"Hannah, you don't need to—"

"A tape recorder. He pushed a button and turned it on. It was a small machine. Then he put inside my body the thing you talk into."

"The microphone?"

"Yes. The microphone. It was small. It hurt but not too much."

"He taped it?"

"You don't believe me?"

"Yes, but I—"

"He was a pitiful, stupid rapist, Alice—"

"With a microphone?"

"Like on the news. But smaller. Mr. Jensen is glad there can be no pregnancy."

I didn't want this to make any kind of sense, but I couldn't keep her revelation from planting a believable, an audible image. The recorded sounds of labia saying (in so many non-words), You're hurting me. And the sounds of a resistant, forced vagina, of a bruised cervix saying, You have no business here, get out!

Hannah said, "I tried to stay quiet. So the tape would be, you know—"

"Blank."

"Yes. Blank."

"I don't know."

Hannah shrugged. "I don't think I was quiet."

"Did you tell this to the police?"

"No. They don't need to know this. My husband thinks so, too."

"This could be crucial evidence, kiddo. The very thing that will help them to catch the guy. An MO—*modus operandi*. That means his particular way of doing things, a pattern, something to go on. You have to tell the police."

"I couldn't tell them. I won't. They won't believe me. It is too—"

"You should have. You will. I'll explain to Mr. Jensen. We'll go down there right now—"

"It is too private. A bad joke of a rape. I should have told you before, but—"

"You have nothing to be ashamed of."

"I'm telling you because you understand things. Because you believe me. So now we don't think about it anymore in this lifetime, okay José?"

Hannah gave me her best, her irresistible smile—the one that declares that there is nothing in the world but pleasure. "I think we should go bowling," she said. "I want to do this game. Do you know some place that we can go bowling?"

"Yes."

"I'll drive us there, with the top down."

Hannah was brilliant.

For the rest of the afternoon we bowled at Tava Lanes, badly, worse than the six-year-olds. We ate greasy french fries, and we laughed a lot.

But it didn't go away, what she'd told me—it clung, it sucked like an octopus on deep-water rock. Still does.

Hannah was brilliant even after Eric showed up at the office with a hickey on his neck that his collar could not hide.

Who else? It had to have been Hannah. It seemed he was over there all the time after the night of the rape. That paper on Burton's *Anatomy of Melancholy*?— don't ask.

I didn't want to picture them necking, but I did. I do. Eric would not have made the first move. I know this the way I know that my heart is still beating. It had to have been that, on the white couch in the Jensen living room, a somewhat-drunk ready-to-doze-off Eric accepted a spontaneous kiss. A jubilant nighty-night mmmwaah that did not appear to be seductive, perhaps was not in fact seductive, though it must be said that Hannah was effortlessly captivating at all times, as far as I could tell. And so Eric would, naturally, I guess, have found himself tantalized, tentatively returning the kiss, then giving in, putting his arms around her, briefly. But even briefly would have turned out to be too much for him, would have set too many questions afloat, produced too many unaligned longings. He would have had to stop, pat her hand, half-grateful, half-naysaying. *My* Eric. He would have said nothing as he curled up with his longings and closed his eyes.

As I see it to this day, Eric was sound asleep when Hannah left her love mark on his neck.

That time, the five months or so following Hannah's rape, shimmers now as if it were only a moment, as if everything were one thing. The Campus Rally Against Rape. The run-ins with administrators. The posting of the composite drawing all over campus, all over town. More presents from Hannah. The changes in Eric, in Richard, in Darrell. The dinner I had with Mr. Jensen at a restaurant I'd never been to, never dreamed of going to. And my looking always for the perpetrator, when I was driving, shopping, walking to my car after a night at the library, daring him to turn on his tape recorder and repeat the attack. Though I didn't know how to determine whether or not it was loaded, at night I carried the derringer in the pocket of my new suede jacket. I was always looking for the perpetrator and always looking at Eric, with his new shirts and his haircut and then one day that hickey on his neck. Not long after that I was looking at Darrell's casketed body, then looking at Richard's pacific, tortured face when he told me that he had volunteered, that he was going to Vietnam. And I was looking at Eric as he told me he would be leaving, going with the Jensens to Vermont.

I made one attempt to get Eric out of the way for a while. No doubt that hickey pushed some button, my "go" button, the green one, the one that flashes "do something, damn it, now!"

I hear the awkward clearing of the throat, the "excuse me" as I approached his desk. I see the fumbling with my glasses or my sweater, and then the feigned ease.

I said, "You know, I've never gone anywhere during spring break."

"Maybe you should go somewhere, Alice. You need a respite from all this. I'm worried about you."

"I'm thinking we should all go somewhere. Arrowhead, maybe. The four of us."

"Which four?" Eric asked.

"The original four. You and me, Richard and Darrell. We could take our books. We could talk about the work in progress, the way we used to do, hours on end. We could make it a kind of all-but-dissertation retreat."

Eric looked at me, and kept on looking. "A retreat."

"Call it whatever you want, but what do you say? Tell me it sounds like a good idea."

He was no longer looking at me when he answered with, "Against such an enemy, true courage consists in fear and retreat, in retreat without deliberation, and without looking back." He sounded, when he said this, as if he were afflicted with every form of melancholy Burton writes about in his long, long book. "Sorry," he added. "I don't mean to sound like a pedant. I came across those words a few days ago and they stayed with me."

"And I don't want to know what enemy that quotation is referring to."

Eric said, "No, you don't."

"But you're saying that a retreat is what we all need, right? Our figuring out some way to head for the hills for a week? Get away from all this detective work for a while?"

"No, I'm not saying that."

I wanted to touch him, but I didn't. "Don't you think that—?"

"You're talking to somebody who does not have true courage against such an enemy."

I have no trouble remembering that quotation, since it was Fénelon's *Telemachus* that Eric left on my desk a few months later, after he'd gathered his things and turned in his key. I guess the book was meant to be a goodbye note, an explanation of sorts. The enemy Fénelon is referring to is love.

Bunny's is not one of the faces I want or need to decipher. She's not part of this. And yet she hovers, she provokes, she knocks on the front door of my heart all the time. Will not let me retreat from loving her.

Bunny's fingernails do a lot of digging in the dirt. She is long-legged and skinny and curious. Squeamish doesn't apply to her. Nor does sheltered, though her father seems to be sufficiently attentive, attentive enough to send her here for better schooling, for whatever mothering and grandmothering I can offer. Bunny tells me that he did his best to be home almost every night for dinner and schoolwork, but couldn't help leaving most all of the child-rearing up to the girlfriends.

This does not, in my view, make him a peach. But I suppose it could be worse. She's not there, not fending off self-deprecation, not wishing she were blonde and tan and tall and rich. California, north and south, is hard on some people, and Bunny is one of them. Me too.

Bunny asks me all sorts of questions, some of which I answer easily enough, others I put off. "Let me sleep on that one," I say. But then, long after she goes to bed, I'm awake, imagining scenarios.

"Am I pretty, Alice? Do I look like my mother? My dad says she was a bombshell. Is that a good thing or a bad thing? Is that why she left? In order to, like, explode?"

"Is it good to be all by yourself?"

"Should I dye my hair when I'm old enough?"

"Do you think I might be a lesbian?"

"My dad always says that most men are dirty rotten scoundrels. And then sometimes he says that most women are dirty rotten scoundrels. Is that true, Alice? Are most people scoundrels?"

"Do girls who are tomboys when they're young stay tomboys when they get old? Are you a tomboy, Alice? Is that why you're all alone?"

"What did you want to be when you grew up?"

TEN

It was a seven-hour drive from that B&B in Utah to Denver, during which I tried and failed to give myself satisfactory explanations. What most troubled me—more than the clobbering I took from my regrets, more than whatever role Marie Lamarque played during that night at Logan's—was my momentary but no-question willingness to call it quits, to get up and move down that hallway, fully prepared to walk into a crypt, mad with the thought that the cross-country trip was about that, the long-overdue crypt, my turn to join the long-dead others in the Jensen story.

I did what any reasonable but half-mad-with-questions woman in her car for a long drive would do: I listened to a marathon call-in radio program about investing your money, planning for the future. Stocks and bonds. Mortgage rates. Charitable donations. Of course you're not really suicidal, I told myself. But just in case, you'll stay in good hotels from now on. And you'll invest in mutual funds. And you won't dwell, period. On anything. You'll remember every morning to fill the gas tank, and get a few groceries and some water, so that you won't have to stop, except to stretch and have a pee, until quitting time.

That was the new plan. It was to go into effect the next day. In other words, on the road to Denver, for the first time on the trip, I had to stop for lunch. Yes, I might have pulled into a fast-food restaurant, spoken my order on the intercom, paid up, and then eaten without once leaving the car. But those places are one of the things I'm grouchy about—and stubborn as they come, now that I'm old enough.

Over the years, I've had my share of occasions to see loners taking their meals in restaurants, reading, usually, as they might at home. Except that they weren't at home, and it showed. It showed in the way they looked up now and then from the newspaper or the novel, a quick am-I-being-stared-at glance around the room. It showed in the way they used their napkins after every bite, and in the way they were especially careful not to slurp the soup or let the lettuce dangle from the edge of the sandwich. It showed in the way they allowed the waitress to pour a third cup of coffee, which they apparently did not want, did not drink, but which might be taken (by any interested party) as a sign that they were all right, perfectly capable of sitting by themselves a while longer.

When it was my turn, in a half-empty cafe just outside of a mountain town in Colorado called Rifle, I followed suit: read the guidebook, ate a small salad and a too-hard roll with the manners of a princess, accepted that third, I'm-fine-no-problem cup of coffee, then let it sit. I paid up and got the hell out of there.

It was dark when I checked into the Brown Palace Hotel in downtown Denver. I was as stiff as the un-oiled Tin Man, despite the guaranteed-to-ease-the-pain mat of wooden marbles draped over the car seat. Good thing my bones can't speak—imagine the repeated When are we gonna get there's, the constant complaints, the whining. I was too cramped and crumbled to take in the hotel's ballyhooed features: the lobby faced with Mexican onyx, the six-story atrium, the stained-glass ceiling. They would have to wait for later.

Before I went down to the bar for a bite to eat, I soaked for an hour in the tub, curling and uncurling my fingers and toes in the hot water, trying to strike a bargain with my back: I will mend my ways, plan shorter drives, I promised, but you must agree to hang in there, to display some old-fashioned team spirit. I took my ability to get out of that tub without calling for help as a grudging acceptance of the proffered deal. Bodies: they can be such demanding sons-of-bitches, always waving the limited warranty in your face, then reminding you how much you need them.

Sitting at a bar, I told myself, would not be nerve-wracking. It would not be like sitting alone in a diner, a truck stop. A bar, a barstool, designed for solos, was meant for the likes of me. A bartender, somebody to talk to, sort of, was meant for the likes of me. No boohooing allowed, I told myself. You're going to have to get used to this. You have a long way to go yet.

"Here on business?"

That was the bartender's question as he set a cocktail napkin on the counter. A tall man, thin, nearly as unattractive as Lyle Lovett.

"Yes I am." I offered this answer without hesitation.

"Beef-growers' convention?"

"Do I look like a beef-grower?"

"Wouldn't hurt. White wine?"

"No. I'll have a Wild Turkey, please. On the rocks." There I was, thinking I'd showed him a thing or two.

"Matter of fact, you look like a school teacher."

"Imagine that."

"But these days," he said, "anybody could be anything. Nothin's clear-cut anymore. The whole country's gone to blazes, ma'am—every man, woman, and child, insofar as you can tell them apart." He handed me a menu.

"In your line of work, you must meet—"

"This isn't a line of work, ma'am. It's a job. If you want a real dinner, you're in the wrong place."

"I'd rather not—"

"You don't look like a barfly. But I can see how the restaurants here might be—"

"I'll just finish my drink and—"

"You need something to eat."

"Yes, but—"

"I can handle it."

"Very well." I glanced at the menu. "I'll have the BLT."

He crossed his arms and sighed a big sigh, as if I had asked for something not on the menu, like stir-fried calamari followed by pasta primavera. "We served the last BLT half an hour ago. Kitchen's short on bacon. There's breakfast to consider."

"Then I'll have the shrimp cocktail."

"Wouldn't if I was you. The shrimp are a week old. New shipment comes in tomorrow."

"Is everything else on the menu edible?"

"Edible, ma'am, but not in every case gettable. We're out of the chicken wings and the fried mozzarella. There may be a few potato skins left, bottom of the barrel stuff. We've got fries but no onion rings. Salsa, no chips. Tuna salad, yep. Chicken salad, no. Whole wheat and hoagies, yep. Pita and white bread, no. The buns for the hamburgers—don't think I'd feed them to a dog. Depending on the dog. Same goes for the mushroom quiche. Another so-called businesswoman in here earlier ordered that, ate one bite. Which is one more than I would've eaten. And we've just run short of the kalamata olives for the Greek salad, but I could give you some green ones from the bar. Martini olives. So it's not the same? So what? Nothing's the same anymore. The soup du jour was homemade tomato with garlic croutons and fresh basil. I had it for lunch. By this time on a Sunday night the soup du jour is Campbell's chowder, seasoned with Lawry's salt. Maybe some bottled parsley. Rocky Mountain Oysters—we got 'em fried, braised, sautéed, but I don't see them in your future any time soon. And don't believe "rib-eye" in the steak sandwich description. If you want a rib-eye, you go to the main dining room. Bourbon I've got plenty of. Ready for another?"

"Not yet." I took another sip and did my best not to wince.

"So what'll it be?"

"The grilled cheese sandwich."

"Whole wheat?"

"Fine."

"You a lawyer?"

"I write cookbooks," I told him. "I'm doing a cuisine tour of the Southwest. But not tonight, as you can see."

He leaned back and looked right at me. "Me too. That's what I do in my spare time. I write cookbooks. Do all the illustrations myself." He didn't say, You wanna make something of it? But that's what the lift in his chin was telling me.

He poured a second shot of Wild Turkey into a fresh glass. "You're on your own," he said.

Indeed.

At the bar there was a small, snappily-dressed man of considerable years—at least eighty—chatting up two young, pretty women (one was wearing a blue suede cowgirl hat) who might, for all I know, have been attending the beef-growers' convention. At the tables for two, close to the fireplace, there was a young couple who seemed to have run out of things to talk about, and there was an older woman putting on the dog for someone we'll call her son. Around a coffee table, in a tight circle of wing-backed chairs, there was a huddle of outdoorsy middle-aged men, gesticulating, laughing, liking each other's company.

At the other end of the room, in a similar configuration of comfortable chairs, there was a grown-up family: the presiding father was my age, white-haired and—not to put too fine a point on it—gorgeous, the kind of man for whom you'd buck the liberated tide and hang onto a positive sense of the word "patriarch." The mother was also my age, but what they call a picture of health, a woman you wouldn't be surprised to see on the tennis court, giving her opponent a memorable loss. Between these two, who were sitting at opposite ends of the coffee table, were three apparently happy and definitely well-appointed women in their thirties, I'd guess, and two lively young men of about the same age, all five clearly siblings, clearly the children of the distinguished couple. If the children were partnered, were themselves parents, then all had agreed, I suppose, to leave the add-ons at home, to make this an occasion for the core group, that baker's half dozen. Cut from one steaming loaf. That's what I really wanted to be when I grew up—any one of them.

I must have emitted a nearly audible buzz of envy, a surge. If I could have plugged myself into a socket, I'd have put all the lights out in that grand old hotel. There was a time, as a girl, when I would regularly find myself staring at fathers. At the supermarket, at school picnics, at Saturday matinees. Particularly, of course, at fathers and daughters. But I wasn't taken over, back then, not at first, by the slit-eyed vexations of envy. What took me, I think, what made me turn to watch and kept me watching, was a kind of awe. I would imagine that it would be both wonderful and a little scary for the daughters to be picked up and swung about, to sit in their fathers' laps, to smell their fathers' sweaters and jackets, to feel stubble against their cheeks. I would imagine that, if the fathers were gentle, the daughters would be in love with them, and so would sleep as sound as kittens for the rest of their lives, no matter what. I imagined that my father would have been the most gentle of them all.

I don't know exactly when the anger that fuels envy supplanted the stories I was telling myself, perhaps I was a young teenager. But it was a relief, whenever it was. Hoorah for the envious glance! No more starry-eyed gazing at fathers, trying to pick out the one who might be my second runner up, my king for a day, my almost daddy. I learned to give fathers and daughters a green-eyed once-over, and let it go at that. True, it took some practice.

My dazzling patriarch at that bar in Denver—he was hard to turn away from, hard to dismiss with a glance, believe me.

"Grilled cheese on wheat." The bartender set the plate in front of me.

The usual grilled cheese sandwich looks as if someone stepped on it, right? Two flattened triangles of thin bread become over-buttered toast. Some melted Velveeta in there, but nothing to stir your appetite.

What he served me was thick with sharp cheddar and basil-seasoned sliced tomato. The bread was buttery but crunchy, perfectly toasted, full of those grains that are supposed to be good for you. For garnish there were three sculpted radishes in a nest of pitted kalamata olives and curled carrots.

"You said you were out of these olives."

"Dipped into my own supply."

"This looks wonderful."

"A woman's got to keep her strength up."

The bartender wasn't smiling. I sat there with my mouth full as he spoke.

"I notice things," he said. "For instance: on an empty stomach, a woman can't lie worth a damn. She says stuff, whatever comes to mind, but there's no backbone in it, no respect. Do you get my drift, ma'am? Mendacity deserves respect. Better to say nothing at all than tell a lie that sounds just like a lie. Yep. A woman has to be careful. Somebody could take it personally, *capisce*?"

He let that sink in for a moment, then went on.

"I've noticed that men don't need food in their stomachs in order to lie the live-long day. Why? Because whatever they say sounds just like the truth to them. There's not a man in this room doesn't believe every word he says. Accuse him of lying and he'll make you feel real bad. Doesn't matter if he's starved or as full as a nailed-down goose. But a woman's different. Accuse her when she's hungry and she'll fold right up. Admit to lies long since over and done with. Accuse her when her tummy's full and she'll go down fighting, lying every which way, laying it on thick as fudge."

I swallowed at last and said, "I'm not full."

He leaned both hands against his side of the bar, crowding me. "By which you mean exactly what, ma'am?"

"You know what I mean."

"'Fess up. You'll feel better."

"I feel fine."

"Coulda fooled me."

"All right. I'm not a businesswoman."

"What else?"

"I don't write cookbooks."

"That it?"

"I've been a teacher all my adult life. At a community college in California. I retired a little over a month ago. I'm on my way to the

East Coast, to see some old friends who probably have a good bit of respect for mendacity."

"You've never been anywhere to speak of, have you?"

"Not to speak of."

"I had you pegged from the get-go, Professor."

"So it seems."

His smile didn't improve his looks.

"You're a real bully, mister, you know that?"

"Yep. But I make a good sandwich."

"That you do," I told him. "Do you write cookbooks?"

"What do you think?"

"I think perhaps you do."

He laughed. "You'd best think twice before you pay a visit to those mendacious folks of yours on your own. So. What's your drink? White wine?"

He had me pegged all right.

They all did.

ELEVEN

Darrell was the first to go. You could smell the bourbon on his breath in the morning. That's how bad it got after the rape, after he began going regularly to the Jensens' house for drinks. He was never a drunken drunk. I mean, he was never churlish or sloppy. There was always that case of pens and pencils in his shirt pocket. The weekly haircuts. He remained a gentleman. And I suppose drinking yourself to death is a gentlemanly way to go. No blood, no mess, no scene. He simply passed out on the couch and didn't wake up.

One could say that it was an accident—one drink too many, too much weight, too weak a heart. One could say "accidentally on purpose," but didn't. Because he didn't mean it. It had to have been an accident. That's what we believed.

It was Richard who discovered what had happened. He'd been fruitlessly trying to help Darrell lose some weight. They would walk to the campus together in the mornings. On the day Darrell didn't come to the door of his apartment, Richard got the landlady to let him inside. Darrell was lying on the couch, fully clothed, fully gone. He was wearing the blue cardigan sweater Hannah had given him. Just above his head, hanging there on the wall, was the Korean saber. "Like the sword of Damocles," Richard told me.

I said, "Damocles flattered a tyrant. That's how he wound up in such a predicament."

I could have held my tongue, could have taken the allusion as it was apparently intended, as merely spatial—though a bit of a stretch, since the saber that had been a gift from Hannah was not hanging by a string directly over Darrell's lifeless head. But I didn't hold my tongue. By that time, I'd had dinner with Mr. Jensen. I was full of him, with questions about his intentions toward me, toward all of us, that swooped and vanished, vanished and swooped like bats in a cave. Nevertheless, I could and should have kept my mouth shut.

Richard glared at me. Only one other time—when he'd first learned of Hannah's rape—had I seen that gentlest of men so angrily red in the face.

I back-peddled as deftly as I could: "Of course I don't believe that Mr. Jensen had anything to do with this. Darrell flattered him, that's all. Mr. Jensen told me so himself."

Richard said, "Darrell was a flatterer. We all know that."

True enough, I thought, but didn't speak.

Richard said, "Mr. Jensen is a lot of things, but he's not a tyrant. We all know that, too."

Richard said, "Case closed."

Here is a rough chronology:

Fall 1965, Hannah Jensen enters our lives
December 1965, Hannah Jensen is attacked and raped
January 1966, Darrell Farnsworth steals the diary
March 1966, Darrell Farnsworth dies
May 1966, Richard Stone enlists, goes to Vietnam
June 1966, Eric Langland leaves for Vermont
August 1966, Eric Langland kills himself
April 1967, Richard Stone becomes an MIA
Fall 1967, Alice Clark begins teaching at RCC

I want this to speak to me, but all it does is bow its head. I want meanings to attach themselves to the differences between the dead and the living, between me and what I'll dare to call my menfolk at the time. I want to know where to put Mr. Jensen—I can't seem to pin him down anywhere, even now.

Here is one difference: Alice Clark was not in love with Hannah Jensen.

Here is another difference: Alice Clark did not let herself become enchanted by Mr. Jensen—though she may have come close.

"I'm concerned about your friend Darrell. I'd like to talk with you. I'd like us to put our heads together and see what we might do to help."

That was Mr. Jensen, a week or so before Darrell died, inviting me to have dinner with him, to put our heads together.

He was a member of the Victoria Club, where Riverside's elite golfed and swam and dined on prime rib. These days, I hear, you can join as long as you can pay the membership fees. In those days, you had to be nominated, you had to be approved. Unless you were very rich indeed, the story went, you'd best be a WASP. I'd never been there, of course. "We'll go to the Victoria Club," Mr. Jensen told me over the phone.

I bought a new dress, a new handbag, new shoes.

I remember his hand on my elbow as we entered the club's restaurant. Ruddy men, fellow golfers in their good suits and awful ties, smiling at him, nodding. Mr. Jensen nodding back but not pausing, guiding me to a table by the window, well apart from the golfing buddies and the gathered families, the little girls in their matching Lanz dresses, the well-bred mothers who looked as if they owned at least one pair of shoes exclusively for sailing.

I remember that he ordered two dry martinis, straight up, with olives, and that he said "To Alice's health!" when he touched his glass against mine.

I cannot think of the conversation that ensued without thinking of me as the "Alice" he frequently referred to, as if she and I were not the same person, as if he were inventing her—with my help?—as we went along.

"You mean to Darrell's health, don't you?"

"I prefer to begin our conversation with Alice as the subject. How is she?"

"She's fine, thank you."

We were looking at each other. I don't know what he was seeing. I was seeing a face too narrow to be entirely attractive, large gray eyes, a slender nose that teetered just a little at the tip, as if he'd broken it, or someone had broken it for him. His lips were thin and full of irony.

"Hannah tells me you're divorced."

"What else does she tell you?"

"She tells me that Alice is lonely."

I thought: they've continued talking about me, though I asked Hannah not to. Why did that surprise me? Why didn't I mind? Was it the linens, the festive martini glasses, the gorgeous view of the golf course, the "madam" of the waiter? Mr. Jensen's look-at-me eyes?

"I'm not lonely."

"You're fine."

"Yes. But Darrell isn't. You said you wanted to talk about Darrell."

"Darrell thinks the world of Alice."

"Darrell is as generous as they come."

"He oughtn't to think so well of you? I'm definitely intrigued."

"He can think whatever he likes. We're friends."

"Thinking is not Darrell's strong point, wouldn't you say? He is all emotion. He is like a child."

"Not the Darrell I know."

I was not going to let Mr. Jensen lure me into patronizing my friend. Or so I thought.

"Tell me about the Darrell you know."

"Well, for one thing, he's the only one among us who's beloved by his students—he spends hours with them, going over their work, listening to their worries and woes, offering encouragement and miniature Tootsie Rolls."

"Not a child, then, but a den mother?"

"In a good way. And he's impeccably fair—no pushover when it comes to grades. Darrell is a good man."

"It must have been for a good reason, then, that he stole something from my house."

"Darrell wouldn't do that."

"You don't know him very well, do you?"

"Well enough. Why do you continue to invite him if you think he's a thief?"

"Hannah invites him. He comes for Hannah. But it's true that I join them. He amuses me—we have nothing he doesn't appreciate, insistently, repetitively. The furniture, the artwork, the ashtrays, the bourbon. And of course Hannah herself. He is, as you say, a good man. I believe that he will return the stolen item."

"How do you know he stole something?"

"I know."

"Have you asked him about it?"

"No. I want your friend Darrell to return it on his own, because he must. Because what he did was dishonorable. A breach of hospitality."

"Was it something valuable?"

"Alice knows nothing about it?"

"Nothing. I'm certain that Darrell doesn't either. When you said that you were concerned about him, I assumed you were referring to his drinking, which has gotten out of hand. This other stuff is not—"

"I have never seen him take more than two drinks. Shall we order?"

Either the two drinks he was referring to were oversized doubles, or Mr. Jensen was lying. So was I, about the diary: it was easy, on Darrell's behalf and on my own, to resist becoming a stool pigeon. It was less easy to resist the ways that Mr. Jensen aroused my curiosity. Why was he lying about Darrell's drinking? What was at stake?

"I suggest the filet of sole."

"Everyone else seems to be lining up at the buffet for the prime rib."

"Is Alice always inclined to do what everyone else is doing?"

"No. Well, not always. Almost always. What about you?"

"Never."

He ordered for both of us, and made an apparently impressive selection of wine, which caused the waiter to take another, longer look at me. A look I felt, but did not return. I was watching Mr. Jensen, wondering who he was, appreciating his good manners, and for some reason imagining the courtship of my parents, the two of them out for a special dinner, my mother in her best dress, a corsage pinned close to her heart, and my father saying "and the lady will have . . ."

Mr. Jensen went on. "What I said about the drinking habits of your friend Darrell: allow me to clarify. It is usually the case that I do not arrive home from the office until eight o'clock, sometimes later. He would have no more than two drinks after I arrived. One assumes that there were other drinks prior to that."

"One assumes correctly, I'm afraid."

I was thrown off track by this clarification, tripped as if by a banana peel I'd tossed in my own way. I wanted him to have been lying to me. Because I was lying to him? Probably. Because I needed to be suspicious of the man whose imagination had toyed with our names? That, too.

"Have you heard anything from the police?" I asked.

"Are you bringing up the subject of Hannah's misfortune?"

"Do you mind?"

"Yes. I'd prefer to talk about Alice."

"For the last several weeks, the Alice you prefer to talk about has been entirely caught up in the subject you don't want to talk about."

"There must be other interests. Your dissertation, your courses, your boyfriends."

"There are no boyfriends."

I was wishing that I had finessed the topic of boyfriends, and no doubt too emphatically turned my attention to the food, the wine, the passing of bread and butter. Why was I ashamed? Why was I afraid that he might think that I was coming on to him?

"Your friend Eric—"

"You mean Darrell—"

"No, I mean Eric. He, too, is at the house now and then. When Darrell is not there."

"Eric doesn't have a car."

"Hannah brings him."

"Oh."

"This troubles you."

"No it doesn't."

"Hannah is a good girl. She has a big heart. She wants to make everybody happy. I don't think she is making you happy, Alice."

"She doesn't need to. I'm fine."

He chuckled at this, and poured more wine. I didn't like the sound of his laughter, it was too inward and private, too odd a combination of bass and treble. I wondered why he wanted me to know that Eric was spending time with Hannah, at their house—and that's not all he wanted me to know.

"Eric and I talk late into the night," he told me, "after Hannah has gone to bed. He has read everything, as you probably know. A late-night conversation with your friend Eric is almost better than sex with a professional, if you'll allow me to say so."

"You put in long hours. So does Eric, it seems, now and then."

"Hannah gives him a ride back to his apartment. In the morning."

If he was trying to make me both envious and jealous, he was succeeding. I wanted those late-night conversations, I wanted to be taking Eric back to his apartment in the morning. I even wanted, for a moment, to be worldly enough to offer to compare something, anything, to sex with a professional. I wanted the Jensens' house, their money, their country club membership, their *savoir faire*, their whatever it was that beguiled Eric, made him talk, made him, apparently, happy.

In the diary, my name appears twice on the same page as Eric's. The first time, we form a kind of L: I am the vertical, he is the shorter horizontal. We share the E with which his name begins and mine ends. I want the L to stand for Love, but I don't think it does. Maybe it stands for nothing, simply the calligrapher's whim. It's no good to consider other L-words, because the ones that come to mind are Lack and Lopsided and Loser and Look. As in, Look Out!

The second time we appear together, the E again connects my name to Eric's, but this time we are crawling across the bottom of the page, a creepy filigreed inchworm.

"Of course, Alice could bring him herself. She could stay, talk, listen in. Consider yourself invited."

That was tempting indeed. But at the same time I was afraid that, should I suggest such an evening to Eric, he would turn me down. Or that, if he didn't, I would witness at the Jensen house an Eric I did not know. The Jensens' Eric— would he still be himself? There were many things I wanted to see for myself, but that was not one of them.

"Maybe I'll take you up on that sometime."

"Good. You ought to know that I have spoken to Eric about the stolen item."

"To Eric?"

"He believes that Darrell will have a change of heart."

"Eric knows what it is?"

"Yes."

"Why don't you tell me, too? Maybe I can get it back for you?"

"Is Alice proposing to steal it from Darrell?"

"On second thought—"

"Are you a woman of second thoughts?"

"I would say 'yes,' except that I'm having second thoughts about giving you an honest answer."

"To all of my questions?"

"Just the one."

He looked at me, almost smiling but not quite—a poker-faced smile, a winner's smile. "I would like to see you again."

"I don't think—"

"Perhaps, next time, you will have something for me."

"I won't. There won't be anything. There needn't be any next time."

"There needn't, but there will be."

There are times—aren't there?—when, like Dorothy, you've had more than enough and what you want is to go home. Except that it's not Kansas you're thinking of, and it's not a house or childhood or Auntie Em. There is no place or time like it because it is neither a place nor a time.

Home is the word you use for a kind of comfort that you've heard of, maybe read about, maybe even experienced first hand once or twice, but when you look in the mirror you all-too-rarely see it, you just can't get there. Perhaps you've been fortunate enough to have known approximations, temporarily adequate semblances, so that when you long to go home your longing attaches itself to certain slants of light, the smell of a treasured book or a patchwork pillow, an old soup pot, an evergreen you once planted, which grew and grew. But for the most part you don't let the sensuous attachments fool you. You know the difference between the light, the books, the touch of someone's fingertips as you almost slept and the home you want to go to—where you are you no matter where you are, and you know almost precisely who that is no matter when or what the circumstances, and you can see her without squinting, without dissembling, without mistaking her for a pillow or a soup pot. Not only that, but you like what you see. You're not some wily man's "Alice."

Did I get home that night, after dinner with Mr. Jensen at the Victoria Club? Not even close.

ALICE and BRADLEY. Our names appear once together in the diary. With me, he doesn't use the short version of his name, as he does with Eric. We are formal together, we make no pictures, no evocative shapes. But we do make a little word. His name is sandwiched between two ALICE's. The final letters of both our names are the largest, the most elegantly drawn. They spell out, horizontally, the word "eye." I take it that we are eyeing each other.

The names ERIC and BRAD appear together three times in the diary. Once, they form a pyramid whose apex is an elaborate E overlaid by an equally elaborate B. The last letters of their names are connected at the base with a delicately cross-hatched line that looks like a fence. Then there is an upside-down or v-shaped version of the same combination. The third time, the names form a cross joined by the second letter—R—in both names. BRAD is the vertical, ERIC the horizontal.

An ancient tomb, a pit, a cross?

I just broke one of my grandmother's teacups. Damn.

Bunny told me that one of the girlfriends (the one who left the cat behind) showed up one rainy afternoon with a just-purchased set of stoneware for eight, eight long-stemmed wine glasses, and two glass candle-holders. She washed everything, then set the table, laid out the cups and saucers, the salad plates, all brand new and shiny. Bunny asked if they were having a party. The girlfriend said "sort of" and advised Bunny to go outside and play once her dad got home from work. But it was raining, so after her father got home Bunny stayed in her room—from where she easily heard the crashing against the dining room wall of everything the girlfriend had just bought.

"Dad said it made her feel a whole lot better," Bunny told me. "And he said it was really thoughtful of her not to break any of our own stuff."

I've never done anything like plate-throwing, chair-tossing, door-slamming. All I do is drop things, and sometimes they're precious.

TWELVE

DARRELL WAS THERE, in my Riverside kitchen, a few days before he died. Eric was there too, that same night, but he didn't appear until well after dinner. I'd asked them to come over, in that order. We needed to talk about the diary. I needed to, that's certain.

I was telling myself that it was time to get practical, get some footing, look out for each other. Together, I thought, we would work out a strategy by which to return the diary or keep it. That done, I would turn my attention to Richard, whose name Mr. Jensen had not spoken in my presence. And this rattled me more than if he had.

It would turn out to be my last conversation with Darrell, and almost the last with Eric—an evening hazy from drink that could nevertheless have happened just last week. Nobody threw any plates, but we might as well have. Do what you don't do, be what you aren't: something like that, I take it, is what my friends were displaying for me that night.

My soft-hearted Darrell, my priestly Eric: they will remain that way with me whether they like it or not. They will be the people I knew them to be, insofar as I knew them.

Before Darrell arrived, I put the diary on the kitchen table, then went about preparing whatever it was I cooked—pot roast, maybe. It was definitely something that required attention, chopping carrots, onions, bell peppers. Which I remember because my attention kept being drawn to that little red book, to the names of my cherished friends, and the names of other people, the Jensens, with whom I was friendly and of whom I was afraid for no speakable reason. It wouldn't leave me alone. Names only, but that book told stories. And it seemed to be whispering to me, but all I heard was the hissing sound of innuendo.

In no time I cut deeply into one of my index fingers.

"That might need stitches," Darrell said when he got there, as he re-did my awkward bandaging. Then he said, "Undoubtedly, without a *doubt,* we both need a drink."

Darrell saw the stolen diary on the table, the diary he'd given me for safe-keeping, for deciphering, for fun? But he made the drinks—first things first—before he opened it to an ERIC and BRAD page and announced, "The guy's a genuine artist, Alice. This is *art.*"

At some point I badgered Darrell into putting down his drink and eating something. Then I told him that I had seen Mr. Jensen, that Mr. Jensen knew about the theft, knew Darrell was the one. I was too humiliated or guilty, I don't know, to tell him about the Victoria Club and the excellent martinis.

Number one: Darrell was unfazed.

"I'm not surprised," he said. "He's smart, smarter than all of us put together."

"We're not put together anymore," I told him. "They've scattered us."

"What happened to Hannah would scatter *anybody.*"

"I'm not talking about Hannah."

"You said 'they.' *They've* scattered us."

"Point taken. But let's drop it. Mr. Jensen told Eric that you took the diary."

"Eric knows?" Darrell put down the book, picked up his drink in both hands and rubbed the icy glass across his forehead.

"According to Mr. Jensen. But I'm not sure that I believe him. He suspects that I'm involved, and I lied, for both of us. He may have been using Eric to lure me. Eric might know nothing at all. I've asked him to come over."

"Eric?"

Number two: Darrell was smiling as he repeated Eric's name—smiling the way you do when you have a secret on the tip of your tongue that you may or may not tell.

"Certainly not Mr. Jensen!" I said.

Darrell got up to make himself another drink. "I don't understand what your problem is with Hannah's husband."

"There's something wrong about that diary, Darrell."

"I'll give it back."

"You're the one who called him a son of a bitch for making your name so pretty."

"I meant it in a friendly way. It was *friendly*. Just guy-talk." Darrell poured some wine into my empty glass. Then he sat down across from me, where Hannah used to sit when we played the game. "Listen, Alice," he said. "I'll admit to finding him strange. Strange is just what I feel when I'm over there, when I'm around him, when I'm around *her*. But for some reason, I like the feeling. I can't get enough of it."

That was number three. A big one.

I didn't want to know what he meant. And I did want to know what he meant. And I wondered whether "Alice" didn't already, since her evening with Mr. Jensen, have more than an inkling. He led, she followed—nothing unusual there. But what was she doing dancing that particular conversational dance with that particular man? Why did she sense that there was something lurid pressing at the edges of their talk? And why didn't she mind? Why on earth did she sit through it, in her new dress?

"I don't like that feeling, Darrell."

"You're fine just as you are."

"Fine?"

Number four: "I'm most fine, finer, finest when I'm with her, with them."

He sounded almost arrogant, as if he were telling me that he'd won a bet. A bet against me, perhaps, that would have gone something like: "Five dollars says I'll admit it before you will." Okay, you win, I said to myself.

To Darrell I said, "One of the special things about Hannah is that she makes us all feel special."

"I didn't say special, Alice. I said strange. Strange as in unfamiliar." He paused and finished his drink. "And finer as in better. I think they love me."

Number five.

I'm counting the jabs—that's what they felt like. Pokes that kept putting me off balance. That seemed to be coming out of nowhere. That didn't hurt, exactly, if you don't count my pride.

"They don't love you."

"They love all of us. You too, Alice, even though you don't go to the house much."

Eric arrived, a little early, preventing the argument I was about to have with Darrell, an argument I was bound to lose because I would not have risked losing Darrell.

Come on, 'fess up, old woman. You were bound to lose that argument because of Mr. Jensen's "Alice"—the part of you that was capable of being part of them, that was envious of her friends' frequent visits to their house, that wanted to be strange and loved, strangely loving. If only for a night.

Eric came into the kitchen and said, "You two are not having a good time."

"On the contrary, *au contraire*!" Darrell got up as if he were weightless and graceful. An antic gnome. A different Darrell. He made more drinks, poured more wine.

Eric saw the diary, but didn't touch it. I put a bowl of fruit on the table. He didn't touch that either. Nor did he ask about my heavily bandaged finger. He was watching Darrell, who was splashing ice cubes into already full highball glasses.

I fetched a dishrag. "You're supposed to put the ice in first."

Darrell ignored me, passed a glass to Eric, and proposed a toast. "To Alice, our beloved fuddy-duddy." Eric was hunched a bit, as usual, his posture a kind of no-trespassing sign. But both of them drank to the toast, I have to say, like boys, like show-offs.

Their beloved fuddy-duddy said, "This isn't a party."

"What is it?" Eric was looking at Darrell, not at me, when he asked this question.

So Darrell answered it. "It's a confession, Father. As you may already know, I am guilty of taking something that belongs to someone else. Alice is guilty of bold-faced lying and harboring the stolen item.

We are prepared to return it, to ask your forgiveness, and to do whatever penance you see fit."

I said, "I'm not prepared to return it just like that. We need to discuss this."

"I will vouch for her, Father," Darrell said.

"No you won't!"

"Yes I will!"

Squabbling in front of Eric: now that was something to be ashamed of. Those long, steady, indoor hands. His dark eyes, unmoving, owl-like from behind the new pair of thick glasses. I wanted to apologize. I wanted him to look at me. But he kept on looking at Darrell. There seemed to be some game going on, and neither of them wanted me on his team.

I picked up the diary and left the room with it, stuck it in a drawer. Did I want Eric to come after me? Yes.

When I returned, they were sipping their drinks. Eric said, "You're absolved, both of you. Don't worry about it. It's not important. If you want to keep it, Alice, go ahead."

Number six. That one, that writing it off, hurt more than my pride. I was no longer sure whom I was talking to. Certainly not *my* Eric.

They went on as if I weren't there.

Darrell stuck out his lower lip and put on a pretend pout, as if the whole thing were a joke. "If she keeps it, then I'll be prevented from doing the honorable thing."

I had all too flatfootedly assumed that Darrell would not be sanguine—certainly not playful—about Eric's knowledge of the theft. That there'd be at least a squirm of guilt. I had assumed that Eric would persuade me to make Darrell return the diary to the Jensens. I had assumed that there were some few things I could count on. "What is with you guys? What's going on?"

Eric said, "Just keep it, Alice. It doesn't matter. I'll cover for Darrell."

I said, "Do you know what's in it?"

"I don't need to know."

I didn't stop. "Our names, that's what. And they're—"

Darrell said, "Leave him alone, Alice. He doesn't want to know."

Eric finally looked at me. "They're what?"

I couldn't speak. There was no good answer. And if there were, it was not within reach, it was crowded out by my desire to get those glasses off Eric's face, get rid of those big eyes that were not his true eyes. I stood there like an inept harridan, a shrew with no finesse, declawed.

I managed to say, "I don't know." And then, "For the time being, I'd like to keep it. There's some kind of story in it, that's about us."

"I won't tell."

"No problem."

I said, "I don't understand why it's not a problem."

Number seven: "That's because you're just you," Darrell told me.

Too true.

I let it go, offered dessert and a round of canasta, kept my friends there with me as long as I could, but couldn't keep myself from wondering whether they would head over afterward to the Jensen house, for different pleasures.

People said that the Jensens were moving away to Vermont because of the rape, because Hannah was afraid that the perpetrator, still on the loose, would try it again. It made sense, people said, that Hannah had been living in fear, though she did her best to hide it, to be as uncomplaining and charming as always. People said that the detectives on the case were lazy, uncaring, and ought to be ashamed of themselves. People said that they would do the same thing, leave town, if they were in Hannah's shoes, if they could afford it and didn't have to worry about getting a good job in some new place, which they wouldn't have to do if they were in her shoes. But they wouldn't trade places with her, they said, not for all the money in the world, though for all the money in the world they would give it a second thought. After all, they said, Hannah seemed to be happy even though she had been so brutally attacked. If you're rich enough, some people said, you can get through anything. No, said others, it's not that simple. What you see in Hannah Jensen is a real trooper. The genuine article.

What Eric said was that the move was Mr. Jensen's idea, that he had long since put in for the transfer to Vermont. Mr. Jensen planned to find a country home with plenty of acreage, no visible neighbors, even if that meant a long commute into Burlington.

"It doesn't have to do with what happened to Hannah," Eric explained. "Brad has had this in mind since he got back to the States. Hannah doesn't want to go, but of course she's going."

There was a full moon. We were sitting in my car on a deserted ridge that offered a view of Lake Elsinore. I'd called him, suggested a drive, and he didn't say no. I suppose he knew that he ought to tell me in person that he was leaving—it would matter to me too much if he didn't. In the long run, it mattered to me too much that he did. "Why doesn't Hannah want to go?"

"She likes it here," he said. "She has friends here. You, for instance."

It was early June, a warm night. We had the windows rolled down. The air was thick with the smell of mustard weed. He was leaning against the door, facing me. I was leaning back against the seat, looking out over the steering wheel at the moonlit lake.

"I'm going with them, Alice."

There were ducks out there on the water, quacking their subdued, nighttime quack, as if they didn't want to be overheard, as if they were afraid of the dark, afraid of being pulled in and under by something they couldn't detect, afraid they wouldn't make it, this time, to that spot on the shore where they liked to huddle together with their beaks buried under their wings until the sun came up.

"But you're so close to finishing the Ph.D., closer than any of us. Is this, what, a kind of summer vacation?"

"I've been granted a six-month leave of absence. I'll be back in January."

"Six months?"

"Please don't ask me to explain." When he said this, his voice seemed to be that of a genuine friend, of someone who liked me and trusted me not to ask too much, and not to say a word about his travelling companions.

"I'll go too."

Eric shook his head. "Not a good idea."

It wasn't an idea at all, not at first, not when I spoke it—it was merely a blip, a heartbeat, as insubstantial as the moonlight that was making the far side of the lake appear to be more blue than black. I closed my eyes and tried to see it, the idea of actually going, filling out the leave-of-absence forms, renting the house, packing a big suitcase, arranging for books to be mailed.

"I wouldn't go with the three of you. I'd just go. I could get my own ce, a room somewhere, close by. I could get a lot of work done."

Eric shook his head again, then turned and looked out the win- w. "Not a good idea."

The ducks were finally quiet, safe, probably burrowing their tum- es into the warm earth of the lakeshore, tucking themselves in for night. Eric was still looking out the window on the passenger side en another car pulled up to my left, some twenty feet away, far ugh not to intrude, close enough for me to see the arms of the boy ching for the girl, and she moving so leniently into his embrace.

I thought: that should be Richard there, courting the first of his wives. Or Darrell, reunited at last with his high school sweetheart. I would beep the horn and wave, wave them on, and they would wave back.

I thought: that should be me there, and this man who is looking the other way, eastward and out over the lake, in the direction of his leave-taking. I put my hands on the wheel, but still they seemed to be more empty than they had ever been.

That feeling we call being broken-hearted: I was feeling it, but it wasn't the kind of brokenness, the kind of bursting apart that demands external expression—moaning, wailing, weeping. No, it was a dwindling, an imploding kind of brokenness.

I didn't want him to see it, this shriveling. Call me what you will: vainglorious to the bitter end would do nicely. But I wanted him to take along a good impression of me, have that good impression neatly folded and preserved in his shirt pocket when he came back.

Light and playful, a veritable moonbeam, like gold to airy thinness beat, I said, "Are you sure you can go six months without my pestering you?"

Eric turned to face me. A desperate, smiling Alice. Darrell's favorite fuddy-duddy. I hoped that he wouldn't see the lovers in the other car. I don't know whether he did or not. But my jocular note seemed to have been off-key, or badly timed. Or maybe he just didn't believe it. In any case, it was the old Eric, my treasured Eric, who looked right at me and said, "I don't want you to go, Alice. I'm sorry."

A couple of days after he was gone, I found his copy of *Telemachus* on my desk, a bookmark indicating the page on which I would discover that the enemy from whom one should retreat without deliberation is love. That's how that word would pass between us, that's how he would speak it, through the remote written voice of an old French priest.

That night in the car, beneath a lover's moon, Eric did not say the word, but I heard it. I heard him almost speak it, about her, or them. I heard me almost speak it, about him. I heard their car doors open, the boy and the girl, then watched them walk down the incline toward the water, with their arms around each other. In the distance I heard the wail of coyotes calling out to each other, calling in the wanderers.

"So you'll be leaving soon?"

"Yes."

"I wish—"

"It's not the right thing for you, Alice. The right thing for you is to get your degree, get a job, and stay put."

"I don't want—"

"Let's not talk anymore, let's just be quiet together, the way we were that day on Mount Rubidoux."

He took my hands in both of his. He was consoling me—with his reference to that day, with those same hands—whether I liked it or not. He had remembered. He had remembered that late afternoon as something good between us, how close we had come to being the lovers we weren't ever going to be. And for those consoling hands, for the no doubt too much I made of them, I did what he asked of me: I stayed put, so help me, like a monument to who knows what.

THIRTEEN

A COUPLE OF WEEKS AGO, there was an open house at Bunny's new school, and she asked me to attend. The walls of her classroom were decorated with student paintings and drawings, all self-portraits, all attempts to render the theme that was written across the blackboard in perfect block letters: FREE TO BE ME.

How consistently we manage to reduce our delusions into such perky phrases, and then palm them off on the kids.

Most of the students represented themselves as smiling stick figures, whose stiff little hands were holding flowers, jump ropes, things that appeared to be baseball bats or beach shovels. There were pink Me's and brown ones, a dark orange sunburned Me. There were buzz-cut and curly, pigtailed and behatted Me's. But they all looked alike: each of the perfectly round heads that topped the beanpole bodies were drawn with the help of a compass. This similarity and exactitude apparently pleased the teacher, Mrs. Chandler, the passer-out of gold stars. The stick-figure posters were full of them.

One boy painted himself as a blue cloud in a gray sky, just as blunt as could be. Only a billow or two distinguished the cloud from a blimp. In tiny black letters, inside the cloud, he'd written the word "Me." Not a star-winning self-portrait. Did the teacher think he didn't try? Didn't mean it? I hope he did—mean it, that is. It seems to me a good thing to see yourself as a cloud. Or even a blimp.

I trust that's not quite the same as wanting to be strange. And it's certainly not as dull as being, at all times, just your plain old self.

I wouldn't have been surprised had I learned from Richard Stone that, when he was ten years old, he drew a portrait of himself as a cloud and spent his evenings, when he should have been asleep, reading the stars, imagining an easier world where there would be no need for certain words to exist—like bombardment, like famine, like genocide, like rape. I wouldn't have been surprised because he conducted himself among us like the once and future king of such a world.

In the meanwhile, on this too-often dreadful little planet, he would single-handedly alleviate what he took to be our woes—whether we liked it or not. He lovingly made projects of us all.

Darrell's weight problem: Richard supervised and participated in the daily exercise program.

Eric's years in an orphanage: Richard—he must have known—touched and patted and hugged, fearlessly ignoring Eric's reticence.

My childlessness: after my divorce, he proposed to donate his sperm, to see to it—"no strings, no sex, strictly on the up-and-up for the betterment of humankind"—that my "lineage" continued. I declined. He went to a sperm bank and made the donation anyway.

For Hannah he set out to find the perpetrator, bring him to justice—week after week, he spent his nights prowling the campus parking lots, going to bars and pool halls, the public parks. He'd been to a cockfight in Fontana, a rodeo out in Redlands. Since that day when the detective came to the office, he'd kept a copy of the loathsome composite drawing in his wallet. He told me these things over tacos and beer at La Paloma, the night after Eric and Darrell had been to my house. What I did learn from Richard was that he was giving up.

"On all of us?"

"Not on Darrell," he told me. "We can get that weight down. That's doable. But you—I've run out of arguments on behalf of your progeny. You're too convinced that your life is all right as it is. And Eric, I don't know, I don't see him much anymore."

"He spends a lot of time at the Jensens."

"That's what I should be doing, instead of looking for somebody I'm probably not going to find. I've looked everywhere. I've been to places no man with even the shredded remains of a humane value in his pocket would be caught dead in. It's time I were on the spot, watching out for her, making sure nothing else happens."

"She's perfectly safe at home, don't you think?"

Richard paused before he answered, ate half a taco, rolled up his sleeves, drank some beer. Finally he said, "Did you see that hickey on Eric's neck?"

"Yes. But—"

"Then you see what I'm getting at. Something's going on. Don't let that smile on her face fool you—she's been through something perilous. Maybe he's taking advantage."

"Eric? You have to be joking!"

Richard said, "Do you mind if we don't talk about it?" He turned his attention to what was left of his food.

"Just one thing, and then we don't have to talk about it."

He went on eating, not so much as if he were hungry, but as if it were simply something to do. I remember thinking that he needed to change his clothes, he needed a bath and a trim, he needed someone who would say a prayer for him and mean it.

That evening, stirring the refried beans into his rice, Richard was like a hero without his steed: disconsolate and inconsolable, a worn-out warrior who had nothing to show for his efforts, no rescues to recount, no enemies vanquished, no white carnation pinned to his chest by the girl of his dreams.

"Just two things, then," I said, "to be honest about it. The first is, Mr. Jensen must have seen that hickey, too. He must know—"

Richard interrupted me. "He doesn't care. I mean, he cares, but he doesn't mind. He likes Eric."

"Are you saying that he *would* mind if it were you?"

"I'm not saying. Maybe. What's the other thing?"

I had to move on, couldn't linger out loud on that "maybe" he had given me the way you give a bum a dollar—you do it quickly, you don't look him in the eye, you hope it'll feed him a little something, but you don't let yourself imagine what. I took it, that "maybe," not ungrateful, and fed myself something like: It's not that Mr. Jensen doesn't like Richard, it's that Richard likes Hannah too much. And Eric, then, doesn't?

"The other thing," I said, "is that I'd like to know about your tattoos."

Richard looked up from his plate, but not at me. Just up, straight ahead, at that space we all seem to have in front of us, about the size of a bulletin board, where we keep the notions that compel a gaze now and then. "The princess knows what they mean," he told me. "That's something special between us, and I'd like to hang onto it. But if she wants to tell you—"

I didn't know the man in room Number Two at Logan's B&B. So, believe me, Richard is the only man I've known who did not do all of his crying in private, or in abruptly stoppable bursts. He looked as though he were about to start.

I put my hand on one of his tattooed forearms. "I won't ask her. That's a promise."

He nodded his thanks, unable to speak for a while. Then he told me that he was thinking of signing up, joining the army, going to Nam, doing something that would make Hannah proud of him. She thought it was a good idea, he said, and that, if he went ahead with it, in spite of the pacifism he still believed in, and in spite of the excruciation it would cause his parents (who were setting up a clinic in what was then Rhodesia), he would do it in Hannah's honor, and he could live with that. And perhaps he could have, if he'd lived.

At the service for Darrell, Hannah was sitting between Eric and Mr. Jensen. Richard was next to Eric. I saw them as I entered the church, and wasn't sure where to put myself—who, at that moment, looking at them, was emphatically, merely Alice.

I took a seat in the back row. An old story, that particular kind of discomfort—wanting, not-wanting; one step forward, two in the other direction—and an old, half-way, half-assed solution. I wish that I had done an about-face, left the church, and said a good-bye to Darrell in genuine private.

The service was dispirited and clumsy from the start, when the presiding minister referred to the deceased as Darren. And no one corrected him—the other mourners, including, it must be said, yours truly, took their cues from the dozen or so blood relatives up front, who listened unmoving, with their heads unbowed, as someone named Darren was sent into the hands of a loving Lord.

The throng of students who had been devoted to their teaching assistant, Mr. Farnsworth, looked distinctly out of place—they'd come prepared to remember the details, to console, and to weep. Instead, they twisted and re-twisted their dry wads of tissue while the minister related, on behalf of the grieving family, a few "personal" recollections that could have been said about anybody, Darren, Darrell, Dwayne, whoever. It was awful. I decided not to go to the cemetery for the burial, not to attend the subsequent reception.

Just as I reached my car, there was that hand on my elbow again, and there was Mr. Jensen's voice in my ear.

I remember that day too clearly: the San Bernardino mountains looked especially high and close. What remained of the wintertime snow, in ribbons and pools of blue-ish white, seemed the work of an untormented artist, with plenty of time on his hands, and no one to please but himself. On a day like that, you don't have to look up to the heavens in order to give the old ego a deflating tweak—an eastward glance at the mountains will do just fine.

That's how it was: the mountains too close, the service too dreary, my apartness too acute. Everything seemed to me picayune, paltry. I was in no condition to handle Mr. Jensen, insofar as that was an option. But there he was, standing right next to me. The skirt of my black dress was fluttering against his legs.

"I propose to ride with Alice."

"Why are you whispering?" Behind him I saw the others leaving, preparing to join the line of cars that would follow the hearse to Olivewood Cemetery.

"Respect for the occasion," he whispered again. "I didn't mean, of course, to startle you."

"I don't think anything could startle me today. But you needn't whisper."

"Alice doesn't mind, then, giving me a lift."

"She minds that you refer to her in that way as Alice."

"Forgive me. I presumed that a certain formality in our relation was pleasing to you."

"Formality, yes. Alice, no. As for the ride, I'm not going to the cemetery."

"It was disgraceful and ludicrous, wasn't it? The service."

"Yes."

"Shall we go to the club for a drink?"

"No. Thank you."

"Some other place, then."

"What are you after?"

"You tell me," he said.

"Now you sound like Hannah. You people keep wanting me to tell you what's going on."

"That remark requires an explanation. Over a good bottle of wine."

"I have no explanation. Only bewilderment."

"And at least a touch of thirst, I hope." With a magician's wave of his hand, Mr. Jensen directed my gaze over the parking lot. "The others, as you can see, have gone. Will I at least get a ride to my house?"

The Jensen house: I'd been there only the one time, on the night that Hannah was attacked. Up in the gracious hills above Victoria Avenue. I'd seen so little then, was too distracted, too distraught for much of anything to stick besides Hannah's bitten and puffy mouth as she spoke private words to her husband. But I'd seen just enough of Mr. Jensen's crossed legs—his sleek, motionless, upraised foot—and the way his eyes looked me over as we spoke in the kitchen to make me "too busy" whenever Hannah invited me over.

It was daylight and the air was clear, and I wanted the picayune feeling to go away, to go join the smog out over the ocean. I told myself what they say about curiosity and cats, but then I put that proverb right up against what they say about cats and nine lives—and so cancelled the warning.

I believed that from the Jensen house there would be a queenly view of the mountains, and there would be the fine furniture that Darrell had admired, provocative artwork, things not only to look at but to get the feel of. I believed that I would find something out. At the same time, I told myself that I oughtn't to think that way, to begin interpretations long before there is any text at hand. But as I turned into the driveway, I knew that if he didn't ask me in, I would make something up—may I use your phone? Your restroom? Yes, in fact, I *am* a bit thirsty.

He did ask me in, after he showed me the rose garden, the small pond encircled with camellia bushes, an elegant little statue of Hermes in the middle.

I said, "I can't stay long."

"We'll have one drink."

"Fine. But then I'll be on my way."

The windows in the living room looked out onto the front-yard garden. There was only a partial view of the mountains, but a preferable one, one that tamed them a bit, didn't invite them to preside disapprovingly over your musings. The ceiling was high and dark, in the Spanish style, beams exposed. Everything else was white: the couch and the chairs, the carpet, the walls, the freshly-cut roses that stood in a tall glass vase as if they were expecting company. There were glass tables and lamps, crystal objects here and there—a ballerina, a hummingbird, an ashtray. The paintings—two above the couch, one above the mantle—were abstract, colorful, probably important, but to my untrained eye they were distinctly unremarkable. There was nothing to look at for long. The living room seemed to have been designed by a decorator whose tastes tended toward the stylish and impersonal and dull.

I did not follow Mr. Jensen into the kitchen, where he prepared the drinks. But I couldn't sit down. I heard a cabinet shut, then ice being scooped into glasses. Next to the couch there was a set of French doors that opened onto a backyard patio. I couldn't unlock them, but I could see out—out to more camellias, a charming birdbath, a weathered bench, and a brick stairway that led to a terrace of grass, more eucalyptus trees, and jacaranda. And out to yet another, smaller fishpond, this one presided over by a bronze rendering of Leda and the Swan.

I heard the kitchen door swing shut, then his footsteps on the wooden floor of the dining room, but I pretended not to hear. And he, for a minute, pretended that he wasn't waiting there at one end of the living room, holding the drinks, letting me stand before the French doors, take in what there was to see, and formulate my phrases: as in, Isn't that statue somehow contemptuous of poor Hannah? Wouldn't it be better, for now, to place it in some remote section of the yard? I turned, more or less prepared, but he spoke first, took the lead. I guess it's no surprise that I let him have it.

"So. Alice. What do you think?"

"I think you must have a busload of gardeners."

We sat down at either end of the couch and sipped our drinks.

"Let me be more precise," he went on. "Did she or did she not put on his knowledge with his power?"

He's showing off to the would-be English professor, I thought. Pulling Yeats out of his hat, turning the question of rape into *explication de texte*. "Leda?"

"Who else?"

He seemed relaxed, and he seemed to be asking a genuine question, as if his wife had nothing in common with the ravished Leda, as if what had happened to Hannah had not happened, or was entirely irrelevant. Genuine question or bait?

"Hannah, of course."

"Of course, she says. Of course."

"Well?"

"You wish to talk about Hannah. She wishes to talk about you. I wish to talk to a graduate student about an extraordinary poem by Yeats."

"I don't understand."

"What don't you understand, Alice? Why it is that a businessman happens to be a hungry reader of philosophy and literature? Why it is that I would like to engage your intellect for the brief time—as you've made quite clear—that you deign to enter our house for a visit rather than a mission of mercy? Why it is that I do not find the topic of Hannah's misfortune as interesting as you apparently do? My dear Alice: Hannah herself purchased that gorgeous bronze only a few weeks ago, gave it to me on our anniversary, as a token of her love and esteem."

I was silenced. If he had told me just then to go to my room, that I would receive no supper, that he expected me to reflect upon my unimaginative, unsophisticated nosiness, I would have bowed my head and obeyed. His questions—and the mild but stinging severity of his tone, and those gray eyes that seemed never to have been averted, downcast, or frightened—had the effect of an incantation, a conjuring. I had never felt so small.

He stretched his arm along the back of the couch and waited for me to reply. He was patient. Finally he said, "You are unhappy with me. I don't want you to be unhappy. Would it relieve you to know that our very bright but not very well-educated Hannah most likely believes that the statue represents a benign and thoughtful swan who has come to offer the girl a magic-carpet ride, as it were?"

"She doesn't know the story."

"Not in any of its incarnations. But don't tell me that you prefer not to imagine the exquisite piquancy, if she *did* know the mythical story perfectly well. Or that you seriously think of Leda as a mere victim, indifferently raped. Poor delicate Leda. Poor little Hannah. Please. Such simplicities are entirely unsatisfactory to the intelligent mind, including yours."

I nodded, obedient. There was another silence between us. I finished my drink.

"You are more astute than you think you are."

I said, "Thank you."

He got up, went to the kitchen, and returned with the bottle of scotch. My "thank you" kept on hanging there over the couch like exhaust smoke from the little engine that could.

I noted that he poured less than a jiggerful into my glass, a splash for the road. He made his point: I was not to think that he was disregarding my desire to make the visit a short one. Meanwhile, he would be the earnest and attentive host, apparently eager for stimulating, speculative conversation of the sort that made for pleasurable late nights with Eric, but quite willing to let silence preside if his dull-witted guest could not rise to the occasion.

He stood at the window, looking out. "It's a pity, about your friend Darrell. As he left here that night, he quoted *Romeo and Juliet*: 'I'll prove more true / Than those that have more cunning to be strange.'"

I didn't ask which night. Mr. Jensen was telling me. He was telling me that Darrell had been there on the night he died. What he was not telling me was what to do with this bit of information—where, in my smallness, to find a place for it.

I said, "I'd better go now."

"Grow?"

What to say?

At the door he took my hand, held it for a moment, then let it drop. "Until next time," he said.

It was late afternoon when I got back home and went to bed.

Bed is sometimes good, isn't it, for creating the illusion of cozy peace of mind, especially on dark days when the outside does not want you out there, when it wants nothing to do with you and your garden tools or your walking shoes, when being merely indoors will not suffice. So you get into bed, and then maybe you get into a book, a cave within a cave. But that was not one of those days. The outside had nothing to do with it. Nor did it have anything to do with it when I pulled the covers over me after I returned from the Jensen house with the mildewed taste of that "thank you" still in my mouth: thank you, Mr. Jensen, for thinking well of me. For allowing me to play apprentice to your sorcerer. Thank you for suggesting that, like yours, my inclinations are not simple, no, not a bit, they are all in favor of the exquisite piquancies.

A couple of days after Darrell was buried, I was in bed with what I called the flu—meaning I felt like hell though I had no symptoms, no fever or sore throat or sick stomach. I called Richard and asked him to cover my class for me.

"It must be bad," he said. "You're the only teaching assistant besides Darrell who has never missed a class."

"Yes. It's bad."

But my plan was to fight it off, get into bed with a volume of Stevie Smith's poems and make some headway on next week's class preparation, jot down some notes, have some worthwhile thoughts. Nevertheless, I was asleep when the doorbell rang and kept on ringing.

It was Hannah.

Hannah in pink, dressed for spring. There was a ribbon tied around her thick ponytail. Closer to thirty than to twenty, married, rape victim, presenting herself as some kind of high school cheerleader. She was carrying a bag of groceries and a milk bottle full of roses from her garden.

"Richard told me you are one sick cookie. This is a new American expression for me. I have not seen what a sick cookie looks like."

"Like me."

"Crumbled."

"Something like that."

"I will uncrumble you. Go back to bed." She handed me the roses, then went off to the kitchen, humming "There's a Place for Us" from *West Side Story*. When I had to tell her that I thought we'd done all we could to improve her grades by talking our way through her version of *Clue*, I had suggested she listen to American musicals. I loaned her my records. She soon had them all by heart.

I went back to bed, too grateful to spend much time wondering why it was so easy to turn myself over to her. If someone else had dropped by to look in on me, I would have properly dressed, I would have made the bed, I would have offered refreshments.

Hannah placed a tray in the middle of the bed: there were two bowls of beefy cabbage soup, some hot rolls and butter, two glasses, and a half bottle of red wine. Then she looked at me and said, "Me, too." She took off her shoes and got under the covers.

"You don't feel well?"

"I feel that I want to be doing whatever you are doing." She moved the tray up between us and poured the wine.

Even though I was leaning against the headboard, my feet nearly reached the other end of the frame. Hannah's made an under-the-bedclothes hillock about halfway. My little sister, I thought. She does whatever she feels like doing—which is admirable, right? Disquieting, but nevertheless admirable. And I thought about Eric—Hannah and Eric, lying down together, necking. The Korean saber, hanging on the wall above the couch where Darrell went to sleep forever. Hannah in pink, bearing gifts, getting into bed with me. I didn't know what to think.

"This is the soup I make that is everybody's favorite." She passed me one of the bowls. "Darrell used to say that I must have Cossack blood inside me, to make a soup like this. But I told him not to call me that word."

"He meant it as a compliment, don't you think?"

She nodded her agreement as she lifted a spoonful of soup to her mouth. When she could speak, she said, "All things to him brought out a compliment."

"I miss him," I told her. "A lot. He was undiscriminating much of the time, but that was part of his goodness, his kindness."

"My husband said that the funeral made you disgusted."

"That's one way to put it. I guess he didn't like it, either. As you know, he asked me to give him a ride back to your house."

We were both holding the soup bowls up under our chins, not

pausing for wine, for rolls. The soup was better than delicious—you'd have taken us for two hungry kids who had gone days without being able to keep anything down.

Hannah went on. "We wanted for my husband to have some time to know you better," she said. "The others, he knows them. But he says that Alice keeps a distance. So we wanted after the funeral for him to go with you."

"We?"

"Me and Eric. Richard said okay José, it was all right with him."

So Hannah and Eric had arranged for Alice to spend time with Mr. Jensen. Hannah, who was in my bed. And Eric, who was never in my bed. I let the word "matchmaking" cross my mind, then banished it. Too sinister. There had to be some other explanation. "Your husband doesn't need to know me in order for you and me to be friends."

"Of course he does, Alice. But that is a good thing, isn't it? He is the kind of man who wants to know people, to talk to them. I told him you were not that way, that you were private and a by-yourself person, but you could be changed, and I think I am right." She set her empty bowl on the tray.

"Maybe so."

She responded with an irrelevant bit of show tune: "'*Getting to know you, getting to know all about you. Getting to like you, getting to hope you like me.*'"

"I like you, Hannah."

"I know you do. And I like you. And so does my husband. You will like him, too, I am sure of it. Have some wine now. You will feel better."

"You told him that I was lonely."

"Everybody is lonely, is what I think. Even me sometimes. Even Mr. Jensen. Nobody is left out. Your bed has a good smell, Alice."

I drank some wine but didn't feel better, felt instead the kind of loneliness that has everything to do with the loneliness of everyone else. It's one thing if it's just you, and in your loneliness you imagine that in rooms all about town there is uncensored friendship going on, intimacies that are a comfort and a joy and that might still be within your reach. It's another thing if in your loneliness you imagine, not rooms where there are carpets and cushions and talk that matters, but pine board widows' walks inhabited by solitary pacers who wring their hands and wait for a sign that this is not the way it is for everybody, everywhere.

I said, "Please tell Richard not to join the army. He'll do whatever you say."

Hannah poured the last of the wine into our glasses. "Richard needs to be a hero."

She knew him all right—and, truth be told, I didn't like it, didn't like the power it gave her, resented whatever crumb of power it took away from me. But there it was.

"I can't argue with that," I told her. "Joining the army, though, going to Vietnam—there must be a better way."

"All the ways we choose to get something lead down the road to the same place."

"You're philosophical today, kiddo. My point is, Richard could wind up dead."

"That's the place I'm talking about, you one sick cookie! I like that expression, don't you?"

Hannah closed her eyes. What does she see, I wondered, behind those mesmerizing eyes? Backstage, as it were? Before long, I took the glass from her hand and moved the tray off the bed. She curled onto her side, with a fistful of bedspread pulled close to her chest.

Hannah's long nap in my bed—she slept like a child for an hour—did not noticeably flatten the ribbon in her hair, took none of the zest out of her ponytail.

"You have a good bed for sleeping," she told me when she finally woke up, her cheeks pink with rest or dreams.

I wouldn't have been surprised had she performed a couple of back-flips on her way out.

FOURTEEN

Two months after that nap-time visit from Hannah, there was a going-away party for Richard Stone at the Jensen house. A May Day party, they called it. There were pastel streamers and fresh-cut heaps of flowers and bottles of champagne.

May Day, what a term. Celebration of spring. Unless you think of it lowercased, one word—then it's what you say when you're in a heap of trouble. I called the day before the party and offered to get there early, help set things up. I wanted the "next time"—as in Mr. Jensen's "until next time"—to be, if it could be, voluntary, independent, and grown-up. Hannah responded to my call with a laugh and an "I love you, my friend Alice. Be here at four."

There was a wily breeze on the day of that party, a skirt-lifter, a hairdo un-doer, a seed scatterer. It was a Friday, no classes that day. After lunch I went for a long bike ride, one that took me down and around Fairmont Park, where a few young mothers in loose, breeze-beckoning clothes were watching their children thrill themselves on the swing sets. Where a trio of young men between jobs were smoking cigarettes and fishing as if nothing depended on it, perhaps taking a glance, now and then, at the wistful mothers. Where a middle-aged woman, neatly nyloned and belted and begloved—a Junior Leaguer?—was riding the kiddie roller coaster, round and around, all by herself, stiff as an ironing board. And where an older man, a Mexican with beautiful white hair, hair as white as the Sunday shirt he was wearing, was sitting on the ground in the shade, feeding the geese and the ducks, talking to them in proverbs, in Spanish.

I paused nearby, on the other side of the tree, to listen. If he knew that I was there—and I think he did—he didn't seem to mind, he didn't stop talking, offering bits of bread, bits of wisdom. The breeze blew a thought into my head: I could love such a man. I ought to be in love with a man like that. A nonsense thought, the thought of a silly goose, for which I thanked the trifling wind.

As I listened to him speak, I furnished myself translations when I could, knowing that I'd have a better shot at remembering the English versions of the sayings he was announcing to his rustling, hungry audience with respectful precision, sometimes repeating himself, as if he wanted to make sure that the gift of his proverbs was as evenly distributed as the gift of his bread. As soon as I got home, I wrote down the few that stuck, and then, with help from my dictionary, translated them back into the more melodious Spanish. They're here with these old photographs and newspaper clippings.

Entre tesoro escondido y oculta sapiencia,
no se conoce alguna diferencia.
There is no known difference between
hidden treasure and hidden knowledge.

Él que está en el lodo
querría meter al otro.
He who is in the mud
would like to get someone else in it.

Si quieres que tu amigo no te tenga al pie sobre el pescuezo,
no le descubras tus secretos.
If you don't want your friend to have his foot on your neck,
don't tell him your secrets.

Coja es la pena, más llega.
Pain limps, but it arrives.

Those gifts, those lucky ducks, that puckish breeze, and the second new dress within a space of three months (a highly unusual splurge, believe me) put me in a mood that afternoon for dancing, for letting go of all the groundless, unphraseable suspicions that had been pestering me for weeks. At four o'clock, I drove up to the Jensen house with the image of the white-haired gentleman at my side, the sound of his voice in my ear, his musical cautions. "Quack, quack," I said to him. I was happy.

And I didn't let myself become unhappy when not Hannah but a dressed-in-white-linen Mr. Jensen greeted me at the door. He told me that Hannah had gone out to pick up the cake, that she'd be back in less than an hour.

I said, "She wants us to spend some time alone together."

He smiled at this with too much pleasure, as if the cat I'd let out of the bag were well known, well stroked, a special favorite. His hand again touched my elbow as we walked into the living room. He said something a bit too complimentary about my appearance, offered me a glass of champagne, and handed me a roll of crepe paper.

"I'm not good at this sort of thing," I told him.

"Which sort of thing, Alice?"

He touched my hair, moved a wind-blown curl away from my face.

I wouldn't have said this at the time, but I'll say it now: it was hard not to nibble on that bait.

I looked up at him—at those wide gray eyes that seemed to know no shame, that were doing whatever it is eyes do when they seem to be licking their lips. Was I flattered? A little. Just enough. Tempted? Yes. But what I was telling myself was: You won't get me into the mud with you, Señor Jensen.

I said something like, "I'm not good at hanging crepe paper. It tends to come out either twisted too tightly or not twisted at all. But I'll do the best I can." I set my glass of champagne on the coffee table and prepared to get down to business. I felt like a Girl Scout, full of mottoes, unseduceable. "You take one end, I'll take the other. Now, where do we start?"

"I have no idea." He was still giving me the gaze, the teasing smile.

"I would have thought you had ideas about everything."

This made him laugh, broke the spell he'd seemed to be working on himself, the watch-me-send-out-heat spell. "You are in a humor of some sort today," he said. "I like it. I'm pleased that you're here before the others arrive. It's as if we were friends at last."

Mr. Jensen and I hung the crepe paper, as if we were friends, from the four corners of the living room to the central lighting fixture, where we let streamers dangle. As if we were friends, we set candles afloat in both the front yard and the backyard ponds. We attached balloons to Hermes' hands. We had the sort of fun doing these things that friends might have—though I was secretly glad that he was not my friend. I was sure that he would have his foot on my neck in no time.

But for the night of Hannah's rape, when I saw so little, I hadn't seen the Jensens together, hadn't seen them as husband and wife. As the wife who had left a tattletale love-bite on the neck of one of her friends. As the husband who seemed to have been making a pass at yet another friend. I expected to see some indication—strain, awkwardness—that these things mattered. But I didn't see one. Hannah and her husband were not only playfully comfortable with each other, they were affectionate and tender, glowing like satisfied lovers.

The thing is, they were the same way with all of us—with Richard, with Eric, with me. Certain images and words from that party are as lasting as my photographs:

Mr. Jensen kisses Hannah, not a quickie, when she returns with the cake. Hannah reaches up to hug me and says, "You look good enough to eat." Mr. Jensen hugs that hug. "You two are my favorite girls."

Hannah asks Mr. Jensen and me to help her choose something to wear. We do not leave the bedroom when she changes her clothes, then changes them again. Eventually, Hannah is wearing light blue layers of chiffon and a flapper's string of pearls. Before long, she takes off the pearls and places them around my neck.

Mr. Jensen caresses Hannah's hair as she gives the arriving Richard a kiss on the mouth. Eric follows Richard inside. He's wearing a lightweight cream-colored suit that Hannah must have bought for him. Mr. Jensen is all smiles. He says something to Eric in German, and then they kiss each other on both cheeks. Eric offers to make drinks, as if he were the host.

Hannah turns up the music and invites me to dance. Mr. Jensen stands with one hand on Richard's shoulder as they watch us twist and twirl in our dress-up clothes.

Eric and Mr. Jensen take their drinks down to the front-yard pond, while I unwrap a tray of hors d'oeuvres. I leave Hannah and Richard slow-dancing in the living room.

I take the tray down to the men at the pond. The breeze lifts the silky folds of my green skirt. I'm a walking lily pad. Mr. Jensen calls me a "darling," then kisses my hand. Eric is grinning, he's beautiful.

It was like that, a love fest, for the rest of the evening. Mr. Jensen was not the same man who had seemed to be coming onto me—he was simply charming and fond. And Hannah was not the same person I thought of as a little sister—she was loving and womanly. Together, Mr. and Mrs. Jensen were quite a team: everyone's adoring mommy and daddy, everyone's sweetheart.

We had a grand time. I didn't think "Mayday! Mayday!" I didn't wonder, as I do even now, what the Jensens were like when they had no company. I went, as they say, with the flow: a stream of affection that seemed to have no weedy, entangling bottom, no sudden, sharp rocks, no muck.

It's a good thing, I suppose, that I was from the start in a mood to enjoy myself, and that my white-haired gentleman did not leave my side, so that I didn't enjoy myself too much.

We made toasts to May Day. To long life. To Hermes. To Hannah. No mention was made of Richard's dreadful enlistment, his imminent departure for boot-camp. No mention was made of Mr. Jensen's plan to move eastward, with Hannah of course, and Eric, as soon as his transfer came through.

We did not refer, even obliquely, to the rapist still at-large. Instead, we devoted ourselves to feasting: we ate shrimp and avocados, we ate scalloped potatoes and leg of lamb, we ate oranges and chocolate cake, we drank whatever was being poured.

I was being so pampered by my rich friends that night that I didn't feel the usual edginess with Eric—the awkward neediness, the wishful thinking. Besides, he was the other Eric, the one who made light of my holding onto stolen property. He was in an odd way good company, though his attention was all on the Jensens.

Richard, sentimental Richard, was like a fish who was finally *in* water, in his natural, lovey-dovey, hard-to-come-by element. But he, too, was not quite himself: over dinner he kept tossing out quotations with a kind of hysterical abandon, the way a wealthy man might give away his fortune at the last minute to all comers.

I remember him giving to Hannah, from *Leaves of Grass*, the line: "A woman waits for me, she contains all, nothing is lacking."

To me he said, with a good deal of take-this-under-advisement, Alice, a line from Frost's "Birches": "Earth's the right place for love."

To Eric, from *The Waste Land*, raising his glass, he produced: "the awful daring of a moment's surrender / Which an age of prudence can never retract / By this, and this only, we have existed."

And to Mr. Jensen, from Eliot's "Gerontion," he offered: "Neither fear nor courage saves us. Unnatural vices / Are fathered upon our heroism."

To us all, as a toast, he cited E. E. Cummings: "i spill my bright incalculable soul." There were many more such displays of his literary memory, of the change that took place that night in our otherwise modest "man of the people." But in the course of that delirious party—could it be that I alone was delirious?—the change in Richard was greeted with everyone's approval. We egged him on. I took part in that, damn it. Applauded the spilling of his incalculable soul.

After dinner, Hannah and Richard and Mr. Jensen danced together in a stumbling clump. I sat with a woozy Eric on the couch. I think that if I'd wanted to, I could have drawn his head into my lap, done a fairy dance with my fingertips across his brow, held him in my arms for a while. But I wasn't sure that he would know who was holding him—there were, at that party, too many options. Instead I leaned close and asked him what Mr. Jensen had said in German at the door, when he and Richard arrived for the party.

"He said *alles ist so wei es sein sollte*. Everything's the way it ought to be." Eric closed his eyes and hummed along with the music.

I draped Hannah's pearls over his neck.

Coja es la pena, más llega.

I think it was around midnight when I left—not before hugs and kisses were handed out all 'round, the party favors of choice on that occasion. Eric and Richard did not leave when I did.

I had danced at least one dance with everyone—a twist and mashed potatoes with Hannah, a waltz with Richard, a cha-cha and a fox trot with the suave Mr. Jensen, and a slow dance with Eric, my arm up around his bony back, his arm around my waist, his breath landing close to my ear. Our free hands were clasped, tucked in against our shoulders. Our bodies were touching.

It must be said that he had just danced the same dance to the same music, albeit more laughingly, with Richard. After me, it was Hannah's turn.

"*Whether you're right, whether you're wrong, man of my heart, I'll string along . . .*"

I was almost home when I remembered something about the words of greeting Mr. Jensen had offered to Eric, in German. They were the same words that Hannah had spoken to her husband on the night of the rape.

FIFTEEN

My señor in Fairmont Park: it's good to have him back, good to be writing him down right now, keeping him with me, a travel companion long before I set out on this recent journey.

Did I take an appreciative look at the atrium in the Brown Palace Hotel? For a minute or two. Did I spend any time in Denver worth talking about, seeing the sites? No. I stayed in bed until ten, sleeping, waking, then sleeping again—more a typical than an anxious night in a new place, I guess. Did I need to work on my mendacity? Probably. Did I think twice before I decided to head north, spend a day in Cheyenne, and go to the rodeo? No.

But going to Cheyenne wasn't entirely a whim. I made up reasons to go there. For one thing, I could be in Cheyenne in only a couple of hours, and so give the old bones a little rest. The next day I could get onto another interstate that would take me, eventually, right into Chicago. For another, I'd never been to a genuine rodeo, and Cheyenne promised the "Daddy of 'em All." What better way to implement the don't-think-about-what's-ahead part of Plan B?

And there was this: Wyoming was the first state to give women the vote. Oughtn't a diligent female voter—who had at least been friends with a real feminist—go there? Step foot? Be proud? True, at the time that women were given the vote, as I learned from one of the guidebooks, the men in Wyoming outnumbered the women about six to one—so perhaps this instance of equal rights had something to do with courting: which is to say, not equal rights but the same old horny thing.

There was this, too: one of my former students at RCC, a young black man who loved literature and wrote poetry, and who made damn sure that he got some kind of college education, was born and raised in Cheyenne, Wyoming. I'd thought, when I met him, "Wyoming?" As if growing up there had to be much worse for him than being one of only four young black men attending my city college.

I wanted to see the town that had produced Lane Francis. I wanted to look him up, if he'd gone back after graduation. And yes, there was one other reason: there was the David MacLean as cowboy, from my dream, still hovering with his cheerful phrases. The only bit of cheer I'd been given during my stay at Logan's B&B. Take it as a sign, I told myself. Even if that *was*, according to Sheila's psycho-logic, my own underbelly's "yippee-ki-yay."

Bottom line: I didn't want to be in the car by myself for hours. Not that day. Not so easily "pegged" as a liar and a white wine drinker. Too much invasive Mr. Jensen in that damn bartender.

Cheyenne, Wyoming—not the outskirts, of course—is stately, Victorian, park-filled, and yet it still has all the feel in the mid-1990s of an outpost on the wide-open frontier. The place is a fantastical mix of the rich man's Anglophilia and the poor man's American West that loves nothing better than itself. I suppose this is true of many of our major cities, but in Cheyenne the combination seemed to me to be peculiarly fraught and fabulous. Or maybe it was the weather that day—the kind that seems to strike a pose and demand your gratitude and applause. Whatever it was, I let it put me in a much-longed-for good mood. Maybe too good.

I'd had a bite to eat in the car—no stops for lunch required. I'd found a good but not exorbitant place to stay for the night, then gone shopping, bought myself a jean dress and some comfortable, lace-up boots. I was going native, come what may. And I'd found my way to the rodeo. I'd done everything just right. No glitches. No thinking about what lay ahead or behind. More or less.

I missed seeing Lane Francis by two days. But I couldn't count the good news about him as a glitch. The "L. Francis" in the phone book turned out to be his brother, Lincoln, who told me that Lane had recently paid a visit but was living now in Taos, writing poetry and waiting tables, "happy as the day is long," Lincoln told me. And then, "Praise the Lord."

Moods: sometimes you can simply turn away from them, let them starve, right? But it's so tempting to feed them. To lay on a banquet for your blues—stuff them with torch songs, with images of what might have been, with mildewed mementos and old letters. You can put some meat on the bones of a good mood, too, with all kinds of unlooked-for delicacies—a breeze in early morning sunlight, a stranger's voice offering praise, the smell of horses and saddlery, or boots that fit right from the start. Do such treats banish your regrets, your anxieties? Not in the least. But if you allow them to nourish a fought-for, fledgling good mood, the rest keeps quiet for a while.

So, that was me in Cheyenne, plump with unexpected peace of mind (I'm guessing that telling the truth did me some good, but at the time that bartender was synonymous with humiliation) when I showed up at the gate of the stadium.

Behind me a man's voice said, "If you'd be inclined to accept an Annie Oakley, I've got one for you, ma'am."

I didn't turn around. I figured he was offering me some manner of drugs.

"No, thanks."

"I'm offering you a free ticket, ma'am. If you stay in this line, they're gonna charge you for more events over the next several days than you're likely to be hankering for."

I looked at him.

"An Annie Oakley?"

"A freebie, ma'am. No strings attached, that's a promise. You're a greenhorn, aren't cha?"

I couldn't tell for the life of me whether, at first sight, he was a kind man or a mean one, but I liked the look of him.

I liked the look of him despite a few telltale uh-ohs—the ragged white ponytail that drooled down his back, and the even more ragged goatee, the long cigar he was puffing on, and the turquoise studs he wore in *both* ears, mind you. But maybe because of the leathered spiderweb his smiling face became when he looked at me: that smile, insofar as I could make it out through the smoke that curled round his face, made him seem to be one genuinely nice man.

"Yes," I told him. "'Greenhorn' about covers it."

"The whole enchilada?"

"I don't even know you, mister."

"You're about to, ma'am."

"I don't think so." I was still in line for a ticket, still inching along, trying to be patient there among the families, the always-in-a-hurry kids, bouncing in place since they couldn't go forward.

"A box seat freebie in the shade is all I'm offering. And my company. Or not, if you'd prefer. No harm intended. I'm not a varmint, ma'am. In case you've heard—"

"About the men in Wyoming?"

"We're here to please." He touched the brim of his hat and nodded—a cowboy's version of a bow—then went on. "So where are you from? Where are you headed? What are you doing in Cheyenne? And where have you been the last—pardon my guessing—fifty years or so?"

"Riverside, California," I said. "Since I was five. I lived there more than fifty years, truth be told."

"So you're not just a tall woman, you're a *grown* one."

"Very much so." I think he saw me blush. "And I'm headed east. I decided just this morning to see your rodeo on the way."

"That explains it," he said.

"What?"

"Why I've been leaning forward in the saddle since sunrise or thereabouts."

"You've been riding your horse?"

"No, ma'am. Today's his pasture day. What I meant was, I've been raring to go since daylight, geared up for no reason I could point a finger at 'til I saw you."

I did my best not to let the flattery stick, not to play toast to his buttering up. "I'm tall, mister, and grown, and old enough to know a come-on when I hear one."

He took off his hat then, bowed a real bow, showed me his balding scalp, and said, "Then lemme put it this way. May I invite you, a newcomer to these parts, to be my guest for the premier bronco-riding event that is about to take place and may well be over by the time we finish all this preliminary how-dee-do?"

"You're awfully kind, mister, but—"

"Angelo Lewis." He presented a sun-worn hand, a patient one that was going to keep its easy grip on mine until I got my etiquette in order.

"Alice Clark."

"Pleased to make your acquaintance, Alice. Lewis and Clark—don't that beat all. You can tell me more about yourself while we're watching the broncs, if that's agreeable."

I looked right at him, determined as could be. "I definitely did not say that I would—"

"Yes you did, señorita." With the palm of one leathery hand, he patted his heart. "In here. You said 'sure thing.' Definitely."

Let's call that a lucky guess.

Our seats seemed to me to be among the best in the stadium, excluding the ones reserved for Cheyenne's elite, where the men were wearing summertime suits, the women sported elegant afternoon dresses and elaborate cowgirl hats, and the drinks were served in real glasses by dandy waiters.

My "date," if you will, was a little too easy to talk to, though for a moment I wondered whether anything I was saying was penetrating the smoke that wrapped about his head like an Arab's burnoose. Mind you, I'd been a smoker, and haven't to this day stopped allowing myself the occasional cigarette. But I'd never seen anything quite like Angelo's method, if that's what it was.

He asked about my job. "You're a school teacher, aren't cha?" (why is this so all-too-clear?). And I told him, among other things, about Lane Francis. He noted my new boots, and I told him about buying a pair for Bunny. "No children of your own, right?" And he asked, with all manner of pardon, what was ailing my hands. "Looks like something hereditary." Then he inquired about my family, appeared to be genuinely puzzled that I had none living to speak of. "You've got cousins somewhere." None I'd ever heard mentioned, I said. My parents' respective families went their own ways, left us to ourselves. He said, "But they're out there somewhere, a slew of cousins." Given what he was able to piece together without my help, I was inclined to believe him about the cousins.

"What about you?" I asked.

"I'm retired, like you, but from all sorts of things—cattle, horses, construction, real estate, insurance, bee-keeping. Now I'm down to one good horse, five acres, a weatherproof house on a rise, money in the bank, and a front porch that faces west, toward the Tetons. My kids are all grown up and moved away. You're surprised I'm a solid citizen, aren't cha?"

"Are you one?"

"Good question, Alice." He puffed away at his cigar, smiling as if he were about to laugh.

My good question wasn't answered. The people around us—mainly beer-drinking men in pairs and threesomes, a couple of frazzled families bearing wands of cotton candy—were suddenly on their feet, unmindful of their fistfuls of food and drink. Something splashed against the back of my neck, our laps were sprayed with popcorn. But no matter. We were quickly among the upright spectators and their exclamations:

"That buster don't even know the guy's there, looks like!"

"Why don't they lasso the sucker!"

"Horse is s'posed to be that crazy when the guy's *on*, not when he's lying on the ground!"

"Shee-it! That was a winning ride!"

"Nah, just a rocking horse 'til now."

"Guy slid off like he was silk pajamas. And now look! Yee-ouch!"

The unfortunate rider had apparently pushed off from his bronc in such a way that he was caught underfoot, between the trampling forelegs and the bucking hind legs—maybe not for long, but too long in any case. They told us later over the PA system that the young man's arms were broken.

"Nevertheless," I said to Angelo, "I'm rooting for the horses."

"'Course you are."

"Do you say that because you presume that women are invariably in favor of the horses?"

"And the deer and the buffalo and the fox and the grizzly bear and all manner of critter, that's my bet. But I'm with you one hundred percent. I reckon it comes from the female side of my nature: my wanting a break-loose, white-eyed bronc to show up who'll give one of these sorry fellahs a ride—not a stomping—he'll never forget. So far, the pickings have been too easy. Cadillacs, not Mustangs. But—"

"Whoa there! Back up. Go back to the so-called female side of your nature."

He glanced at me, maybe embarrassed, maybe a little offended. The look was too quick, and the air between us too hazy for me to tell.

"I didn't mean to—"

He was looking out over the stadium, not at me, when he grinned a private grin, then said, "No harm done, Alice. Go easy on yourself. There's some folks known me all their lives, and still can't believe what-all puts me together. I'd like a look through those opera glasses of yours, if you don't mind."

I handed him my petite binoculars. "I'm sorry, Angelo, about my saying 'so-called.' It's just that—"

He looked at me, finally, and gave me a full dose of that wonderful smile of his. "That's the first time you've used my name. Things are looking up, I'd say." He peered through the glasses. "Hot diggety damn! They're having some trouble in the chute with the next bronc."

"And that bodes well for our side?"

"'Our side.' I'm liking the sound of that, too. Yep, they may have an unbustable bronc on their hands. They're trying to calm him down a little, least so's the rider can climb aboard, but they're getting nowhere fast. Take a look."

There were four or five cowboys on the railing around the chute.

On and off the railing—they kept leaping to the ground, out of harm's way. One of them was trying to mount the red-and-white horse while the others tried to keep its head down, keep it from rearing up. But that horse was having none of it. He was an explosion going off in that pen. "You watch," said Angelo. "They'll give themselves a little time, bring out the clowns, try to cool that animal down a bit. But I'll wager it won't pan out worth a nickel. Good thing I'm not a betting man. I'd get reckless and rich on this one."

He was right. The clowns came out to distract us from the delay. "I didn't know this was a betting sport." Angelo laughed the way he smiled, as if he'd just discovered a star. "You are one unworldly school teacher, Alice. Always have been, haven't cha?" He was getting such a kick out of this that I couldn't jump to my defense—did I have one?—and deny him the pleasure.

"What you bet on, if you're a betting type of person, is the time: how close to the buzzer can the rider stay aboard a kick-ass bronc, or how many seconds after the buzzer can he keep on taking those bony-withers jolts to the scrotum from an easy one. Time with a capital T is the story here. The longer he stays on the bronc, the more it's gonna dish out whatever it's got. So what's your take, Alice, on our young rider who's not been able to get his sorry butt onto the back of rampageous ol' Red there? Where are you putting your money?"

"On the horse. Two dollars."

"You're wanting me to bet against you, which'll be the same as betting against my own horse sense?"

"Yes."

"Odds?"

"Two to one."

"Let's make it dinner for two if you win—Dutch treat, so you won't keep on believing that I'm only trying to seduce you. And, if you lose, we'll make it drinks only. Deal? A little of your time is all I'm asking. I don't want you sending me home with nothing but the barbwire garter." He must have seen the "what?" in my expression. "The boobie prize, Alice. You never heard of the fur-lined bathtub?

The porcelain hairnet? The barbwire garter? Jimminy, woman!"

He put his arm around the back of my seat and gave my shoulder a pat. "Look, señorita bonita, he's *on*." For a moment, the pat turned into an easy squeeze. At my age, I was being squeezed by a handsome, funny-boned older man, who wasn't shy about laying claim to "a female side."

The chute flew open and all of us were again on our feet. Rampageous Red, as Angelo dubbed him, was finally mounted. The clowns dispersed to various edges of the arena. And then the bronc lived up to his name. He was all unearthbound legs and rubberband back and unpredictable twists. He threw the rider a solid five seconds (that's a long time, I learned, in these things) before the buzzer went off, and even then refused to be subdued. It was as if that horse was against the whole enterprise, wouldn't become a doable bucking bronco if it killed him. When he was finally herded into a small corral, still kicking and carrying on, the people around us left their seats. I guess that bronc gave our fellow spectators the kind of thrill that calls for more hot dogs, more soda, more beer.

"Looks like I lost. So will a steak house suit you?"

"That depends."

"The place I have in mind, I guarantee you, is no hole-in-the-wall."

"My welching on the bet depends on whether you'll answer a couple of questions."

"Is it time for me to whip out my résumé?"

"No. But I'm curious about a thing or two."

"Then shoot."

"For instance, how is it that you came to have an extra ticket in your pocket today?"

"Fate was looking out for me."

"You're a rascal, but not trouble. Right?"

"For chrissakes I was born and bred a *man*, Alice. I'm gonna be worrying my ass off about you, what's left of it, you asking a question like that. Shall we get a move on? Take my word, we won't see a better bronc than the one we just saw."

"Are you going to tell me about your extra ticket?"

"Over dinner, if that's all right with you. I'm hungry as all get out."

It turned out that Angelo Lewis had been married four times, twice to the same woman, Muriel, who was the mother of his daughter, Amoretta, and the three boys, Bandit, Cameron, and Diego. And it turned out that his most current woman-friend, who remained nameless, had recently jilted him for a younger man just passing through—a cowpoke connected to the rodeo "administratively."

"This is mighty humbling, Alice. But you asked and I'm telling you. I've had those same box seats going on two decades. Last time I was stood up—that was back a few years, and that was on account of a genuine cattleman even I would have ditched me for, not some crew-cut in a suit and tie—I did the same thing I did this afternoon. Showed up at the gate and gave my extra ticket to somebody else, a teenage boy that time. This time, I got lucky."

"Don't count your chickens—"

"They're counted. You're here. That's all there is to it."

"You are one slick ladies' man."

"Yep." He pushed his plate aside and lit another cigar. "But nope, too."

According to Angelo, all of his women—there were clearly more than he'd specified—were crazier than hell about him, and he about them, but none could for long abide his sometimes knowing exactly what they were about to say before they said it. Nor his sometimes knowing what they had no intention of saying, ever, to anyone.

"It's a curse," he said. "This knowing things about women. Came upon me the first time I fell in love. Zap! It doesn't happen with men. Sometimes I've wished it did. I've wished I could hear their hearts talking, the way I do with the ladies. But they talk too soft, those hearts, barely a whisper. What I'm hearing right now is that you want me to come east with you."

Picture it: Dinner is over. You're resting your elbows on the table. You're enjoying the smell of his cigar. He takes your hand. The two of you are glossy with good food and drink. Now he has asked for the check. You haven't had anything resembling a date in, say, fifteen years. And you like Angelo Lewis enough to want to spend some time finding out whether or not he's trouble with a capital everything.

But you, Alice, are committed to an end of something, closing an old door—will it close? Will you be outside or in? Will you be alone? Will you wish you were? Will there be music? Will you ever know more than you know?

So even though you'd be inclined to linger in Cheyenne with this man, you're wondering how to say goodnight, goodbye, how to organize, in a hierarchy, the attractions of the here-and-now in relation to where you've been and what has to come next, whatever that is.

"Are you listening to me, Angelo, or to you?"

"You."

"I don't think so. But be that as it may. A friend of mine, a long time ago, when he was leaving for the East Coast on this same journey, told me: It's just something I have to do. You stay put."

"You stayed put for a long time, didn't you? Waiting for your friend to come home."

"Too long, yes."

"He wasn't a lover of yours."

"No, he wasn't. Now quit pretending to be rummaging around like an antique dealer in my head, all right? I like you best right here."

"Then we are of one mind, cowgirl. That's where I'm liking you, too. But you're looking ahead to your travels. And meanwhile you're still wondering whether or not I'm a solid citizen."

"I'll keep on wondering."

"Okey-doke."

He wrote his address on one of the cocktail napkins.

Angelo Lewis
#1 The Bluff
Cheyenne, Wyoming

"You need me, I'll be there," he said. "Don't have a phone, but the telegraph office still works in this town."

I looked at the napkin.

"Don't you be thinking what you're thinking now, Alice," he told me, reading my mind again. "I mean it. I'll be there. And you're not exactly—"

"I know. I'm no Wonder Woman."

While we waited for the check, he massaged my hands as if their gnarls were his own, as if he could feel it from my end. And then without any fuss or fumble, he kissed me right there in the restaurant. Not for long, I should say, but it was enough of a smooch to provoke a few laudatory hoots from the young men gathered around the bar.

"I'll stay put, señorita," he told me from inside his smoky cloak. "Waiting your return."

"I don't believe you for a second, señor." He laughed then. We both did.

"Good thinking," he told me.

SIXTEEN

THE LONG DRIVE from Cheyenne to Omaha was a drudgery, a bleakness through and through. I must have thought I needed to put a considerable distance, fast, between me and the man who'd called me a "humdinger."

In any case, I was rested and well-provisioned when I left Cheyenne, glad for the time I'd spent with him, and even more glad that I'd resisted any entanglement with the old rascal, and not glad at all that I'd never see him again. So there was some mooning about Angelo sooner rather than later, and a good bit of telling myself to get over it. Both of which made me now and then grip the wheel (something I'd been keen to avoid doing, lest my hands be all the more demanding at the end of the day) as I crossed and crossed and crossed the cornhusker state.

And there was the drought-dry Nebraska landscape, the thirsty and unbecoming Platte River, the road signs that kept on featuring forts and old graveyards and "Wild West" towns. Sites of battles with the Indians, gunfights among the settlers, infamous lynchings. I remember a sign that read: "See the Gomorrah of the Plains." And another that encouraged us to get off the interstate in order to visit "Carhenge: The Only Stonehenge Replica Made From Old Cars!" These things didn't lift my spirits.

Top that off with Mr. Jensen.

At some point, I felt him occupy my mind, move the furniture around, so to speak, so that he could spread out and make himself comfortable. He was coming along for the ride at that point.

You again, I thought. Can't this wait until I get there? Until we're face to face? And why you? Why not Hannah? Why does it have to be you, your voice, your ironic smile, that is as constant as bad weather, year after year after year. Why can't you leave me alone?

Because Alice can't leave *me* alone.

Of course I can, Mr. Jensen. I've been doing so for years.

Why must you continue to lie to me?

I don't know.

You want me to like you, though you want to be free not to like me in the least.

I think it's the other way around. You're confusing me with you.

Am I?

This isn't about you. I'm not doing this for you.

Alice doesn't know what's she doing.

Point taken.

I can't wait to see you.

That kind of thinking made me feel a little crazy, and *that* segued itself in no time flat into what you might call distress or shame or self-doubt or guilt or chagrin or humiliation or dejection or pensiveness or gloom or heartache. Waves of all the above, and not necessarily in that order.

Seems I can kid myself about it now, but at the time I was a definitive mess. More than a little crazy. I wouldn't have been surprised to see a thick cloud of locusts coming my way across that seemingly treeless prairie, in order to finish me off.

Perhaps I should have paid a visit to Carhenge.

I was within an hour or so of Omaha when I pulled myself together enough to get off the interstate. There was no town to speak of, but there were some worn wooden houses with yards and trees, and there were children outside playing some kind of ballgame. I stopped at a house-become-convenience store, whose relationship to its foundation was iffy at best. A hand-painted sign attached to the roof of the porch read: "Sandwitches, Sodas, Cures."

A sandwitch: I didn't want this to be a misspelling. I wanted there to be such persons inside that store. I wanted a sandwitch to help me get through the rest of the trip. And I got one. Two, in fact.

There were a couple of middle-aged men sitting in chairs out front, drinking sodas and smoking. They were far more long-legged than the Native Americans I used to see in Riverside—who were there, incidentally, because the Sherman Institute was there, which was there to un-Indianize them. I was out of my car when I heard one of the men tell the other a locals' joke, the kind a passer-through like myself is not supposed to laugh at: "Why's it so windy in Wyoming?" "I dunno." "Because Nebraska sucks." They tipped their hats to me as I stepped up on the porch.

Inside I was greeted by a young Native American girl, in her early teens, I guessed, who struck my dull imagination as too lovely to be a witch of any sort.

"Welcome, lady," she said. "What do you need today?"

"Do you have bottled water?"

"Yes, we have some of that."

"Your sign outside—it says 'cures.'"

"We have those, too." There was a stack of pamphlets near the ancient register. She handed me one. Her smile was perfection.

"I know one thing you need already. I'll get it, and the water, while you look at our book, okay?"

"Okay, child," I told her, in that voice that sometimes oozes out of me, as if I were every young person's auntie.

She paused, turned back to me. "I am twenty years old, lady. My son, Donny, is about to be two."

"You're twenty?"

"Everyone in my family says I look too young for my age. Sometimes the elders mistake me for my younger sister." She glanced up at me then in a way she hadn't before, lingering a bit. "Let that be a pleasure for you, lady. Not an embarrassment."

You know how, when you are upset but stoical or tight-lipped or outright afraid to let the floodgates open, and then someone, almost always a woman, touches you—and what happens is, your throat suddenly feels as if it had a dumpling caught in it, your eyes get teary, and you wish she hadn't touched you, but at the same time you're not sorry that she did. You do your best to swallow that dumpling, open your eyes wide to keep any tears from forming the rivulets they want to form. Then you speak a non sequitur, if you're able to speak at all.

My non sequitur was: "Sparkling water, if you have it."

"Carbonated? We have that. Are you okay, lady?"

"I'm fine." She disappeared then, left me with that pamphlet in my hand, and the lump in my throat. That particular lump is long gone, but I still have the pamphlet. It's a kind of recipe book, herbal remedies for the most part. It takes the precaution of calling itself a "supplement" to white man's medicine, but it includes a descriptive list of the flowers and herbs one ought to grow in one's garden, since white man's medicine is so often "no good for you." I now cultivate some of these medicinals: along with the relatively ho-hum chamomile and comfrey, there's mallow and motherwort, cinquefoil, feath-erfew, sweet flag, dove foot, shepherd's purse, and wood sorrel. I suspect that saying the names of this stuff is part of the cure. And there's a young sassafras tree, too. We keep everything in pots, so that they can come inside during the long Vermont winter.

At the shop outside Omaha, I thumbed through the booklet slowly, looking for a cure for something, I wasn't sure for what: not piles, not "bloody flux," not worms, not "king's evil" or "gleet" (whatever those are), not gout, not palsy, not warts or corns. Then I came upon a recipe called "Balsam for All Kinds of Pain." That's what I wanted, some of *that*:

> Take laurel leaves, wormwood sprouts, marigold flowers and leaves, of each two handfuls, cut them all very fine, sprouts of fine sage and rosemary flowers and leaves, each of three handfuls, and eight handfuls of juniper berries; put the whole in a glazed earthen pot, and after having poured over it a quantity of sweet oil so as to cover the whole amount about an inch, cause it to infuse amongst some very hot horse dung, during several days, then you will cook it over a very slow fire, and af-

> ter it is done, you must add to it a small quantity of new yellow beeswax, a small glass of brandy, and one dozen cloves; stir well the whole, and let it take a boiling over the fire, and then strain it through a strong linen, pressing the ground well, and keep it for use in an earthen pot.

When the young woman returned, I pointed to the page in the pamphlet and asked, "Do you have some of this balsam?"

"Yes, good choice. You have pain in a lot of places. But you must do this cure, too, lady. It is for your hands."

I thought: I must look a fright. Either that, or she's a sandwitch after all.

"It's almost time to end the day here. Where are you going?" she asked.

"There's an inn in Omaha. According to one of my guidebooks, it has a room with an especially large clawfoot bathtub. I reserved that room before I left Cheyenne this morning."

"The Offutt House?"

"That's the one."

"When you get there, do this." She took the book out of my hands, turned the pages, found what she wanted, then pointed to a recipe "Against Rheumatism." What she was putting into my plastic grocery bag, along with a bottle of carbonated water, was a thick jelly jar for me to pee into. The simple recipe goes like this:

> You must boil on the fire a glass of the urine of the person afflicted with it, then bathe the afflicted part; afterwards, dip a linen folded double in the urine, apply it on the pain and tie it up.

"How will I boil the urine?" I asked her.

"You will order room service, okay? Pay the extra. In special cases, they will do this. Ask for a candlelight dinner. There will be linen napkins, I know, because the father of my son and me, we made our baby there, on our honeymoon. Donny's father is gone now, but there will still be linen napkins at the Offutt House. Be patient. Hold the jar over the candle. It will boil. This jar will not break. Tie the napkin around your hands. Leave it on all night."

"But the smell—"

"There are many things worse to smell than ourselves. We are not so bad. I think for a white person you smell good on the outside, so maybe you do on the inside, too. Don't be afraid. This works. Wait now while I get you the balsam. We made it a week ago, but its power lasts, the old people say, six months or more. How much do you want?"

About a month's worth of being in your presence, I thought. But what I said was: "Does it come in grams, ounces, or what?"

"We have this in quart pots and half gallons. And it's very expensive."

"How much?"

"Seven-fifty for a quart."

"Seven hundred—?"

"Seven dollars, fifty cents. Where are you coming from, anyway? Hollywood, California?"

"Near there, yes."

"I'll sell you two quarts for twelve dollars."

"I'd be more than willing to—"

"I know you would, lady." She went away again, to fetch the balsam, just as a gray-haired woman came into the store. "Sally in the back?" the woman asked me, as if I were a neighbor, a friend of the family.

"Yes. She's gone to get me some of this." I showed her the relevant page from the booklet.

"Good for everything." She looked me over, curious and kindly, like a decent doctor, assessing my everything. "You are a tall person for a woman," she said.

"That I am." She was probably a foot shorter than I am.

"Your upset is taller than you are."

"I'm in a state, yes."

"Men," she said. "You need the urine treatment on those hands."

I reached into the plastic bag and displayed the jelly jar.

"Good. Do this first," she tapped the jar. "Don't mix with the other."

"Hi, Mom." Sally placed two clay pots on the counter, then gave the other woman a quick hug.

"I told her not to mix the cures."

"You're the boss." Sally and her mother both laughed at this.

"Open the pots. I wanna see how it looks."

"She's staying tonight at the Offutt House." They laughed—whatever the joke was, it tickled them no end.

I leaned in for a peek while Sally's mother dipped a finger into one pot and then the other. What I saw looked something like honey, only darker and thicker and speckled. "Bend down," she told me. "So I can reach you."

With the tip of her balsam-covered finger, she made a line across the center of my forehead, then rubbed it in. "To cure your thoughts," she said. "But wait until after the urine treatment to use this on your hands. Good for your back, too. Do you have someone?"

"No."

"Maybe you'll find somebody at the Off—"

She couldn't finish. It seemed that the very word had long since become the focal point of a story that mother and daughter thought hilarious. Me too, I couldn't help it: was the balsam on my forehead already working? We laughed like goofy schoolgirls. When it seemed, at one point, that we were getting hold of ourselves, Sally said, "That was the worst time of my life there, at the Off—." And she and her mother cracked up again, as if they would never be able to stop. The worst night? I was a little lost, as you can imagine, but their laughter was like a downpour, and me, I was like the drought-stricken plains, wide-open and grateful.

It took us a while to get back to the matter at hand. But when we were finally more or less composed, I asked, "Can I apply this anywhere?"

Sally's mother said, "Anywhere on the hard pains. Leave the soft ones alone. And never put it into your mouth or near your sex."

Sally must have sensed my next question. She said, "The soft pains come and go on their own. They come in exchange for special favors we ask of our bodies. They hurt, but they're good. The hard ones are there in exchange for living. They're good too, but they hurt more."

Her mother was nodding, smiling, putting the lids back on the pots. "We have to close the store. You feel okay?"

I was about to, but didn't, say that I was fine, thank you. "I'm a mess." I told them the truth. "But it seems to be a better mess than it was fifteen minutes ago."

"Mess is normal. You need to let you hair down." Her eyes told me that she knew, in so many words, that she was making a metaphor, but also that the metaphor had quickly turned into a plan. "Sit here. I will give you a braid. Sally, you close things up."

Sally's mother took the pins out of my hair and swept her smooth, rounded nails against my scalp. I decided then that, if I ever got settled someplace, I would get my hair done on a regular basis. Maybe pinned back up—but the point would be the massage, those combing nails, the desire to purr. Am I a silly old woman? So be it. "What's your name?" I asked her.

"Official tribal, it's Broken Wing Dove. Official American, I'm called Sue Fire. But I'm of the Sioux nation, so that name is always ready to be turned into a joke. If they don't want to joke with me, people call me Dove. Your hair is too thin. It needs to come down more, breathe some air."

I had a long—not as long as Dove's—loose braid down my back when I left that store. And a sack full of remedies and reading matter. And no more Mr. Jensen for a while—he'd been ousted, evicted by more powerful squatters.

Mother and daughter were there on the porch, waving as I pulled away. Again, it seemed we were neighbors. I found myself rolling down the window, giving them the peace sign. I don't know what came over me, I hadn't done that in a thousand years. And they gave it back, laughing their charms in my direction. The men on the porch laughed, too, and offered the peace sign, not just to me but round and about.

As I drove away with their V-shaped fingers at my back, I remembered that it used to be a warrior's salutation, chiefly Churchill's, and then the Allies' at large. V for victory. I was a pre-teen when I stood around as if I were being helpful while my mother and grown-ups I didn't know worked the soil in a Victory Garden—that was over on Ramona Drive, in a nice part of Riverside, near my old city college. My mother told me that the opening of Beethoven's Fifth (. . . —) was Morse code for V, and therefore for Victory, and she'd wave those two Churchillian fingers above my head while she sang out a da-da-da-daah. I suppose that for some, like Nixon, the V remained a symbol of triumph (though his hands-raised, two-fisted way of doing it made him, poor thing, seem all too vulture-like, didn't it?). But for the most part, in the sixties, victory was somehow or other taken out of that sign. Poof! Just like that, the two-fingered wave came to be about a world in which there ought to be no victors, no losers, no generals, no war. Same sign, entirely different meaning: a lasting appropriation, apparently, which was not initially pleasing to my mother (no doubt she was not alone in this). But I suspect that she would have joined in there—wherever we were, me and Sally and Dove and their friends, between Lincoln and Omaha, Nebraska—waving the peace sign as if there had been a different story of American history among us.

I called my mother by her first name. Lydia.

She was thirty-three and I was four when my father was killed in an accident in front of the building where he worked in the garment district, New York City. He was crushed by a truck that was not supposed to be backing up.

We moved to California a few months after the accident. There was nothing to keep us in New York, she told me later, when I was old enough to begin to hear bits of her story.

Lydia's immigrant parents, both factory workers in Syracuse, had gone back to the old country, to Poland, once their children were old enough to get jobs of their own. Her brother, Peter, followed them after six months or so of trying to take care of himself. Peter had a decent job as a salesman for Kodak. But according to Lydia, he too-achingly missed his mother's impatient tendernesses, her overcooked potatoes, her devout arguments with this Pope and that one. He lived with his parents—and brought his Polish wife to live with them, too. I never met any of these relatives. As for my father's kin, they disowned him for marrying a Catholic, no matter that she hadn't entered a church in years.

On the plane to Los Angeles, someone spoke to my mother about Riverside. More affordable than L.A. It was decided. We'd make our new life in Riverside. She had been a salesgirl in a department store in New York. She was a salesgirl in a department store in Riverside. We lived in a viewless two-bedroom apartment in New York. We lived in a viewless two-bedroom apartment in Riverside. And in both places the sound of trains—underground in one, above ground in the other—became as integral to the rhythm of our days as the rising and the setting of the sun. Riverside's plushy palm and orange and magnolia trees may as well have been New York City's throttled little maples. Different climate, same life. Except that we no longer walked by the spot where my hug-giving, happy father was killed, as if, if we did that often enough, we would discover that there had been some mistake, that it never happened. He'd be standing there, unloading the truck, my tall mustachioed daddy. He'd be waving at us, smiling an adoring family man's smile.

I never told my mother about Eric, about the others, about Hannah. She knew their names, she knew I had friends, a "peer group," as she put it. But I didn't tell her the rest. For all she knew, I slept soundly and longed, as she did, only for my handsome father, Nathaniel Clark.

She was tall, my mother, and thin but not bony. She wore her brown hair in upsweeping pioneer twists that would make you wonder what it looked like at night, when she would release it for private brushing. You would appreciate, too, her large dark eyes, the way they paid attention, and the seriousness of her mouth. When Lydia smiled, you knew that she meant it.

Once, before I was married, and not politely, I asked her not to treat me like an honorary widow. She decided it was time I had a place of my own. It was me who was treating myself like an honorary widow. And Lydia sensed it. She didn't sit back and watch. She cashed in her savings and put a big down payment on the house I lived in for all those years.

If she were with me here now, we would have one hell of a time holding hands, Lydia and I. And she would get such an old-world kick out of the balsam that promises to cure everything.

My mother wouldn't allow anyone to stand in for my father when I married Ted Fisher. Take my word for it: that was vintage Lydia.

"I'll be doing the giving away of the bride," she told the minister when we went to speak to him about the ceremony.

"It's unheard of in our church." He was a Presbyterian named Stewart something-or-other. I remember him as an elegant dresser whose face was too soft, too like a babydoll's. Lydia, though lapsed, still harbored far too much respect for the Catholic Church to want us married there.

"Everything starts out by being unheard of."

"Mrs. Clark—"

"Adam and Eve, for example."

"I'm sure we can find someone—"

"Turning water into wine."

"Mrs. Clark—"

"The locomotive, the TV dinner, nylon stockings."

"Wouldn't your husband have preferred—?"

"He is not replaceable. I can carry out this duty with a pure heart, knowing all the while that I am not taking his place. Find me a purer heart, and I'll reconsider."

Of course, he couldn't find one. So it was Lydia who was standing outside the church with me on that warm afternoon, who would escort me down the aisle when the music started up. Or not, if she'd had her way.

She took my arm and whispered, "The car is right over there. You say the word, and I'll take you wherever you'd like to go, within reason. We could drive to San Francisco, if you want. I've got some extra money on me."

"Everything's ready," I told her. "Everyone's waiting."

But there was no stopping her. "I have a bad feeling about this. It just doesn't sit well."

"Are you sure we shouldn't get someone else to walk me down the aisle?"

"How about heading up to Yosemite? We could rent a cabin. You could take a long walk and think twice."

"I'm going through with it."

"You can do better than this, Allie. This relationship is too so-so. Not bad, not good. I'd give it a C-minus if I were tipsy, a definite D if I hadn't touched a drop."

"I'm getting married to Ted."

"It's one thing to nurse a stray back to health, the way you've always done. Pigeons, puppies. And now this pre-pubescent boy—"

"Ted is hardly pre-pubescent."

"We'll see. But what I meant was, you're attending to the boy, Ted's son, what's his name—"

"Daniel."

"Daniel, yes. Poor baby. But you—your track record goes that they get better, then they fly away, go find somebody new to play with. Fine for them. Remember that girlfriend of yours in high school who—"

"Charlotte. She got better and stopped being my girlfriend."

"Loneliness is not a good enough reason to marry somebody."

"I'm not lonely," I told her. And, God bless her, she didn't call me on it.

Instead she said, "When they make me say that I'm freely giving you to that man, I won't mean it."

"Fair enough."

We heard the music. It was time. "Last chance," she whispered.

Lydia died at seventy-two, her insides so worn out by the side-effects of arthritis medication that she had to surrender. I was there with her, in the hospital, and the last thing that she said to me was "think twice." I reminded her that I hadn't asked for any advice. This made her smile a fond mother's smile. The kind that tells you that she continues to enjoy knowing you better than you know yourself.

Along with my most recent bottle of arthritis medication came a white slip of paper that should be fiction, but it isn't:

> Side effects that may not go away during treatment include nausea, vomiting, diarrhea, gas, constipation, stomach cramps, dizziness, lightheadedness, drowsiness, or headache; if these are bothersome, check with your doctor. If you experience depression, fatigue, blurred vision, ringing in the ears, swelling of hands or ankles, fever, sore throat, vomiting material that looks like coffee grounds, blood in the stool or in the vomit, or stomach pains, check with your doctor. Contact your doctor IMMEDIATELY if you experience seizures, swelling of hands, face, lips, eyes, throat, or tongue; difficulty swallowing or breathing; or hoarseness. If you notice other side effects not listed above, contact your doctor.

Imagine those *other* side effects. I have. And I've decided that, should I ever have to take one of those pills, I'd better get some kindly somebody to prepare to shoot me afterwards.

SEVENTEEN

In Omaha, I woke in a lovely room, in a mahogany sleigh bed, with my hands wrapped in damp napkins, reeking of piss.

Lydia would have cheered me on.

Did it work? What I'll say is this: Try it. But try it at home.

After I bathed again—there was easily room for two in that tub—I turned the sheets around on the bed, so that what remained of the odor would be discovered at the foot, not up by the pillows. In other words, I decided to grin and bear my letting the housekeeper think I was incontinent. The grinning was no problem for me that morning. But I'd rather have worked the cure in my own bed.

I'm not saying that, once again, lo and behold, I was in a good mood. The thing about moods, good or bad, is that they're transient—indeed, their changeability seems to be what's beguiling about them. It's what puts you in their service, makes you feed them whatever they want (picky eaters that they are). But that morning was not about a mood, not about anything that comes and goes. It was as if I'd found or been given something that I was to take hold of, keep, and act upon. It was a smallish something, in its infancy—and I'm uncertain about what to call it—but it was there all right, sprung up like a blossom, a perennial. Its one clear feature was that it was not something I'd planted all on my own. This was what I had to call a community project.

Yes, it had at least a little something to do with the fireworks smile of Angelo Lewis that had found itself a front-row seat into my crowded memory. And with the buoyant kindness of the hostess at the Offutt House. (She was surprised by my request for room service—these days, for the guests, she makes only breakfast—but without missing a beat she offered to fix me up with some leftovers, which turned out to consist of a soft local cheese and homemade dinner rolls and a French-style veal stew: it was the best meal I had on the trip.) And it may also have had something to do with the hypnotic effect of waiting for my urine to boil over candlelight, then falling into a good sleep while reading about catnip and horsetail and dandelion. But mainly it had to do with the neighborly laughter of Sally and her mother, who would not be daunted by any "worst nights." They reminded me whose daughter I am.

There was this, too—pardon the vanity: I liked my loosely braided hair. It moved, it swooshed between my shoulder blades, it slipped around my neck when I leaned over to lace up my new boots, surprisingly companionable.

At breakfast downstairs—where nearly every table was noisily occupied, and the cinnamon rolls were being gobbled up as if everyone were having a last meal, and a vibrant recording of Ella Fitzgerald was coming through the speakers—I wrote a note to Bunny, told her a little about Sally and Dove, said a lot, for the first time, about how much I missed her.

Then I consulted my maps: I could cross Iowa and be into Illinois by midday. But where to from there? Chicago? Was that my kind of town? No. I set my sights on Peoria.

I should have gone to Chicago, despite the heat wave. Big impersonal hotels everywhere. Air-conditioning, check in and then out. No questions asked.

Peoria was far more a city than I had expected, and a fine one: perched above the river, park-laden, considerable charm to many of the buildings—more Old World, less western than the places I'd been to at that point. But it would have nothing to do with me. And it was personal.

I had been so sure about my destination of choice that I didn't call in advance for a reservation. A big mistake.

At a gas station, the pregnant young attendant, a curly redhead who hadn't yet outgrown a bad complexion, asked seemingly cordial questions, but kept responding to my answers with undisguised contempt:

"*Vermont*? Why would anyone want to go *there*?"

"You're driving there *by yourself*? Aren't you too *old*?"

"You're staying *here* tonight, but you don't know *where*?"

And much more of the same. I guess she hadn't outgrown some other things as well.

It was raining when I found a quaint mid-sized hotel downtown, and I was soaked when I presented myself to the desk clerk. Maybe it was the pinkness of his mainly bald head, or the starchiness of his white shirt, I don't know, but he was the cleanest young man I'd ever seen. Not just spotless but positively scoured. He put on his glasses and looked at me, and then leaned over the counter to see if I were dripping. I was. His response to my apology and request for a room was: "Ordinarily, unaccompanied women, well, we'd rather not, in the past we've had, this is a men's, our policy is, even at your age—I'm afraid all of our rooms are taken for this evening."

At the second hotel, the proprietor, a burly and bespectacled woman in a business suit, had this to tell me: "The sign may say 'vacancy,' but in fact there aren't any. We'll change the sign once the rain stops. Meanwhile, you need to get yourself an umbrella. A body can just about see right through your blouse." She let me use the ladies' room in the lobby before I set out again. There was no pleasure to be had there from my appearance, but there was this gratifying bit of graffiti dialogue scratched into the stall door:

PRAY FOR ME.

Will do, hon.

I drove in circles for a while, passing the imposing mental health center three times before I found a drugstore, where I bought an umbrella. A boy of about six years old in a wet yellow slicker was standing behind me while we waited in line for our turn with the cashier. He gave my braid a couple of quick pulls, the way you do when you're signaling a bus driver.

"What do you want, young fella?"

"Nothing."

When my back was to him, he did it again. "Please stop that."

He put his hands on his hips and said, "Why should I?"

Outside, I put up the umbrella against what by that time was a driving summer rain, a Mack truck of water coming right at me. The umbrella was a joke, its delicate ribs reversed and bent within a minute. I was quite a joke myself, no doubt, and more soaked than ever.

At the third hotel, a much-sideburned man, maybe twenty years my junior and with a tag that said "Manager" pinned to his black shirt, said: "You lookin' for love in all the wrong places?"

At the fourth one, there were vacancies: "No problemo," the man said. His white cowboy hat was pushed back, so that he seemed part-boy, part-man. But he was all boyish smiles as he went on to say, "But I've got a hotel full of carousing dairy men tonight. You'll be the only cow among a bunch of bulls, pardon my saying so. I'd see about getting one of the rooms at the Old Church House, north of the city, if I was you."

I stood there, nothing but udder, while he gave me directions and advised me to pick up some food before I got there.

At the Old Church House, there were two guest rooms, one bath, and a ladder that led to a library in the loft. The place was cozy despite the high ceilings, and filled with antiques. A perfect getaway for lovers—or loners, if there were no other guests, as was the case that night. I had to forgive the man who'd called me a cow.

The owner I spoke with seemed preoccupied as I checked in. And this was a blessing—he was the only person I'd run into in that neck of the woods who didn't give me the once-over. I told him not to bother with the breakfast. He said, "Fine. You can pay me now and leave whenever you want." He, too, seemed to be having a difficult day. He drove off, left me there by myself. I don't remember what he looked liked, except tired.

There I was, just north of town, alone in the Old Church House. Not another soul in the immediate vicinity. I drew a bath and reminded myself that I knew precisely how to get to the mental health center.

The *Spoon River Anthology*—I'd crossed that river earlier in the day—was among the books in my room, and my choice for dinner reading. While I ate some fried chicken and coleslaw out of a box, Edgar Lee Masters' people did keep me company, but they are a fretful lot, for the most part, who say things like:

> I saw myself as a good machine
> That life had never used.

and

> That much-sought prize of eternal youth
> Is just arrested growth.

In other words, not good company. So after what I'm loosely calling dinner, I settled into a cave of feather pillows on the bed with a volume of Carl Sandburg's poems—he grew up in Peoria—and did my best to find a few lines to remember and appreciate.

Enough said.

I was asleep by nine and out of there before the sun came up. Ready to break all promises to my back and tackle a ten—(at best)—hour drive to Buffalo, New York. I'd made an overconfident, maybe hysterical, hotel reservation as soon as I was settled in the Old Church House.

Here was the route: from Peoria to Indianapolis, northward to Cleveland, then on to Buffalo. I'd have to keep at least a couple of my wits about me, but it was doable, I knew. I had already put in almost as many miles in one day, when I crossed Nebraska. And the balsam for all kinds of pain was something to write home about. After a night in Buffalo, I would head into Western Vermont. I made a pre-dawn stop for coffee and no-stops-along-the-way supplies (I arrived at that convenience store at the same time the bagels and donuts did; the delivery man was carrying a significant pistol in the holster around his waist), then drove right into the sunrise.

It's a shame that I was for all those flexible years such a homebody. I've found out far too late how much I like sipping lukewarm coffee through a straw, at dawn, with the car windows open, heading out to someplace I've never been. And that sunrise as I crossed the state line into Indiana was spectacular. The previous day's brief but ostentatious rain, which had been so successful at embarrassing yours truly, seemed intent on making apologies by providing me with a cool, cleansed morning air, the smell of wet grass and summertime weeds, and a clear canvas for the sun's plumey showgirl rising, for the puffs of cloud that prismed the increasing light.

A few weeks before I left Riverside, Bunny convinced me to let her have a "sleepover" at my house one night. If she'd had in mind to bring some schoolmates with sleeping bags in tow, the convincing would have been easy. But she had in mind that she, alone, would sleep in my spare room.

"I smell a rat," I told her.

"It's more like a mouse."

"What does this mouse want?"

"To show you what a really good roommate she can be."

In other words, it was about my leaving, about her wanting to come with me. The thing is, I had no doubt that Bunny would prove to be a good roommate, and I was impressed with her efforts to persuade me. Worried by them, too—why was she so determined to go with me? But I gave in without much struggle. Not, however, without setting some rules: No discussion of Vermont. No clandestine candy bars. You eat properly. You're in bed by nine. You can read for an hour. Lights out at ten. No flashlights for surreptitious reading under the bedcovers. You're up at six-fifteen.

"I *never* get up that early."

"You mean to say you've never seen the sunrise? Not ever?"

"So?"

"Ask me that insolent question, young lady, after you see it."

With a curtsy and a "yes, your majesty," she took all the sizzle out of my tone and made us laugh.

Turns out I slept through the alarm (which is uncharacteristic—maybe it was the presence of someone else in the house?). Bunny, pleased as could be, had to wake me up. But I was ready in a jiffy and drove us over to the Mission Inn, for sunrise followed by breakfast. Bunny hadn't been there before—she was clearly taken by its peculiar enchantments, especially the life-sized figures who circle in and out of the clock above the patio. No one was up and about at that hour except a few gardeners and a dozing receptionist, so we walked right in and took the elevator to the top, where the chapels are, and the views.

The sunrise that morning was a letdown. That's an understatement. It was as if Aurora were simply tuckered out by the same-old-same-old, didn't give a hoot that her reputation was on the line. I was hoping that she would show Bunny the whole works, a fan of golden-pink rays reaching up over the mountains, and then a stunning first glimpse at the bald pate of the sun, which on a good day looks, well, sunburned. What we saw instead was just an ordinary sun, a yellowish, sluggish globe rising into a smoggy haze.

"That's it?" Bunny asked.

"On some days it's gorgeous, trust me."

"Maybe you have to be closer to where it comes up from," Bunny offered. "Like on the eastern side of the country."

"They have so-so sunrises there, too, I'm certain."

"If I was there, I'd get up early every morning. That way, I wouldn't miss seeing a gorgeous sunrise at least once in my entire lifetime. And I'd follow all your rules. Even if that means watching boring stuff about animals on the TV. And I'd help with the gardening. And I'd get a job babysitting. And I'd—"

She didn't seem to be paying any attention to the tears that were leaving their snail-trails on her cheeks, but I was.

On the way to Indianapolis, there was a man driving a truck that was full of white chickens. He kept on wanting to get his big truck alongside my aging little Accord. I'd pull ahead, and he'd speed up, feathers flying. He'd wave, I'd speed up. Then I'd slow down, to let him pass. But he, too, would slow down. For long stretches he followed me, not dangerously close, but always within reach. This went on for miles and miles. Every now and then he would pull up ahead of me, though he was in the right-hand lane, and wave again, fingers downward and fluttering, the way you impatiently strum a tabletop.

I might have abided his menacing presence more easily (along the lines of, it's a free country, I don't own the highway) if it weren't for that wave, which wasn't really a wave. He wanted me to take a good look at the artwork that decorated the cab of his truck: a detailed and weirdly beautiful portrait of a drowning woman—Ophelia, I think. All that golden, beflowered hair floating among lily pads and dragonflies. And her girlish body draped in a sheer white gown, as relaxed as if she were bathing. But the eyes in that rendering were neither peaceful nor resigned. They were surprised, as if she didn't mean it at all, as if she were being pulled under.

At one point I got in front of him and signaled my intention to exit the highway—but so did he. That's when I finally went way over the speed limit. It took me a while to lose him. I have yet to lose the image of his terrified Ophelia.

Outside of Cleveland, I settled into the slow lane (which these days travels at 65 mph) and turned on the radio. Then turned it off. Too many bombs, too many bodies, too many children killing and killed. The O.J. trial everywhere else. That, and all the rest, which is to say the truck driver—not his artwork alone, but also his aggressive insistence, and the pleasure he took, I presume, in my distress—turned me once again into an older lady than I really am. Utterly bewildered. What world is this, anyway?

Young people don't much like to hear older people say that things used to be better. "We know more now," they'll tell us, cocksure that the world we grew up in was as mean-spirited and deadly as theirs is. And not nearly as nifty in its technology. So we say, perhaps, "You win." But my guess is we don't mean it.

My mother used to tell me that things were different for me—she meant better, and she wasn't wrong. But she was thinking about student loans, civil rights, jobs for women. She had no reason to think that I might one day be harassed on the road, or robbed at gunpoint in a parking lot, or blown up in an airplane, or raped after spending an evening in the college library. I'm sure that she never saw the baker's delivery man armed as if we lived in the wildest parts of the Wild West. And I'm glad that she's not alive to worry about these things, and more. Something else is in the air now, we all know this. Even some of the young people know this. And it's not better.

Did I make it all the way to Buffalo? No.

I got as far as Westfield, New York, which is smack dab in the vicinity of Lake Erie and Chautauqua. A good place to end an arduous day that began with a sunrise who offered herself as if she were jewelry—saying, wear me for a little while, every bit of me is real, priceless, and not for keeps.

This time I planted myself in a gas station phone booth and called the Buffalo hotel to cancel, then started in on finding a good place to stay—no going from door to door, no suffering the disapproval or roundabout insults of sundry innkeepers. You could say that I was rewarded for having learned my lesson: there had been a cancellation at the well-appointed William Seward Inn, which serves dinner as well as breakfast. I could look out at the water of Lake Erie while I had an early dinner, and then collapse.

But I didn't, as it turned out. I ordered room service. My room was lovely, but the view was viewless. I'd brought up to the room the bag that contained the game of *Clue*, Mr. Jensen's diary, the derringer, the large envelope filled with my newspaper clippings, photographs, chronologies, and the like. I didn't have a plan, only an urgent sense that I'd best gather those things around me and do some thinking.

On the last page of the diary, Mr. Jensen has drawn the names of HANNAH and ERIC. Drawn them and transformed them. They appear vertically on each side of the page, ERIC on the left, HANNAH on the right. The names are vertical but intricately redesigned and encased within figures that resemble peacocks: so that Eric's C, for example, has become the focal point of a fabulous, fanned-out he-bird tail. From the tip of Hannah's final H there is a sweep of folded-in female tail feathers. The first letters of both names are crowned with what look like bejeweled balloons on strings. Yes, Darrell my friend, this is art.

In the space between the formidable creatures that are HANNAH and ERIC are several miniaturized one-syllable words—miniaturized and aflutter, like a flock of startled chickadees. They float, they fly—words on the wing, so to speak. I didn't need Darrell's help to see that these words were formed by combining letters from each of the names: can, hear, rain, her, chain, ache, rich, nice, he, are, ran, niche, near. Baby birds aloft in the center of the page, as the pair of peacocks look on.

There's a scrap of paper tucked into the diary here, Darrell's attempt to turn these birds into words of poetry:

he can hear rain
her chain, her ache—
rich are nice
he ran near her niche—
he can hear her

And there is a recipe of sorts among these keepsakes, on yellow notebook paper. I must have composed it on one of those nights—I let there be far too many of them—when I had finished all tasks for the day and was thinking about my office-mates, needing to talk to somebody, wanting to call one of them, but not doing so:

Stew:

* Gather into one bare-bones graduate-student office a handful of young ascetics. At least one of these should be a genuine, "organic" ascetic; the others may be uncommitted, or chicken shit—which is to say, simply losers.

* Maintain moderate temperature.

* Allow them to settle into their ways.

* Keep them busy. Don't let them think about whatever they might be missing out on.

* After three years or so, add one Hannah Jensen: a goulash of dependent child, married woman, girlfriend, cheerleader, acolyte, drinking buddy, Tinkerbell, ballerina, foreign princess, pouter and enthusiast and sexpot.

* Stir.

* Now turn up the heat.

* Keep one eye closed.

* See if you can see what happens.

I told myself: I am too grown up now to let them truly frighten me. And I told myself: Or maybe still young enough to be foolhardy.

EIGHTEEN

When I got to Vermont, to a town called Brandon, the summer evening was more dark than light and I was more tired than hungry. I saw a lit-up "vacancy" sign and pulled in—my only dirt-cheap highway motel. I don't remember the name of it. But I do remember the conversation going on in the adjacent room—the walls must have been like cardboard.

She said: "I still can't get those people out of my head."

He said: "What people?"

"The ones in that building. In Oklahoma. All the little kids there for day care."

"Don't talk."

"I can't help it."

"That was months ago. And that shit has got nothing the fuck to do with us."

"I can't help it. *Jesus*!"

"Put a lid on it, goddamnit. I was almost there."

"Okay."

"Fuck your 'okay.' 'Okay' isn't good enough. All it tells me is that you're not into this."

"I'm into it, baby."

"Do more of that."

"More what?"

"More 'baby.'"

"Okay."

Okay? That's it? More *baby*?

It's not only the Jensens, I thought, who can make me feel as though I am not of this planet.

For a while the next morning, her more-girl-than-woman's voice and his gruff one followed me like stray puppies as I breakfasted on waffles at an always-open diner. I was too groggy and too hungry to be self-conscious about eating alone in public. Too groggy, too hungry, and too unprepared. So to hell with it. Besides, there was no "public" except me, the waitress, and the cook.

It was still quite early and gray when I drove through the town of Chittenden, Vermont and finally came to the sign, then turned onto the narrow, unpaved, tree-thick road that would take me to the reservoir where, according to the newspaper clipping, Eric had unmade himself. That road: a throbbing hole, a tunnel with a heartbeat.

No. That first time it was like a leaf-covered bridge that whispered only loudly enough to make it clear that stories were being told, but I couldn't hear them. I was hearing Eric's voice when it was telling me that he was no match for the enemy Fénelon had named, and I was thinking that he would have had to travel—on foot? late at night?—the same distance on the same road. Was I seeing some of the same trees arching toward each other? I wanted to stop the car and get out and then touch everything there on that road with all of me. Because he was the love of my life?

That's not it.

Eric wasn't the love of my life. But maybe he could have been?

Grief and longing: we know how those beleaguering twin sisters operate. One of them pulls you back toward the irretrievable, the other pulls you forward toward what you cannot and will never have. They are naked and sallow, forever feeding on the wrong things, on mere echoes and scents, on the mealy roughage of words almost spoken, on images both remembered and hoped for.

I soon came to a small parking area, where there is a boat ramp (only canoes are allowed on the reservoir) and the posted entrance to a hiking trail. There were no vacation homes in sight, no motorboat noises to be heard, no swimming children, nothing but tree-covered hills and a gorgeous body of water, even on a cloudy morning. I walked the hiking trail until I came to a sandy clearing, just big enough for two people to sit comfortably, barefooted, contemplating a chilly swim.

I thought: They must have come here that summer, right here, the two of them, Eric and Hannah. Their special place, this comma of a beach among the few that punctuated the otherwise rocky shoreline. They would have spread a blanket right here under the trees, among the ferns and shrubs, at the water's edge. She would have produced a picnic of thick, meaty sandwiches, seasoned potato chips, and chocolate cake. She would eat her entire portion and talk. He would eat some of his and listen.

And I wondered: Was it in fact here, where I was standing, on this particular bit of clearing, that he knocked himself out with whiskey before he drowned? Am I standing where he last stood? Am I looking at the same too-lovely amulet of water? Did he have this view of the encircling mountains? Or was it too dark? And what books did he have in his pockets? Did he read from any of them before he died? Did he think any thoughts about doing something other than dying? Like coming back to Riverside, finishing his doctorate?

A suicide would, I suppose, keep the arms from flailing, would put up no resistance against the desired downward pull. Ophelia did no flailing. Neither did Virginia Woolf.

I can understand taking an overdose of sleeping pills—chicken shit that I am. Or letting carbon monoxide lull you into a limp foreverness as you sit at the steering wheel of your car in your tight garage: Going someplace? Indeed. I can halfway comprehend putting a gun to your head, or to your heart—blasting away at the parts of you that have long been broken but have never shut up. I assume that people who lie in the tub and slit their wrists are more than a little angry that they have no garage, perhaps no car, and thoroughbred stomachs that will not put up with an overload of pills or booze. Circumstantial insults added to scores of psychic injuries. The wrist-slitters have to settle for a little pain and a lot of visual effect, without too much of a mess—this, too, as a suicide method, makes a kind of sense. As does, almost, letting your presumably worthless self be pounded by heavy surf, minusculed by the deep vastness of the ocean.

I do not at all understand drowning yourself in a reservoir, a man-made lake. You'd have to be blind drunk or drugged up before you would enter the stillness of a lake with the purpose of letting it take you over, pour into your mouth and fill you up, turn you into a bloated and rubbery log, a body of water. You'd have to make sure that your body had no mind of its own, no will, no fight left, no instincts that would drive even the bad swimmer to empty his laden pockets and get back to the shallows, just over there, where the lake is doing its dove-like flutter against the shoreline.

What I'm getting at is that I want Eric to have been out of his mind with drink, not himself, utterly unfeeling and forgetful, too out of it to notice, and definitely unwaving—no cries for help, no struggle, virtually fast asleep long before he stepped into the Chittenden Reservoir to die.

I didn't stay long that morning at the reservoir. Nor did I indulge any visible, audible expressions of grief. My being fearless on that score would have to wait. I drove back through town within twenty minutes or so, then onto the highway, where I'd seen a police station.

The local state policeman gave me no "there, there." That is, he didn't treat me as if I were a child, nor did he treat me as if I were a bit of old lace.

Officer Burt Gonzales: a patient and articulate young man, good-looking, just a little gray in his thick black hair, probably has the world by the tail, you would think at first sight, but then you would see something else and think no, he doesn't have anything by the tail. You would see that he was afflicted with a tic of sadness. Not a grief exactly, and not depression, but something had happened that showed itself in his otherwise content face—there was a shadow there, a distracted flicker, as if a low-lying powerful magnet were giving a yank now and then to his eyes and mouth.

I noticed, dare I say, that he wore no wedding band.

I told Burt Gonzales a considerably abbreviated version of my relation to Eric Langland. (I did not tell him that the relation, such as it was, could be characterized by abbreviation itself.) He did not take any notes, but I could tell that he would remember everything I told him. He had that look, the look of a good listener, a rememberer, a cousin of mine, of sorts.

When I finished, Burt Gonzales got up and found Eric's file in a collapsing cardboard box, took a more-than-cursory glance, then drove me in his police car back to the Chittenden Reservoir. On the way, he reported that it was the constable's Labrador—"He swims with his dog every morning at seven. The dog I'm referring to is long dead, of course"—that had found Eric's body. The constable, Tobias Stockwell, then took upon himself the role of chief, if only semi-official, investigator.

"The state police run the show here," he told me, "when it comes to people dying when they aren't supposed to. But the constables are the guys everybody usually calls first whenever something happens." Burt Gonzales went on to explain that the constables are part unofficial police, part unofficial sheriff, part official postman or bartender, key players in the town's goings-on, since they know nearly everyone and all the gossip.

"Is Mister Stockwell still alive?"

Burt Gonzales laughed a little. "He would live through a double dose of arsenic, ma'am. Then go fishing the next day. And yes, he is still the constable."

"You don't like this man?"

"I love him. But he's a lousy cop. Always has been."

"Should I talk to him?"

"I have to say that talking to him is an opportunity you won't regret. But if your loss is—"

"I can handle it."

"On a scale of one to ten, how is your sense of humor feeling these days?"

"Two point five or so."

"Barely middling."

"Will that do?"

"It might do." We pulled onto the road that leads to the reservoir, that leafy tunnel, that bridge, that whatever it was, that road taken by both the living and the dead.

"Talk to the man," Burt Gonzales said to me. "He'll tell you whatever it was he kept to himself. Word is, he kept something. But I'm guessing he'll tell you what it was. Not that that changes the case. This case is exactly what it looks like."

Burt Gonzales walked ahead of me on the hiking trail until we came to a spot that was not the same place from which I had whispered out to Eric in the early morning.

"This is where they found the whiskey, so one has to assume—"

"I see."

There were trees close by, but nothing that looked like a good venue for a picnic. The bit of beach was tiresome, too rocky and bug bedeviled, no place to sit comfortably.

"I'll wait in the car until you're done," Burt Gonzales said to me.

"Thanks. I won't be long."

Eric walked into the water from that spot. The official story. And probably the true one. As I stood there, looking at the water, looking at the pictures in my head, I remembered something Angelo Lewis had said: "Some things are part of a person's true story, some aren't but they're still true."

I waved away the bugs while I let myself, briefly, go back to the young people who were in the car above another lake, in Riverside. Back to Eric's taking my hand, telling me to stay put, telling me that he would, before long, return to the West Coast, to his studies, to me.

That is, he indicated that he intended to resume his work on late medieval literature, take up his hunched position at the same old desk in our same old office. Which is to say that he would have seen me nearly every day. He intended to do that, I'm sure of it. Is that part of the true story?

Afterwards, at the state police station—where there were posters of famous skiers on the walls—Burt Gonzales and I sat across from each other at one of the desks, drinking chocolate-flavored coffee.

"You were an infant," I told him, "when this young man died."

"Thereabouts. Let me see. August, 1956. I was five."

"Was there, according to the file, any serious investigation?"

"I can't imagine there wasn't. Not in this town."

"You implied that the constable was an iffy—"

"A failure of precision on my part, ma'am. Stockwell is a lousy cop from a professional point of view. But he's a good man."

"Does that make him qualified to conduct the investigation?"

"Most people here die because they get too worn out to keep going. As for suicides, we have old people, all alone and sick of being sick, who now and then take all their medications at once, to get it over with. And we have our share of stupid young lovers now and then. This case of Mr. Langland doesn't square with the norm. So somebody would have investigated, just to make sure, and anybody who had something to say about it called Stockwell. That makes him qualified, wouldn't you say?"

"May I see the file?"

"I'd have to check with the man himself, Tobias, and he's fishing this morning."

"All right. You don't have to hand it to me. But can I ask you some questions?"

"Suicide plain and simple, says here."

"Does it say what books he had in his pockets?"

"He had books?"

"That's what the newspaper claimed. A clipping about Eric's death was sent to my university, where we were in school together. Years ago. Graduate students."

"Local paper?"

"Yes."

"Then he had books. Let me see. Here it is. He was wearing a heavy jacket, top quality—that would mean deep, zippered pockets, a removable down lining, probably a hood. The pockets were full of stones and books."

"That's what it said in the newspaper clipping. Is there a list of the titles?"

"No, ma'am."

"I don't understand. Wouldn't they, the books, be evidence?"

"Of what?"

"I don't know."

"It was an open and shut case, Ms. Clark. It says here that he was stone-cold inebriated, and the rocks found in his pockets were hefty. Even a seasoned swimmer with that alcohol content and those weights would have one hell of a time struggling against—"

"I'd prefer to see him sinking quietly, if you don't mind. Passed out before he could feel it. No struggle whatsoever."

"I believe that is exactly how it happened, ma'am."

"Thank you."

"As far as those books you're interested in—well, they can't be what you'd call a deciding factor. That must be why there's no detail here."

"You're speaking only of the literal weight of them—"

"Anything else is irrelevant."

I was about to reply that it was their *contents* that might have told us something, served as some sort of witness. But Burt Gonzales beat me to it, with a gentle reminder that I was certainly old enough, maybe even smart enough, to know better.

"People have been known to set the bottle of sleeping pills they've just swallowed on the bedside table, right next to a copy of *Cinderella*."

"The happy ending."

"Yes, ma'am."

"And reading Ernest Hemingway or Virginia Woolf doesn't make you kill yourself."

"Didn't me."

"Nor me, sir."

"Call me Burt."

"Nor me, Burt."

Burt went on: "Says here the jacket was returned to its owner, after he positively ID-ed the Langland fellow. No question of theft in regard to the jacket."

"It belonged to Mr. Jensen?"

"That's the one. You know him?"

"Yes, and his wife, too. They were acquaintances of mine," I heard myself tell him, "back in California. It must have been one of them who told the police about Eric's ties to the university in Riverside. I mean, that would explain why your local paper sent us the clipping."

"No mention of that here that I can see. But the Jensens I know."

"Eric was living with them at the time of his death. Is that in the report?"

"All the necessary particulars are in the report, Ms. Clark," he said, though he'd long since stopped looking at the file.

"Are Hannah and her husband friends of yours?"

"No, ma'am. In my teens, after my family moved up here from Providence, I used to go over there, to the Jensen house. Just to hang out after school. The older brother of one of my friends rented their studio apartment for a couple of years."

"Was that where Eric—?"

"I can't tell you for certain whether he lived out in the studio or in the house. It's a big house."

"So you saw them frequently—the Jensens?"

"He was almost never around when I was there. But she was. Not that she spent time hanging out with us. She'd bring us a couple of six-packs, then leave. My friend's older brother, Tony, got to be tight with both of them."

"What happened to Tony?"

"I don't what he's up to these days, if that's what you're asking me."

"He was all right when he left them?"

"I never heard otherwise. But I'd stopped going over there before he left."

"Because of them?"

"No, ma'am. I got my first car during that time—a junk heap. I spent all my free time with her." As if at a road sign, he seemed to look both ways before he went on. "You suspect the Jensens of something, don't you, ma'am? I take it this isn't your first inquiry into the death of the Langland fellow?"

It was my turn to stop, look both ways, see recrimination coming at me from all directions. "At the time, I did nothing."

There. I'd said it out loud. Only six words. Burt couldn't of course know that they contained decades of nightmares, of rememberings and rehashings, of avoidances and complacencies.

I went on to try to make some minimal sense of it. "The Jensens would have found out had I made any noises about Eric's death. I didn't want to talk to them. I didn't want any contact at all at the time. I might have—I don't know. Besides, I had nothing to go on but inklings."

"That's changed?"

"No. Inklings are all I've got, but they're vivid and insistent. And the years have made me immune to the Jensens' charms." I hoped this would prove true. "I'm no longer afraid to stir things up."

"You haven't told me what you think they did to your friend."

"Eric was in their midst when he was driven to suicide."

"Ma'am—"

"Please call me Alice."

"Alice, pardon me, but it goes like this: some people kill themselves. And they're in the driver's seat when they do it. Now, if law enforcement has information that leads us to believe that a suicide had, say, the lowdown about someone else's criminal activity, then we hound-dog the someone else. But that won't tell us why the dead person committed suicide instead of just spilling the beans and staying alive. All we can say is, he had his reasons. If you think about it, there are reasons by the truckload that could make a person decide to call it quits. Some close to home, some not. There's not a one of us walking completely free and clear, day after day, of some reason or other to throw in the towel. Could be that's why suicide doesn't sit easy with the rest of us, who keep on living despite all the reasons not to."

"So I should give it up? My desire for some explanation?"

"Honest answer?"

"Yes."

"Then you should have given it up about thirty years ago."

"I tried to. And I succeeded intermittently. But these inklings: I'm the old boat to their barnacles. I've got time now to try to do something about them. To give those barnacles a scraping, clean things up. Close the case."

"As a case, Alice, this is suicide. And it's as closed as they come."

"Officially, yes. I know. But what if the suicide in question were someone you loved?"

Burt Gonzales smiled a smile that would delight a dentist. "I'd probably be doing what you're doing. Hoisting the boat—"

"At last."

"Getting her sea-worthy."

"I hope that's possible."

"It'll take a while." He tapped the file folder with his pencil. "I'll talk to the constable, find out if it's all right for you to read through this. Where are you staying?"

I couldn't tell him the name of the place, but my description brought out a low "whoo-eeee" from his otherwise restrained demeanor. "You must have been more tired than the Wandering Jew, ma'am. Alice, I mean. You need to get yourself some human place to put your feet up for a spell, until you're satisfied. Can you—if you don't mind my asking—afford to move out of that motel?"

"Yes. But you've made it clear, young man, that a satisfactory explanation is more than likely to be an impossibility."

"You might have to settle for some other kind of explanation."

"I might, yes."

"I suggest you check into the Churchill House. I'll call ahead, tell them you're coming. The owners are good friends of mine. I think I can get you— what?—two or three weeks' worth of a cut-rate deal?"

"Perfect."

And if I were thirty years younger, Burt Gonzales might have struck me as pretty nigh perfect. So of course, when the time came, I introduced him to Barbara Dulaney.

From the start, Kay and her husband Reese, the owners of the lovely old Churchill House, did their best to turn me into an insider, even though they were more than a little curious when I arrived for my longer-than-usual, arranged-by-Burt, discounted stay—partly, I think, because my "contact" was their friend the policeman, and also because I was clearly not Burt's out-of-town sweetheart. But we got along as if we had shared old times together, simple times, as if we were the cousins Angelo Lewis had imagined for me.

Neither of them seemed to mind that I sidestepped the touchy questions, like what exactly are you doing here? If they remained curious, they appeared to appreciate the condition of curiosity, didn't want it to go away, didn't want me in some outburst of bluntness to release them from imagining what I was up to (as if I knew!). By the end of my stay at their inn, I was sharing with them what was left in the first container of the balsam for all manner of pain, and they were sharing with me the exuberant friendship of the local vet, Doc Marion, who had a house to rent, with an option to buy. This very house.

NINETEEN

In a couple of weeks, Bunny will go out to California to stay with her dad for the rest of the summer. She's been here with me since last fall. I want to say that it was for her that I decided to stay, but that's not the whole of it. There was Barbara Dulaney too, not long after. And there was me—and a chance to do more than simply muse about my community project.

Bunny's father decided last year—at the last minute, after Labor Day, and after a good bit of persuasive pestering, I'll wager, in addition to his daughter's so-so grades—to send Bunny away for her schooling, without sending himself to the poorhouse. Bunny was on the phone the very day she received the letter in which I told her that I had rented a house. She had already found out on her own that there is a small, progressive school within a longish bike-ride of this town. Classes would begin on September the tenth. So in a rush the three of us arranged over the phone that she would live with me and give this new school a try. I didn't say that I had rented the house for only a month. Instead, after my conversation with Bunny and her father, I called Doc and told him that I just might be the buyer he'd been looking for.

In that week before she got here—that's right, I had only a week to prepare, to visit the school, to fix up her room, to get just the right groceries, to calm down—I had dreams every night, not nightmares exactly, but complicated, and they invariably involved everything going wrong. But when I finally picked Bunny up at the airport in Burlington, she was wearing those red cowboy boots. Her dancing shoes, she called them. I told myself to forget about the bad dreams and try to believe that there'd be good ones.

Now and then, but not often enough, that kind of telling yourself how to behave does the trick.

Barbara let us know she was coming for more than a short visit via a postcard that featured bathing beauties on a Southern California strip of sand. I showed the postcard to Bunny.

Brabra's had it up to here with the siliconed imitations. She's talked to your people, including the tempting but no-dice daddy-o. She knows where you are, is coming for a long visit, and hopes this is okay.

Bunny said, "Is your friend's name really Brabra? She didn't say so on the phone. Not to me anyway."

"And not to your dad either, honey bun."

"She calls him daddy-o. I like the sound of that, but I don't get it."

"There's nothing to get. That's old-timey talk, from long before you were born. Her name is Barbara. She's making a joke on her name."

"I know she is. But is it funny?"

"To some people, I guess. But it's not funny to her, not really. Nor to me."

"Do we want her here? I mean, she was okay when we talked, but that was only for a minute or two."

"You'll like her."

"If all your new friends come to live with us, can we make me a room in the barn?"

"We can make you a room out there even if they don't."

"I knew you'd say that."

"Don't be a wiseacre."

"I wouldn't live out there or anything."

"No, you wouldn't."

"It would be my office. Like the one you have here. Even though you're always in this kitchen space."

"Fair enough."

"If I ask you what a siliconed imitation is, am I being a wiseacre?"

"Yes."

"So we'll talk about it when I'm—?"

"Twenty-five or so, okay?"

Barbara told me that I was nuts, in fact "mixed nuts," for turning up at the Jensens' house the way I eventually did.

We were sitting across from each other at the long kitchen table—not an antique by any means, but it surely predates the invention of coasters. I'd been telling her what seemed to have had happened back in '65 and '66. Barbara smoked and listened, now and then scratching at her new perm or adjusting her shoulder pads, as I told her about what happened when I was in graduate school. But when I began to speak of my unannounced visit to the Jensens here in Vermont, she couldn't keep still.

She said, "Not one living soul informed of your whereabouts or your wherewithals or what you were up to, am I right? You bet I'm right. Did you, like, lose your thinking cap along the way? Leave it in a bar somewhere? On a bedpost? We all know that your thinking cap was pretty much raggedy to begin with, dear lady. But you're not supposed to leave it lying around somewhere. I mean, those people sound world-class strange. They could have buried you in the backyard or something, Miss Take-the-Law-into-Your-Own-Hands, and nobody'd ever know."

I tried to get a word in. "But they didn't. They weren't—"

"A Mountie is what you needed at your side, lots of hat and cheekbones. Pecs to die for. Standing there in his shiny boots, just a decent ways behind you, while you knocked on the door. Those people would have been, like, okay, we don't mess with her."

"They didn't exactly—"

"It's a good thing I decided to show up. I mean, you need a seasoned swimmer around to let you know how deep the deep end is."

"I'm not a very good swimmer."

"Am I, like, shocked?"

"You turned up because you decided to change just about everything. And because you weren't too uppity after all to contact the father of my ten-year-old 'people' and find out where I was. Lucky for me, you brought a record player as well as one of those CD things, and an electric food processor, and a curling iron, and way too many pillows and blankets."

"You left out all the new sweaters and the really good kitchen knives and the even better nose, which can almost always—give or take a couple dozen stupidities—tell the good guys from the bad guys."

The snow was knee-high when Barbara showed up with all of her stuff and "boo-koo bucks in the bank," as she put it, since she had sold everything else. And I mean everything: she told me that the elderly man who bought her condo in Santa Monica offered an irresistible sum of money for the furniture, almost all of the kitchenware, the appliances, the sheets and towels, the movie prints on the walls, everything. Even the wedding albums (there were two of them) and other memorabilia that Barbara was ready to toss.

This house is wooden, painted a dark barn-red with glossy white trim around the windows and doors. It's two-story, not large by California standards, though there are three bedrooms, virtual cubbyholes, good places for readers—each bedroom has a cushioned window-seat and a view of the sloping, partly wooded acre behind the house. Downstairs there is a small wood-paneled room, which has its own small fireplace. This is the room, where I've been holed-up since lunchtime, that Bunny refers to as my "office." The rest of the downstairs space is taken up by the kitchen and dining area. There's room for a couch and two rockers near the wood-burning stove but no living room as such. When I first saw this layout, I thought, well all right then, I must learn at last to be a real cook, to make my own bread and pasta from scratch.

From one of the large windows in the kitchen we can see the

old covered well, whose tarred roof is so pitched that it resembles a witch's hat—you can imagine the fanciful tales we've spun around that well, of wishes granted and denied, of transformations for the better or the worse.

Last August, after I'd rented this house, I spent probably too much money here at yard sales and outlet stores. I planted some herbs and flowers, ordered a load of hay for the barn. I sent for the books and the good china that I'd put into storage.

But I didn't know at first, while I was busy making this place my temporary own, that I was soon to have roommates and regular guests, that I'd be exchanging my expertise at living alone for the hit-and-miss hubbub of sharing a house, a bathroom, a record player. That I'd be taking in hefty doses that medicine which didn't come in a jar, and which I'd picked up in various places along the way here.

Kay reminded me recently that when I unloaded the car on my first day at the Churchill House, we didn't talk much. I inquired, "brusquely," she says, about a local Laundromat. She told me that I could use her machines any time after three.

I'd said, "You're making this so easy for me."

"The laundry?"

"The whole move."

"You're moving here?"

"It looks that way, yes. For a while."

She then handed me a message from Burt Gonzales. "The constable awaits you at the stationhouse."

For a moment, according to Kay, I was quite the personage: given my involvement in police business and all that. She had wondered, since I could not be explained as Burt Gonzalez's sweetheart, if I were in the FBI's relocation program, a fake-identitied snitch on the mob. And I left her wondering. Dumped everything in the room that would be my home for a while and drove back to the police station for my meeting with the constable.

"Madam," he said, "I extend my considerably post facto but heartfelt condolences."

"Thank you."

"And I expound my readiness to lay your restless mind to rest concerning the untimely death of your long-ago acquaintance."

Thus spake Tobias Stockwell. Somehow stuck in a goofy eighteenth-century novel? Putting on the rhetorical dog for the English professor?

Picture a seventy-year-old Glenn Ford lookalike who, without his boots on, is only a little over five feet tall. As we stand in front of the desk shaking hands, his mouth is directly in front of my chest, which I might not have taken memorable note of had he not been such a puckerer and smacker of lips.

He has a bit of a belly, but is otherwise as lean as a mink. And that belly seems to be proud of itself: it protrudes between the brackets of his suspenders as if to say, I can eat whatever I want, drink whatever I want, but take this taut tummy's word for it, I spend next to no time in front of the TV. What you see here is an all-seasons outdoorsman.

One other thing: his thick gray hair is close-shaven on the sides and lifted forwardly on the top, in what resembles a mohawk cut. I used to wonder who convinced him to adopt such a style, until I ran into him and his pierced and tattooed girlfriend at the market.

I thought that, from the start, I had the upper hand on that comical old rooster. Surely he was going to let me look at the file. But I was wrong.

After the handshake I took a seat, the same one I had been sitting in when I discovered little else except that Burt Gonzales was a good man and that I was still capable of being schoolgirl-foolish about some things.

Tobias Stockwell sat in front of me, atop the desk. That is, I was to look up at him. We had the place to ourselves.

"I'd like to see the Eric Langland file."

"I am informed of your wish in advance of the expression of it, madam."

"You've spoken with Burt."

"To be sure. Officer Gonzales put the matter into my hands, which at present are teeming with apology, for I am bound and beholden to be non-obliging. Next of kin you are not. Widow you are not. Law enforcement you are not. In a word, and without ado, entitled, madam, you are not."

"Please call me Alice."

"That would be a pleasure, madam."

"Alice."

He let the heels of his boots tap against the desk as he cleared his throat. "I was, Alice, in on the investigation of this unfortunate case from the very moment it became one. You are looking upon the man at the scene of Mr. Langland's undoing, though I was wearing only a speedo at the time. You are looking upon the subsequent inquisitor of pertinent persons and collector of data turned over to the state police for their professional perusement. And you will, my dear lady, forgive my attraction to the allures of alliteration. You are looking upon a man you can trust."

"I do." And this was true. He was an odd duck all right, a concoction, but a sincere one.

"*Bueno*," he said. "The gist, the marrow, the hard heart of this case is that there is nothing here but a desire on the part of a young man to do himself in."

"Yes, that's what Officer Gonzales told me. But there must be some explanation. Something that suddenly drove him—"

"Excuse me, Alice. But suddenness as such is inapplicable if we deposit into the account of this woeful event the fact that your young man had been failing to attach much value to himself prior to the fatal Chittenden Reservoir incident, as you must already know."

"No, I don't. Do you mean that he had—?"

"There were clear indications of a prior commitment on his part to detach himself from this vale of tears. Indications which, I surmise, you yourself, an intimate friend, would surely have espied."

"When he left California, he told me that he would be back. He had arranged for a six months' leave of absence from the university. That doesn't sound suicidal, does it?"

Tobias Stockwell put on a pair of reading glasses that had bright red frames and began to look through the file. "I was referencing heretofore the scars on his forearms. The sorrowful tale they tell is etched just above both wrists by some devoutly wished-for blade. My coroner—theirs, the county's, to be precise—adjudicated the age of said scars at five to seven years. Forgive me, Alice," he said as he removed the glasses. "I appear to be telling you something unbeknownst."

"You are, yes. Eric and I were friends, fellow graduate students, office-mates for about three years before he came here with the Jensens. He always wore long-sleeved shirts. Even when it was hot."

"There are grown men in this beloved country of ours, too many, if I may say so, who hold an unfounded grudge against crying females, but the person below which you sit is not one of them, Alice. So, *mangia*!"

"*Mangia*?"

"That's Italianate for 'have at it,' 'go for it,' 'dig in'! To wit: let the weeping commence." He hooked his thumbs in his suspenders and gave them a pedantic snap.

Given that invitation, any crying on my part was out of the question. Instead, I had to stifle a giggle that was all too close to all-out laughter—of the off-balance, hysterical sort.

"I'm all right."

"There is no need to indulge stoicism—"

"I'm fine."

"Let me therefore say that I am of the opinion that human character types formulate themselves, primarily but not exclusively, into those who die for love and those who live for love, which opinion leads to the furthermore that your gentle self, Alice, is of the latter group, as is, you will be pleased to know, yours truly."

"Are you saying that Eric Langland died for love?"

"No. His typology dies for death—"

"Then why—?"

"I am a staunched admirer of anyone who can carry an unrequited torch o'er the years. We are a dying breed."

"I wouldn't say that I—"

"Of course not. Humble is the patrimonial name of all such torch-carriers."

"Did you speak to Mr. and Mrs. Jensen?"

"I did." Tobias Stockwell put his glasses back on and thumbed through the papers in the file. "They, the Jensens to whom you have made reference, bespoke themselves highly of you."

"Why would they have mentioned me?"

"Another man, a lesser man, would not enter the privacies mapped out by your inquiry."

"But you will?"

"As a member of the romantic race, I will proffer a fitting response. However, as a member cum considerable seniority of the constabulary, I must abridge my inclination to speak to you as if you had been a friend of my youth."

"Fair enough."

"On the occasion of my official visit to their home in Rutland, your name arose firstly when he, Mr. Bradley Jensen, requested that I relay by post the sorry tidings to the university where the deceased had been a graduate student. She, Hannah Jensen, served chocolate éclairs. Both disclosed knowledge of the young man's previous attempt to put an end to the question of his continuing to be. With considerable hospitality vis á vis drinks that came upon the heels of the éclairs, she explained that they had offered the young man a sabbatical, a respite from the storm of despair. But the care they extended could not, alas, remove the burdens that can weigh a young man down and down."

Respite from the storm: if you ask me, that éclair-eating, drink-fixing couple *were* the damn storm.

But what I said was, "Are you referring to his love for Mrs. Jensen?"

He looked at me then over the top of his glasses—"peered," I should say, gave me the thrice-over.

"You quite point-of-factly do not know, do you?"

"Know what?"

"Allow me to reflect for a moment, since a love that can ne'er be expressed ought not to be expressed by a party whose role in the matter is circumsized by official protocols."

I leaned my face into my hands for a moment. His wanton way with words was making it difficult for me to get hold of myself. I wished that Burt Gonzalez had given me a more explicit, more detailed warning about what to expect from this old gent. Did I truly want this Dickensian "member of the romantic race" to confirm any of my suspicions? Yes, I suppose I did. But at that moment it was as if I were standing at the open door of a plane without any parachute. And at the mercy of a pilot who couldn't read a navigational map without adding a few longitudes and latitudes of his own invention.

"What don't I know, Mr. Stockwell? Just give it to me straight."

"I like that in a woman." His heels tapped against the desk. "You must understand that the relevance of the information you are exacting is irrelevant with respect to the actual demise—"

"I understand. Now, please, tell me."

"Perchance I should begin at the beginning, insofar as it was made known to me by the enchanting Hannah and her kindly husband."

"Begin wherever you like."

The story he finally told me was about a young man who from childhood until his death at twenty-nine was preyed upon by a recurrent and increasingly hungry depression, which even as a boy he called his "ghosts," and for which the cures at the time were drugs that reduced the patient to the vivacities of a concrete block.

Eric's adoptive parents, good Quakers the both of them, defended against the onslaughts of the ghosts with tenderness, hope, lavish kindnesses. But these proved weak weapons time and again, and Eric could do nothing but watch over the years as Mr. and Mrs. Langland began to sink, to stoop under the weight of their inability to help.

When he was old enough to make such a decision—and to know himself as a creature always stalked, forever unable to turn a corner that would leave the ghosts baffled and empty-handed—he decided to refrain, no matter what, from entering into any relations of the heart. He would allow himself companions but no close friendships, no intimates, no loves who might call upon him to be something he was not and could never pretend to be.

Eric believed that he would be able to guard himself against falling in love, so fierce was his desire not to inflict his despair on anyone he cared about, as he had cared about his parents, who by the time he left home for college had grown silent day and night, and prone to tears. But according to this story, it happened nevertheless. Eric fell in love with Alice Clark, and was compelled to absent himself from the object of his devotion, lest she find him out and find herself adored by a young man already more dead than alive.

This story, the story Tobias Stockwell learned from the Jensens, goes on to insist that it was not Eric's unspoken love for Alice Clark that took him by the hand and led him into the foreverness of the nighttime waters of the reservoir. No, he had long since been called to the grave by beasts he could not name. He would have died the first time, back in Riverside, before he'd met Alice, were it not for the solitary landlady who kept track of all the comings and goings of her quiet, college-student boarder—so that when he did not head out for class at the usual time, she went to his room, spare key in hand, and found him dying but not yet dead.

As I understand it, the story goes that, death having been defeated by an attentive little old lady, Eric's ghosts went into a long, faintly audible huddle. They let him go on to graduate school while they strategized. They kept up their constant and tormenting hum, but toned it down enough for him to hear, eventually, shy other things—the fledging peeps of an affection that would soon soar. According to the Jensens, Eric's ghosts gave themselves a few years to prepare for round two, and they did a good job of it. They made sure that they wouldn't lose. Despair is never a good sport.

This is what I meant, the constable explained, when I said that Eric had not died for love but for death.

As I listened to Tobias Stockwell tell me this story, I tried to believe the part about Eric Langland's love for Alice Clark, and I tried to ignore the shame of it—the shame of my eagerness to believe it, the shame of wanting him to have died because he could not live with or without me, the shame of my coming all this way to be told by anyone, even a self-regarding raconteur, that Eric loved me. But I couldn't ignore it. And I knew that the Jensens' story about Eric and Alice was a lie.

There had been no time during the trip east—not the distressful drive across Nebraska, not the discouragements I encountered in Peoria, not even, though this comes close, the night in Aurora, Utah—when I more wanted never to have left my bougainvilleaed Riverside home than on the day Tobias Stockwell concluded his tale with another snap of his suspenders, put the box of tissues in my lap, and produced a plate of stiff but edible scones. He unlocked one of the desk drawers and poured each of us a shot of whiskey. He touched his glass to mine and was clearly about to make a speech. But I stopped him.

I drank my shot.

I thought at first that I would confront the Jensens the next day, tell them that I knew they had lied to the constable. Eric may have been clinically, irreparably depressed, I was prepared to say. But that's no reason to go off with you two, is it? And what happened to the other young man, Burt's friend, Tony?

I went down this road for a while and saw myself turning back, selling the car and getting the first plane out of Burlington to New York and then home, back to California, to a retired life in Riverside.

But that same night at dinner, Kay and Reese seated me at their table, along with their friend Doc Marion, who told me about this house he had for rent. And he told me about the horses he tended, and the goats, and the cattle, and the occasional broken-winged pigeon some young girl would come upon in the woods or just outside the windowpane. He told the story about his name. (His mother had named him George, after her favorite nineteenth-century novelist. He changed it to Marion when he read George Eliot in high school and found out her real name, Mary Anne, not to mention his own real sexual preference.) I was liking him a lot, and Kay and Reese, and my old house in the West, and the prospect of a new one in the East, and somehow these good things made me decide to wait until I had more than a room in an inn before I knocked on the door that belonged to Mr. and Mrs. Jensen. Doc Marion's rental, now our home, was just the thing.

So it was just after Labor Day when I made the visit I had come here to make, shortly before Bunny came to stay. In the meanwhile I worried that I would run into one or the other of them at the market or the post office or the bank, but I saw no trace.

TWENTY

When the day came, it was Mr. Jensen who opened the door.

He was wearing a plaid flannel shirt, mainly blue, with a white turtleneck underneath, though it was a late-summer afternoon. He was narrower in the chest than I remembered him, bonier, as if his body didn't want to have much to do with him if it could help it.

His big gray eyes were giving me an "assessment smile" (thank you, Peoria, for all the lessons in that gaze) behind glasses that didn't fit properly. And his posture was tilted slightly to one side, as if he were now forever unmoored. But he was not a bit stooped by age—he could still look me straight in the eye.

"Alice Clark," he said. "At last."

He took both my hands in his: we stood there for a moment, taking it in—what was between us, and what was not.

"I thought perhaps you had changed your mind," he said, as he removed his glasses. "About coming to see us."

"Changed my mind? I never told you that I—"

"I've known you were here. It's been—what?—three or four weeks now?" He gave my unwilling hands a squeeze. "Come in, come. This is a fine tribute to our Hannah's marvelous intuition. She has maintained for years that you would come to us, and here you are. You've changed your hair, haven't you?"

I said to his Alice Clark: Be careful. Be *mindful.* Be happily *tall.*

He brought me forward through a small, elegant hallway and into the living room, where there was a wide swath of ceiling-to-floor windows, a gorgeous view of the mountains, and a modern arrangement of two sleek white couches and four matching chairs. Hannah was nowhere in sight.

So they had known for weeks that I was in the vicinity. Right from the start, and yet they had waited for me to come calling.

"Tobias Stockwell. Did he—?"

Mr. Jensen chuckled at this. "He couldn't wait to tell us of your arrival. Tobias has for years now been a great fan of Hannah's. He thought she would be pleased to know that her old friend had finally appeared in these parts. You round us off, you complete the rhyme scheme—that's how he put it. You made quite an impression on him, Alice. 'The thing itself,' he called you, though only he might know what he meant. Please don't say that you mind that he told us."

"I mind that you talk about me. And I don't want to complete the rhyme scheme."

"Do you have a choice?" He was gearing up to put on the insinuating charm.

If we had been a couple of well-bred young dogs, we would have been circling each other, sniffing each other's important parts—not so much preparing to fight as establishing seniority, determining know-how, sizing up each other's courage.

"I wouldn't be here if I didn't. Is Hannah at home? If not, I'll—"

"She's out there." He directed my gaze out the windows, to the yard that swooped sharply downward from the house and became a child's dream of a meadow, small and flower-filled, with a hide-and-go-seek weeping willow and an oak that offered itself for climbing and a gazebo that also served as a bridge across a brook. On the other side of the brook there was what looked like a large dollhouse. The studio apartment Burt had told me about.

"You have a brook."

"Of sorts. 'By June our brook's run out of song and speed . . . A brook to none but those who remember long.' Like you, Alice."

"You've been reading Frost."

"One cannot abide in these parts and avoid him, I'm afraid. You must stay for a while. Hannah has become an artist. She'll be in soon."

"Are any of these hers?" I gave the room a glance. The paintings I'd seen in their California house had been so unmemorable, mere streaks and lines, that they might well have been hanging in this one, too—I wasn't sure. But I was certain that the few canvases on the windowless side of the room were equally not worth a second look.

Mr. Jensen laughed. "That's a Mondrian, Alice. Those others are Rothkos, minor Rothkos, but still the genuine article. I got them very early on, before the art world decided to price these modern masters out of my range. Perhaps Hannah's work takes some cue from these. I have no idea. She has declared herself a painter of some sort, that's all I need to know. We used to rent the studio—it's small but quite suitable for a young bachelor."

"Did it look like that when Eric lived there?"

"Like what?"

"A bachelor pad designed by Barbie."

He stepped back, to take me in again. "I don't recall that you were inclined to deliver witty, perhaps even cruel observations. It becomes you."

Why did I want to curse like a gangster?

I do know why I didn't curse like a gangster—no practice whatsoever.

He went on: "For the last many years, Hannah has been spending every afternoon out there, working away. If you can get her to show you her work, you will have pulled off a small miracle."

"Aren't you the least bit curious?"

"More than a bit. But my policy with Hannah has always been not to interfere. With you, Alice, I have no such policy. Please, do sit." He pointed to my shopping bag and smiled. "What have you got there?"

"Presents for Hannah, mainly. Chocolates. And an old game we used to play together during her first term at the university, when I volunteered to be her second tutor."

"Did she have a first?"

"Didn't she?"

"Not that I know of. Why would she?"

"She told me that she was doing poorly in her classes."

"Not straight-A work, as I recall, but it does seem odd that our Hannah would have required a tutor, much less two!"

"Perhaps I misunderstood? I proposed that we spend some time together at my house, so that she could practice her English."

"She hardly needed that, now, did she? I wish you had made *me* such a proposal," he went on to say. "We spent far too little time together."

"Far too much, Mr. Jensen."

"Please call me Brad."

"No thank you."

I'd like to think that that little thorn stuck. But he seemed to have disregarded it.

"What else have you brought back with you from the grave?"

Whatever he saw in my response to this question, it made him offer a tepid reassurance. "A joke, Alice."

I set the game on the coffee table.

"Ah, cops and robbers. One of my favorite genres. I watch it on the television."

"This is strictly BBC stuff," I explained, "smart detectives and smarter but careless murderers. No cops and robbers."

"Hannah would be excellent at such a game."

"She made up new rules and won every time."

"And she would now, too. Not only make up new rules but win. What else have you brought us?"

"This pretty derringer that Hannah gave to me. She seemed to think I needed a gun. I didn't think so. What could I possibly shoot?" I wasn't aiming the gun at anything, at anyone, just holding it, I'm sure.

But he said, "Me?"

"I don't know whether or not it's loaded." This was true.

"Let's not find out." He guided my hands as together we put the little gun down next to the game.

I said, "I don't recall that you would be inclined to be fearful. It becomes you." I was half-way thinking *touché* when I said this, despite the anxious wasps in my stomach, the stage-fright.

He stood up. "I'm being a forgetful host. There's some very good scotch. I'll be right back." And then, before he left living room, he turned back to me to say, "You are different, Alice. Good for you. But you are still extraordinarily dim."

I may be dim, I thought, but my batteries are still charged. Dim lights are nevertheless lights on. You are not going to make me small, make all the lights go out, make me want to get under the blankets.

With the drinks and a tray of hors d'oeuvres, Mr. Jensen came back to the living room. "What else is on that mind of yours, Alice?"

"I brought back the diary, the book with our names in it."

"That was to be yours for keeps. And it is not a diary. It's a—"

"A message of sorts?"

"Don't be silly."

"Darrell Farnsworth called it artwork."

"Darrell. Yes, that is precisely what he would have called it. Poor old Darrell."

"He never had the chance to get old."

"Lucky him, wouldn't you say? Getting old has its myriad downsides."

"Even so."

He clinked his glass against mine, but did not launch into whatever toast he'd been about to make. "Are you all right?"

"No."

"An honest answer. Brava!"

"I'm not all right because I'm *here*."

He proffered the cashews. "And *here* is this lovely bowl. Do you remember?"

"I gave it to Hannah, for Christmas, in 1965."

Still vying for alpha dog, he again touched his glass against mine. "To your excellent memory! Mine has gone the way of my eyesight. The up-close remembrances are as clear and as readable as your welcome face. The far-away ones are mere presences, which does not, of course, take the potential sting out of them. Hannah's memory has become a little thick around the edges. She remembers things that never happened."

Was he setting Hannah up? I didn't want to know.

"Is my face all that readable?"

"Absolutely. It was always one of your best features. You are a distinctly inept prevaricator. And that hasn't changed."

"Unlike Hannah."

"Don't be so damned abashed, my dear Alice, about the tutoring business. It's a trivial matter."

"Prevaricating is?"

"Doing it as poorly as you do renders it so." His laughter was either easy-going or derisive. Not at all readable.

"When will Hannah be in?"

"Most days, she works out there from two until five. Unless Ben gets home early and pesters her into coming back to the house for conversation."

"Who is Ben?"

"Our current boarder. He's an assistant professor of philosophy over at Middlebury. It won't surprise you that he adores Hannah."

"No, it doesn't."

"Do you want to know what I read in your face at the moment?"

"No."

"Fair enough. I understand you've found a place to live in Chittenden."

"Mr. Stockwell told you that, too."

Mr. Jensen began spreading paté on crisp rounds of French bread, smiling like an advertisement housewife who enjoys a good appetite in the people she serves.

"What are you going to do with yourself, Alice? Apart from spending time down at the state police station? Will you be looking for a teaching job?"

"I went to the police station and talked to the constable in order to inquire about Eric's death."

"So we're done?"

"Done?" I asked this even though I knew that he meant we were done pretending, badly, to be old friends, at least for the moment.

"With these cordialities, which you continue to disregard. Rudely, I must say."

"We're done." The word "rude" and I had never before been introduced in the same sentence. Now that we had, we shook hands.

"Good. I want you to tell me why you're here. I take it that you are before me now not to shoot me but to hear me talk of then."

"I have questions that I should have asked a long time ago."

"I suggest you ask your questions before Hannah comes in."

I was both over-prepared for this and far from ready—like the student who spends hours studying for the final exam, only to discover that she was supposed to study that *other* book.

"Well?"

"I've been to the reservoir several times," I told him.

"So this elaborate undertaking of yours has only to do with Eric Langland."

"I wouldn't say 'only,' since Eric in some way has to do with Darrell and with Richard."

"The three blind mice. Have some more paté." Mr. Jensen passed me the hors d'oeuvres. "'See how they run.'" He sing-songed those words.

I didn't sing, "'Did you ever see such a thing in your life?'"

"Never."

"Those mice should have known better."

"Knowing better. It is marvelously like the former you, Alice, to believe in scraps of un-nuanced common sense."

"I should have seen what was going on."

"Forget the mice for a moment and think about that farmer's wife, her agility and cleverness, the admirable delicacy of her aim. Such a woman might very well have pocketed the tails of perfectly sighted mice."

"Such a woman would be Hannah."

"You don't have a clue, do you? I mean, during those months when you saw her virtually every day, were you so taken by her that you never once suspected?"

"I suspected."

"What?"

"That she and Eric had become lovers. And that either you didn't know or didn't mind, given how much you enjoyed his company."

He patted my hand in a "there, there" way that threatened to disarm me.

"I'm going to fetch the decanter," he added. "Help yourself to the paté." He was away from the living room again for a few moments, during which time I did not help myself to the paté but did help myself to a large dose of get-on-with-it, ask your questions and get out of there.

"You're troubled," Mr. Jensen said as he reseated himself and freshened his drink.

"I think I've figured out the rape. Up to a point."

"You haven't. But tell me nevertheless. Your version is bound to be—"

"Too simple?"

"Of course."

"My guess is, Hannah staged the rape lest she turn up with a pregnancy otherwise awkward to explain, a pregnancy the ardent father would insist on claiming as his own. Whichever 'he' it was that she had slept with. I'm assuming it was Eric."

"Far too simple, Alice. But it has its charms. Like a plot from one of the old black and white films. Hannah has never been pregnant."

"What the hell happened?"

"A rude *and* snappish Alice! I love it."

"Tell me."

"Our Hannah saw the essential needs of you and your friends, and she attempted, in her way, to satisfy them."

"In her way?"

"What I observed is that she moved all of you, as if you were chess pieces. Richard, the knight, of course—an inveterate trooper whose aggressive forward movement is always sidetracked. Darrell, a bishop—incapable of going in a straight line, but doesn't seem to know it. Eric, a castle, far more fragile than he appears. You, Alice, sturdy, reliable, and often quick to be captured—a pawn."

I side-stepped the pleasure he took from that jab. "I didn't die. They did."

"Don't be prosaic, Alice. At least pretend for a moment not to be. Hannah did not 'kill' anyone. She helped Darrell to be the character he had fashioned for himself, she helped him to *be* Darrell Farnsworth. To play his part. Even as she helped Richard, though that was more complicated."

"She pushed them—"

"She didn't push. Pushy people seek to change your behavior, try to make you 'well,' according to norms that may have nothing to do with you. Hannah simply provided space, ease, let all of you stop beating around the bush and feed the famished parts of yourselves. If that meant drinking yourself to death or dying in battle, she would see this as a happy ending."

"And you?"

"Just a member of the audience."

I wanted to slap him. "And the producer. The stage manager."

"You won't give me any credit for set design?"

"I hate this."

"Sparring with me? What did you expect?"

Good question. I reached for the decanter, but he beat me to it and poured me a modest two fingers. Handed me a fresh cocktail napkin. Took the pause to play the gentleman he could play so well.

What did I expect? That Mr. Jensen would have offered some words of regret, remorse, some tincture of guilt? A moment of commiseration? That he would not, in other words, still be Mr. Jensen?

"I expected that you would tell me why I didn't die."

This brought out a distinctly ungentlemanly laugh from him. "You're an impossible woman, Alice. Ask me a question I can answer."

That would leave out most of my questions. But not all of them.

"Why did you tell Tobias Stockwell that Eric was in love with me?"

"That was Hannah. She told him a version that would most suit him, that he would be glad to hear. A tragic love story. He didn't inform us that he had repeated it to you. Do I assume correctly that you were not glad to hear it?"

"You assume correctly. Eric was not in love with me."

"Nor with anyone else, Alice."

"Surely he and Hannah—"

"We both loved Eric as a friend. After a while, he gave in, gave himself one last shot at being taken care of, though he warned us many times that he was a hard case. And he was. That's all, there was no affair. I'm certain she would have told me."

I would have been more certain of his certainty had he looked at me. But Mr. Jensen was looking down at the drink in his hands. If I'd never met him, never talked with him, if I'd walked into his living room at that moment and seen him for the first time, staring into his drink, I would have taken him for a man whose burdens cling like vines—twisted tight, inexpungeable—to his aged bones. I would have taken him for someone else.

"After the three of us settled here, Hannah soon found that she could move him only in the direction he had long since decided for himself."

"Suicide."

"He had tried before, and not half-heartedly. For a while, I thought—we thought, I should say—that perhaps a new family—"

"*You two*?" Without expressing any explicit suspicions, I somehow expressed them, emphatically, years of them.

Mr. Jensen took gentle hold of my chin and turned my face toward him. His eyes did not coincide with his touch—they were smoky gray with anger. "We thought that we might save him from himself and we failed. That you could for even a moment think that we would endanger him—" He still had me by the chin, still gently, though there was a tremble in his fingertips. "Hannah is right about your friends' stories, about the parts they were destined to play, and you know this, Alice, whether you like it or not."

"I don't like it at all."

I removed the hand that had me by the chin. A bony, trembling old-man's hand. There was not more than a foot between us, though miles of lifetime—marked by dozens of "Do Not Enter," "Wrong Way," and "Dead End" signposts.

Mr. Jensen saw me looking at his hand.

"I have a touch of Parkinson's," he said. "It will get worse, but it's not much trouble so far. Hannah says that it is quite fitting—me with the trembles, the gradual loss of balance, the—"

We heard Hannah's footsteps crossing the deck that met up with the living room, then saw her appear at the sliding glass door.

I stood up, squared my shoulders, and smoothed my skirt. You could have taken me for an old soldier who comes upon the American flag. An ally no matter what.

She was still dazzling: her hair, more blond than gray, was caught up loosely at the top of her head with a wide turquoise barrette. Her tunic and pants were a series of blues—I would call them tie-dyed, but they looked much more expensive than that. A painter's smock was draped over her arm. She was plump, but not a chocolate eater's plump. Indeed, she moved toward me like a dancer, utterly unafflicted by age, barefoot and tiny.

We gave each other an awkward hug while she stretched up to whisper, "I thought you would come to see us a long time ago, Alice."

I moved back and looked at her. If her face were as readable as mine evidently was, then there was nothing to see right then but a sheen of contentment. I waited for some sign, some hint, something that would help me to know what to do with that brilliant smile other than let it give me my marching orders.

"You are shivering, Alice." As she rolled up her smock and set it on one of the out-of-the-way chairs, she spoke to her husband without looking at him. "Make her a fresh drink, would you? She would like some ice, wouldn't you, Alice?"

I reached for my bag. "I'd prefer some tea at this point, if that's all right. I've brought some with me, homemade. The recipe says that if you 'drink plentifully of it, it is a most certain remedy.' It doesn't say for what."

"We must all have some of that remedy," Hannah said. She hadn't taken her eyes off me. She was glowing, a virtual floodlight. "But first I will have some beer."

Mr. Jensen hopped to like a butler.

"It has taken a long time for you to visit. Too long. But now your job is all over and done with?"

"Yes, I'm retired. I've sold the house in Riverside, and I'm renting one in Chittenden."

"Everything is over with, and you come to us right away. I'm so glad."

"I need to know what happened."

It was not a glowing Hannah who hesitated, then said, "If you are talking about Eric, there is only that he went for a walk one night and did not come back. He did not want to live anymore. Have you been here long, at this house?"

"Less than an hour, I think."

She leaned up to whisper again. This time she said, "Don't believe anything bad that Mr. Jensen has told you about me."

I found myself whispering back, "I won't." And that was almost true.

Hannah had one more thing to pour into my ear. "He is the one."

"The one who what?"

Mr. Jensen returned to the living room with a small mug of beer in time to see this whispered exchange, and to look right at me with a lopsided grin on his face.

"Old girlfriends and their secrets." He was doing his best to beam. "Wonderful. Come, sit. The tea will be ready shortly. I bought some of that paté you like, Hannah."

They occupied the two corners of the couch. I sat across from them. "He does all of the shopping, all of the everything." Hannah said to me. "Are you happy to be here in the Green Mountains?"

Before I could answer, Mr. Jensen said, "Of course she is!" He raised his glass for another toast. "To this long-awaited visit."

Hannah said, "We get older, Alice, but some things stay the same. Like you. Like me. Aren't you glad?"

"I'm not the same."

"Your hair!" said Mr. Jensen, as if he could with a twirl of fingers "poof" away our conversation.

Hannah's smile was still brilliant, but rough around the edges. "It is so nice a thing to see you again. Are you still all by yourself?"

"In a few days, I'll have a roommate. A ten-year-old girl from Riverside who is coming here for school."

"No more lonely old Alice?"

"I wasn't planning on it, it just—"

"What were you planning on?" Hannah asked this the way a magistrate would, as if she were weighing a question of intent, of precisely how guilty I might be of something.

Mr. Jensen rescued me from having to answer that question. "You haven't given Hannah her presents," he said.

Hannah, still be-robed, so to speak, still presiding, uttered a sound that was both a laugh and a purr. "You have presents for me?"

"Yes, well, this is a present." I reached into my bag for the box of chocolates. "The other things are—I'm not sure what to call them."

"Keepsakes," Mr. Jensen offered.

"Things I want to you to have, instead of me."

I pointed to the game and the derringer on the coffee table, next to Mr. Jensen's diary. A silent Hannah was sitting Indian-style in the corner of the couch, the box of chocolates in her lap. The chocolates were not having their usual effect. There was a glossy stiffness on the surface of her dimpled face.

"More paté, anyone?"

"Not for me," I said to Mr. Jensen.

Hannah shook her head and finished her beer. "Use one of the larger mugs this time." She waved her empty mug at her husband, who got up without a word and left the room again.

An angry Hannah was something I had never seen during our

time together long ago. "The things you have brought me are all about a time that is over. But you are not letting it be over. You are afraid to let things finish. That is not the story here, Alice."

"Then what's the story?"

"Happenings take place. They are meant to, and then they do. We go on to the next day."

"You mean deaths, suicides."

"There is nothing to say about Eric except that we loved him as friend and brother and he killed himself. Especially my husband. I wish that you had not brought me these things. This little gun was a gift for you."

"You gave each of us weapons of one sort or another. I still don't know why."

"You are the one who had this game with all the weapons in it. Revolvers and ropes and poisons. You thought this was a fun game."

"There weren't any poisons."

"I never owned such a game, Alice. You did."

"That doesn't explain—"

"They were gifts, that's all. For your imaginations."

"Food for thought?"

Hannah smiled at me. "You still use those expressions I like." She picked up the derringer, opened the barrel, then clicked it shut.

"It's loaded," she said. "Food for thought, yes? Did you put in these bullets?"

"I've never even done what you just did with the barrel, Hannah. I assumed that it was empty."

"What is the good of an empty gun? Do you think they still work? The bullets?"

"My guess is that after all this time they'd sputter or backfire."

"You look so tired, Alice, like you want to sputter and backfire."

"Your husband and I have been talking for a while. He told me about the rape and—"

"You and your long-ago. I hoped that you would come to us some day, but not for such talk."

"He told me that you inflicted yourself—"

"Don't believe him."

"Had Richard become a problem?"

"Nobody has ever been a problem."

"Eric?"

"I have nothing to say about Eric. He did what he chose to do. You all did. I am sure that Richard was doing a good deed when he died, aren't you?"

"He should not have gone over to that goddamned war."

"How do you know that?"

"I'm not sure. But—"

"What else did my husband speak of? He has been giving you wrong ideas about everything, I think. You and your 'goddamned.' Not like you, Alice."

"We talked about Darrell."

"Darrell the Barrel," she said. "His nickname for himself. A barrel of booze-oh-la, he used to say to me, with a pretending accent. Very funny. We had so many times of laughter together. He needed me more than any of them. More even than Tony. Or Michael. Our boarders for a while. Darrell was such a kind man, but not content with himself, don't you think?"

"Have there always been boarders? Your husband mentioned Ben—"

"Don't make conclusions from what Mr. Jensen told you. He—"

"Are Tony and Michael, your boarders, still—?"

"Say the rest of your question, Alice."

"You're pointing the gun at me."

I didn't know whether or not the woman I was talking with would pull the trigger. She was not at all *my* Hannah. She was, just then, a person I would have to call Mrs. Jensen, eyes flickering with power.

"I did not mean to do that." She tucked the derringer between two throw pillows that she then set in her lap. Her gun now. "We have too much room here. So we have boarders. Eric was the first. Ben has been with us for five years."

"In the studio?"

"In the house. The studio has been for me for, I don't know, a long time. For my artwork. Ben won't get home from work tonight until eight o'clock. You will be gone from here by then, I think."

Hannah's husband returned to the living room carrying a tray laden with more beer, cups of tea, and three steaming Oriental soup bowls. Hannah spoke to him the German phrase I had half-heard her speak on the night of the so-called rape, the same phrase Eric had spoken in greeting Mr. Jensen at the May Day party.

"Yes, darling," he said. "All is as well as it could be under the circumstances. A happy reunion! I bring you ladies your libations and some hot and sour soup."

To Hannah he said, without changing his chipper tone, "Has Alice told you that she has been to the reservoir?"

"She has not told me anything. I think you have made her mad at me by telling her things."

"I'm not mad, Hannah. But this is not a happy reunion for me."

"He should have told me you were here. He makes things up that make you unhappy."

The Jensens looked at each other, a lingering look that made the distance between them on the couch irrelevant. "I merely tried to explain—" he began.

"Do not believe him, Alice. I am as simple as ABC."

"In a language no one knows but you, darling."

"You know it, too. Don't pretend in front of Alice—"

"Even now I'm just a beginner. My vocabulary is nothing next to yours."

They were having some sort of good time with this exchange—toying with me as much as they were with each other, taking my perplexity playfully in hand and adding a few more knots. The heart's ease tea would be no match for them.

I wanted out of there. Out of their house, out of their story.

I ventured a change of subject, said to Hannah, "I would love to see your work."

This caught his attention, drew it away from his wife. "Ah, Alice, you are indeed, despite your shortcomings, surprisingly fearless."

Hannah appeared to be thinking this over, and as she did so she almost looked her age, more dull than bright, brittle despite her roundness.

"You may enter the studio," Hannah finally said, "if you take back these old things I do not want. This *Clue*, that book there. I don't want to know about it. You keep the old days for yourself, Alice. That is not what we do here, is it?"

The last question was directed to her husband, who might as well have bowed, if you ask me, when he answered, "We do, we are, whatever you want, dear Hannah."

"He is making that up," she said to me.

"On the contrary—"

"Don't listen to him, Alice."

"Perhaps I shouldn't have come."

"You had no choice," she told me. "You are just you."

"A long time ago you said that was one of the things you liked about me, that I was always just Alice."

"That was a long time ago."

Perhaps nothing so unequivocally told me that I was no longer the Alice of old than this verbal slap in the face. Because it didn't hurt in the least, didn't shame me, didn't make me feel small, apologetic, and constitutionally unsophisticated. We'd changed, Hannah and I: she had become capable of being unadorable. I had become capable of being unembarrassed by who I was, and wasn't.

"If you'd rather I didn't see your work—"

"You will take these things with you. Away from this house. And everything else. All of your questions, all of your stories, all of this talk."

"Yes."

"Then you may see my private artwork, Alice."

They were standing together at the sliding glass door as Hannah handed me the key to her studio and gave me instructions. I was to take a quick look around, lock the place back up, then return to the house, where we were to have another drink, a bit more food. And

I was to watch my step when I crossed the gazebo that served as a bridge. They didn't say so, but I took it that I was to be gone well before their current boarder showed up.

"Be careful," Hannah told me. "The bridge out to the studio is much older than we are."

"It's my age." Mr. Jensen put his arm around Hannah's shoulders, emphasizing her littleness.

"Which means that the bridge is ancient, Alice," she said.

"Old as the devil," he laughed.

At the gazebo I paused, not for long—lest they were watching—but long enough to see that to my left, in the middle of the brook, upon a shelf of flat stones, stood their exquisite statue of Hermes, the messenger and guide. To my right, tucked among periwinkles, was Hannah's anniversary gift to her husband, the bronze Leda and the Swan. I understood then that, when I first saw the Leda piece at their Riverside home, I didn't take a good look at it. Why look? I knew the story. A glance was sufficient. Leda, swan, rape, Hannah. The imagery was what it was.

But in fact the bronze that Hannah purchased portrays not a ravaging swan, wings outstretched, talons prepared to grasp and subdue, nor a disheveled Leda. She is standing, leaning slightly forward to touch the feathery head of a seated swan whose long neck is lying seductively upon the folds of her heavy skirt. She's Leda all right, but she could pass for a young Mother Goose. Except for this: she is clearly stunned by the hungry look in his eyes.

The windows in Hannah's studio had been painted over, black, but the overhead light was more than adequate. I could see what there was to see. There was nothing in the way of art, no easel or canvases or brushes, no sculptor's or weaver's materials. There was only another lie.

A galley-type kitchen led to a small but well-appointed bathroom. In the main space there was a blue corduroy sofa-bed, a rocking chair draped with an afghan, a coffee table on which there were several magazines. Above the sink was a door-less cupboard in which—along with tea things and biscuits and a child's set of acrylic paints, red, yellow, green—there was a bottle of bourbon. Not large, not a heavy drinker's bottle. The couch, I thought, would well suit her small, curled-up body. Perhaps she just sleeps the afternoons away.

The whole set-up was more dreary than cozy—or maybe it was imagining her, day after day, spending hours with this secret emptiness if that's what she did, that made the place seem acutely bleak. Nothing dollhouse about it on the inside. No wonder she welcomed the boarders' interruptions.

Did her husband truly have no idea? And why did Hannah allow me to see this? This grim portrait of her seemingly barren afternoons? What had brought this on? Had she come to need a hideout? To get away from her husband for a few hours? Or was this a place for trysts? Was she, was he, were they, carrying on out here, secluded but within sight of the house?

Don't come up with the tried-and-true-and-boring, I reminded myself. Mr. Jensen must know precisely what's going on, whatever it is. It may be nothing. It may indeed be afternoon naps. But if he does know, I thought, then the artistry that goes on in this somber dollhouse is collaborative. Maybe all of it is. And maybe all of us—the friends, the acquaintances, the boarders, the local constable—constitute their medium.

You, too. Don't forget that. If Hannah—if the both of them—tell people what they want to hear, what suits them, what encourages them to live out their supposed stories, then they would try to do the same with their "Alice."

Childless spinster: don't forget how she cast you in her play, which turned out to be your role for most of your adult life.

"I am as simple as ABC."

"In a language no one knows but you, darling."

Listen to their teamwork.

Standing there, trying not to be extraordinarily dim, as he'd put it, I wondered: have we given you two the means to craft the artwork that is the long relationship you call a marriage.

And this: I could be entirely wrong. You may in fact be evildoers plain and simple. If so, you're too good at it. Not plain, not simple. Nothing can stop you. You can't be arrested for generously indulging the self-destructive impulses of your friends, can you? Should I drive up to Middlebury and pay a visit to your assistant professor? Maybe. But to warn him about what? That he might become implicated in helping the Jensens to find each other endlessly interesting?

In any case, I decided to keep the studio's secrets, to play along, to say to Hannah when I returned to the house that her "productions" were exceptionally colorful, and to say to him, "You'll have to cut your own deal, Mr. Jensen."

On my way out I saw the nearly empty bookcase. Had the few books not been so bedraggled, had they instead been, say, a tidy set of classic novels on display, I might have ignored them. But these books were by no means "displayed." They were just there, by themselves on a middle shelf, leaning awkwardly against each other on damaged, weathered spines. Aquinas, Dante, Augustine, Burton, Hopkins.

Eric's books, they had to be. Once heavy, quality hardback editions. The very books he must have had in the deep pockets of Mr. Jensen's fancy jacket on the night he went for a walk and didn't come back. Tobias Stockwell must have given them to her, privately, chivalrously.

Despite Hannah's hurry-up, be back in ten minutes instructions, I had to sit down. I had to resist touching those books. Why? I had to be able to walk away from them, to lock the door of Hannah's studio and leave them there, not hide them in my clothes and take them with me. Why not just ask for them? I had to be able to wear a face when I returned to the Jensens' living room that showed nothing of my longing to open each book and see Eric's name studiously penned on the title page.

Those books, as a kind of suicide note, tell me that he was still, that very night, he was still my Eric, the young man I had known and loved, not very well at all in either case.

You could say I would not be here in the East, in a green valley, with roommates and visitors and a barn and hard snow in the winter, I would not be so—what's the word? *familied?*—were it not for Hannah and her husband. You would be wrong.

True, I wouldn't be here if they weren't. They might have moved to Florida instead, reeled me in from there, a disappointing catch in any case. No longer appealing to their appetites.

They won't be getting any thanks from Alice Clark.

But Dove and her daughter will, and Angelo Lewis, and Marie Lamarque, and even those bullies I met along the way who got me to take another and then another look at myself. And of course Barbara Dulaney, now one of the roommates, refugee from the kind of Southern California marriage that requires breast implants.

I'm kept busy being more than a former neighbor to Bunny. Now I'm an eat-your-breakfast nag, a packer of school lunches, a supervisor of homework, and a would-be stern setter of rules. I can manage the setting of rules but not the stern part, to tell you the truth. I seem to be a bit too enthralled by that young girl's every moment. Have I been a grandmother-in-the-making all my adult life?

Not entirely, it seems. Since I'm also busy being more than a sidekick to Barbara. Now I'm an older sister, a girlfriend, a would-be pedantic setter of taste and tone, if I weren't so taken by her own variety—such as it unpredictably is—of taste and tone.

"You're not, like, outfitted, Alice," she told me a couple of months after her arrival.

"Outfitted?"

"That's what they call being properly dressed in these parts."

"I'm always properly dressed. Outfitting is for mountain climbers."

"We're going shopping. You need to get out of those old tennis shoes. They're so retro."

"Retro is what I do, Barbara."

"What you *did*, woman! You're about to become post-retro. Whatever. You need some cleaning-up goat-shit wear. It's time you got for real."

Lately she's been encouraging me to contact Angelo Lewis, invite him to visit this mainly (except for the constant Burt, the dog, the cats, and one of the goats) female menagerie, though I've told her time and again that he may well be a scoundrel.

Bunny, who has overheard some of this girl-talk (as Barbara calls it), also wants me to invite him, but only if he is in fact a scoundrel. She wants to meet one.

"So I can see for myself if there's a difference between my dad's dirty rotten ones and your plain-old old ones."

"He's not exactly Methuselah, sweetie."

"But he's a lot older than you are, you said. I mean—"

The youngsters: They have little to not one iota of notion how anachronistic one's own actual age can sometimes feel—when you're sixty-something and being chatted up, for instance, or kissed in public. Nevertheless, for now, I've resisted giving my roommates any satisfaction on the topic of Mr. Lewis. I've sent a postcard to former-stepson Danny and have written a short you-must-see-for-yourself note to Sheila, hoping she can get away from her good works for a week or two and witness an Alice who isn't resigned to being her own sorry company.

I tend to the garden, to our half-dozen Nubian goats, to my roommates' young collie and three hilarious Halloween kittens—a black and orange comedy troupe, all stiff-tailed style and harmless hissing. I think that both the roommates and those kittens are trying to teach me something about mock ferocity, about how to get on with it, come what may.

We lock the door only before the last of us goes to bed. I make cookies and keep a kettle warm for the folks who drop by now and then for tea or drinks, for supper or dessert—my roommates are a draw, believe me. Doc Marion is here for a meal every Wednesday, and for drinks at least three days a week. Burt is around more often than that. And Kay and Reese often come over after they go to church on Sundays. Their two preteen girls huddle in the barn with Bunny, consulting the Ouija board about what lies ahead, while we have our coffee and conversation and one too many sweet rolls.

Doc has allowed Barbara to trim his beard and bleach the yellow out of it. That was after she first met him and scolded him with, "What kind of an actual gay man lets his looks go to hell?" Doc answered with a question: "A veterinarian?" The two of them have been thick as mud ever since. Doc melts—and I mean visibly comes undone—whenever Burt walks into the kitchen space, but he's nevertheless an effusive supporter of the Gonzales / Dulaney courtship, full of advice for his "Babs."

On Fridays and Saturdays, I work in Barbara's beauty parlor—that's how she proudly refers to it in this day of unisex studios and salons—as the receptionist. We call it a family business. Bunny—who puts in an hour after school every day and works with me on Saturdays—has become an expert shampooer and an almost expert manicurist. On Sunday mornings, early, if the weather is friendly enough, I spend an hour or so at the Chittenden reservoir, mainly but not always at Eric's spot. There are wider views elsewhere, good places for those times when gratitude is part of the mix.

I have paid only one other visit to Hannah—an edgy dropping-by with a casserole, nothing but weather in our brief, at-the-door chitchat.

Once or twice, that's all, I've run into Mr. Jensen at the reservoir. I have assumed that his resumption of the vigil has to do not with Eric but with me—with keeping me intrigued. But so far, he has nodded a greeting and continued on to some other spot. If he now and then puts himself in my way in order to keep me guessing, he seems to believe that his mere presence will do the trick, will continue the haunting. And he's not wrong. But it lasts for only the few minutes it takes him to stroll my way, then continue on his own. I don't let his "exquisite piquancies" or those gray eyes follow me home, keep me locked into their story. I've at last got one of my own to work on.

ACKNOWLEDGEMENTS

The recipes for the Native American cures are from a small pamphlet I found many years ago called *Indian Doctor: Nature's Method of Curing and Preventing Disease According to the Indians*, distributed by Aerial Photography Services, Charlotte, North Carolina. No date of publication is provided.

Pushcart Prize-winner **MELISSA MALOUF** is the author of a collection of short stories, *No Guarantees*, and a novel, *It Had to Be You: The Joan and Ernest Story*. She earned her PhD at the University of California at Irvine, and teaches literature and creative writing at Duke University.

MICHAL AJVAZ, *The Golden Age.*
The Other City.

PIERRE ALBERT-BIROT, *Grabinoulor.*

YUZ ALESHKOVSKY, *Kangaroo.*

FELIPE ALFAU, *Chromos.*
Locos.

IVAN ÂNGELO, *The Celebration.*

The Tower of Glass.

ANTÓNIO LOBO ANTUNES,
Knowledge of Hell.
The Splendor of Portugal.

ALAIN ARIAS-MISSON, *Theatre of Incest.*

JOHN ASHBERY & JAMES SCHUYLER,
A Nest of Ninnies.

ROBERT ASHLEY, *Perfect Lives.*

GABRIELA AVIGUR-ROTEM,
Heatwave and Crazy Birds.

DJUNA BARNES, *Ladies Almanack.*
Ryder.

JOHN BARTH, *Letters.*
Sabbatical.

DONALD BARTHELME, *The King.*
Paradise.

SVETISLAV BASARA, *Chinese Letter.*

MIQUEL BAUÇÀ, *The Siege in the Room.*

RENÉ BELLETTO, *Dying.*

MAREK BIENCZYK, *Transparency.*

ANDREI BITOV, *Pushkin House.*

ANDREJ BLATNIK, *You Do Understand.*

LOUIS PAUL BOON, *Chapel Road.*
My Little War.
Summer in Termuren.

ROGER BOYLAN, *Killoyle.*

IGNÁCIO DE LOYOLA BRANDÃO,
Anonymous Celebrity.
Zero.

BONNIE BREMSER, *Troia: Mexican Memoirs.*

CHRISTINE BROOKE-ROSE,
Amalgamemnon.

BRIGID BROPHY, *In Transit.*

GERALD L. BRUNS,
Modern Poetry and the Idea of Language.

GABRIELLE BURTON, *Heartbreak Hotel.*

MICHEL BUTOR, *Degrees.*
Mobile.

G. CABRERA INFANTE,
Infante's Inferno.
Three Trapped Tigers.

JULIETA CAMPOS,
The Fear of Losing Eurydice.

ANNE CARSON, *Eros the Bittersweet.*

ORLY CASTEL-BLOOM, *Dolly City.*

LOUIS-FERDINAND CÉLINE,
Castle to Castle.
Conversations with Professor Y.
London Bridge.
Normance.
North.
Rigadoon.

MARIE CHAIX,
The Laurels of Lake Constance.

HUGO CHARTERIS, *The Tide Is Right.*

ERIC CHEVILLARD, *Demolishing Nisard.*

MARC CHOLODENKO, *Mordechai Schamz.*

JOSHUA COHEN, *Witz.*

EMILY HOLMES COLEMAN,
The Shutter of Snow.

ROBERT COOVER, *A Night at the Movies.*

STANLEY CRAWFORD, *Log of the S.S. The*
Mrs Unguentine.
Some Instructions to My Wife.

RENÉ CREVEL, *Putting My Foot in It.*

RALPH CUSACK, *Cadenza.*

NICHOLAS DELBANCO,
The Count of Concord.
Sherbrookes.

NIGEL DENNIS, *Cards of Identity.*

PETER DIMOCK,
A Short Rhetoric for Leaving the Family.

ARIEL DORFMAN, *Konfidenz.*

COLEMAN DOWELL, *Island People.*
Too Much Flesh and Jabez.

ARKADII DRAGOMOSHCHENKO,
Dust.

RIKKI DUCORNET,
The Complete Butcher's Tales.
The Fountains of Neptune.
The Jade Cabinet.
Phosphor in Dreamland.

WILLIAM EASTLAKE, *The Bamboo Bed.*
Castle Keep.
Lyric of the Circle Heart.

JEAN ECHENOZ, *Chopin's Move.*

STANLEY ELKIN, *A Bad Man.*
Criers and Kibitzers, Kibitzers and Criers.
The Dick Gibson Show.
The Franchiser.
The Living End.
Mrs. Ted Bliss.

FRANÇOIS EMMANUEL,
Invitation to a Voyage.

SALVADOR ESPRIU,
Ariadne in the Grotesque Labyrinth.

LESLIE A. FIEDLER,
Love and Death in the American Novel.

JUAN FILLOY, *Op Oloop.*

ANDY FITCH, *Pop Poetics.*

GUSTAVE FLAUBERT,
Bouvard and Pécuchet.

KASS FLEISHER, *Talking out of School.*

FORD MADOX FORD,
The March of Literature.

JON FOSSE, *Aliss at the Fire.*
Melancholy.

MAX FRISCH, *I'm Not Stiller.*
Man in the Holocene.

CARLOS FUENTES, *Christopher Unborn.*
Distant Relations.
Terra Nostra.
Where the Air Is Clear.

TAKEHIKO FUKUNAGA,
Flowers of Grass.

WILLIAM GADDIS, JR., *The Recognitions.*

JANICE GALLOWAY, *Foreign Parts.*
The Trick Is to Keep Breathing.

WILLIAM H. GASS,
Cartesian Sonata and Other Novellas.
Finding a Form.
A Temple of Texts.
The Tunnel.
Willie Masters' Lonesome Wife.

GÉRARD GAVARRY, *Hoppla! 1 2 3.*

ETIENNE GILSON,
The Arts of the Beautiful.Forms and Substances in the Arts.

C. S. GISCOMBE, *Giscome Road.*
Here.

DOUGLAS GLOVER,
Bad News of the Heart.

WITOLD GOMBROWICZ,
A Kind of Testament.

PAULO EMÍLIO SALES GOMES,
P's Three Women.

GEORGI GOSPODINOV, *Natural Novel.*

JUAN GOYTISOLO, *Count Julian.*
Juan the Landless.
Makbara.
Marks of Identity.

HENRY GREEN, *Back.*
Blindness.
Concluding.
Doting.
Nothing.

JACK GREEN, *Fire the Bastards!*

JIŘÍ GRUŠA, *The Questionnaire.*

MELA HARTWIG,
Am I a Redundant Human Being?

JOHN HAWKES, *The Passion Artist.*
Whistlejacket.

ELIZABETH HEIGHWAY, ED.,
Contemporary Georgian Fiction.

ALEKSANDAR HEMON, ED.,
Best European Fiction.

AIDAN HIGGINS, *Balcony of Europe.*
Blind Man's Bluff
Bornholm Night-Ferry.
Flotsam and Jetsam.
Langrishe, Go Down.
Scenes from a Receding Past.

KEIZO HINO, *Isle of Dreams.*

KAZUSHI HOSAKA, *Plainsong.*

ALDOUS HUXLEY, *Antic Hay.*
Crome Yellow.
Point Counter Point.
Those Barren Leaves.
Time Must Have a Stop.

NAOYUKI II, *The Shadow of a Blue Cat.*

GERT JONKE, *The Distant Sound.*
Geometric Regional Novel.
Homage to Czerny.
The System of Vienna.

JACQUES JOUET, *Mountain R.*
Savage.
Upstaged.

MIEKO KANAI, *The Word Book.*

YORAM KANIUK, *Life on Sandpaper.*

HUGH KENNER, *Flaubert.*
Joyce and Beckett: The Stoic Comedians.
Joyce's Voices.

DANILO KIŠ, *The Attic.*
Garden, Ashes.
The Lute and the Scars
Psalm 44.
A Tomb for Boris Davidovich.

ANITA KONKKA, *A Fool's Paradise.*

GEORGE KONRÁD, *The City Builder.*

TADEUSZ KONWICKI,
A Minor Apocalypse.
The Polish Complex.

MENIS KOUMANDAREAS, *Koula.*

ELAINE KRAF, *The Princess of 72nd Street.*

JIM KRUSOE, *Iceland.*

AYSE KULIN,
Farewell: A Mansion in Occupied Istanbul.

EMILIO LASCANO TEGUI,
On Elegance While Sleeping.

ERIC LAURRENT, *Do Not Touch.*

VIOLETTE LEDUC, *La Bâtarde.*

EDOUARD LEVÉ, *Autoportrait.*
Suicide.

MARIO LEVI, *Istanbul Was a Fairy Tale.*

DEBORAH LEVY, *Billy and Girl.*

JOSÉ LEZAMA LIMA, *Paradiso.*

ROSA LIKSOM, *Dark Paradise.*

OSMAN LINS, *Avalovara.*
The Queen of the Prisons of Greece.

ALF MAC LOCHLAINN,
The Corpus in the Library.
Out of Focus.

RON LOEWINSOHN, *Magnetic Field(s).*

MINA LOY, *Stories and Essays of Mina Loy.*

D. KEITH MANO, *Take Five.*

MICHELINE AHARONIAN MARCOM,
The Mirror in the Well.

BEN MARCUS,
The Age of Wire and String.

WALLACE MARKFIELD, *Teitlebaum's Window.*
To an Early Grave.

DAVID MARKSON, *Reader's Block.*
Wittgenstein's Mistress.

CAROLE MASO, *AVA.*

LADISLAV MATEJKA &
KRYSTYNA POMORSKA, EDS.,
Readings in Russian Poetics: Formalist and Structuralist Views.

HARRY MATHEWS, *Cigarettes.*
The Conversions.
The Human Country: New and Collected Stories.
The Journalist.
My Life in CIA.
Singular Pleasures.
The Sinking of the Odradek.
Stadium.
Tlooth.

JOSEPH MCELROY,
Night Soul and Other Stories.

ABDELWAHAB MEDDEB, *Talismano.*
GERHARD MEIER, *Isle of the Dead.*
HERMAN MELVILLE, *The Confidence-Man.*
AMANDA MICHALOPOULOU, *I'd Like.*
STEVEN MILLHAUSER, *The Barnum Museum.*
In the Penny Arcade.
RALPH J. MILLS, JR., *Essays on Poetry.*
MOMUS, *The Book of Jokes.*
CHRISTINE MONTALBETTI, *The Origin of Man.*
Western.
OLIVE MOORE, *Spleen.*
NICHOLAS MOSLEY, *Accident.*
Assassins.
Catastrophe Practice.
Experience and Religion.
A Garden of Trees.
Hopeful Monsters.
Imago Bird.
Impossible Object.
Inventing God.
Judith.
Look at the Dark.
Natalie Natalia.
Serpent.
Time at War.
WARREN MOTTE, *Fables of the Novel: French Fiction since 1990.*
Fiction Now: The French Novel in the 21st Century.
Oulipo: A Primer of Potential Literature.
GERALD MURNANE, *Barley Patch.*
Inland.
YVES NAVARRE, *Our Share of Time.*
Sweet Tooth.
DOROTHY NELSON, *In Night's City.*
Tar and Feathers.
ESHKOL NEVO, *Homesick.*
WILFRIDO D. NOLLEDO, *But for the Lovers.*
FLANN O'BRIEN, *At Swim-Two-Birds.*
The Best of Myles.
The Dalkey Archive.
The Hard Life.
The Poor Mouth.
The Third Policeman.
CLAUDE OLLIER, *The Mise-en-Scène.*
Wert and the Life Without End.
GIOVANNI ORELLI, *Walaschek's Dream.*
PATRIK OUŘEDNÍK, *Europeana.*
The Opportune Moment, 1855.
BORIS PAHOR, *Necropolis.*
FERNANDO DEL PASO, *News from the Empire.*
Palinuro of Mexico.
ROBERT PINGET, *The Inquisitory.*
Mahu or The Material.
Trio.
MANUEL PUIG, *Betrayed by Rita Hayworth.*
The Buenos Aires Affair.
Heartbreak Tango.
RAYMOND QUENEAU, T*he Last Days.*
Odile.
Pierrot Mon Ami.
Saint Glinglin.
ANN QUIN, *Berg.*
Passages.
Three.
Tripticks.
ISHMAEL REED, *The Free-Lance Pallbearers.*
The Last Days of Louisiana Red.
Ishmael Reed: The Plays.
Juice!
Reckless Eyeballing.
The Terrible Threes.
The Terrible Twos.
Yellow Back Radio Broke-Down.
JASIA REICHARDT, *15 Journeys Warsaw to London.*
NOËLLE REVAZ, *With the Animals.*
JOÃO UBALDO RIBEIRO, *House of the Fortunate Buddhas.*

JEAN RICARDOU, *Place Names.*

RAINER MARIA RILKE, *The Notebooks of Malte Laurids Brigge.*

JULIÁN RÍOS, The House of Ulysses.
Larva: A Midsummer Night's Babel.
Poundemonium.
Procession of Shadows.

AUGUSTO ROA BASTOS, *I the Supreme.*

DANIËL ROBBERECHTS, *Arriving in Avignon.*

JEAN ROLIN, *The Explosion of the Radiator Hose.*

OLIVIER ROLIN, *Hotel Crystal.*

ALIX CLEO ROUBAUD, *Alix's Journal.*

JACQUES ROUBAUD, *The Form of a City Changes Faster, Alas, Than the Human Heart.*
The Great Fire of London.
Hortense in Exile.
Hortense Is Abducted.
The Loop.
Mathematics: The Plurality of Worlds of Lewis.
The Princess Hoppy.
Some Thing Black.

RAYMOND ROUSSEL, *Impressions of Africa.*

VEDRANA RUDAN, *Night.*

STIG SÆTERBAKKEN, *Siamese.*
Self Control.

LYDIE SALVAYRE, *The Company of Ghosts.*
The Lecture.
The Power of Flies.

LUIS RAFAEL SÁNCHEZ, *Macho Camacho's Beat.*

SEVERO SARDUY, *Cobra & Maitreya.*

NATHALIE SARRAUTE, *Do You Hear Them?*
Martereau.
The Planetarium.

ARNO SCHMIDT, *Collected Novellas.*
Collected Stories.
Nobodaddy's Children.
Two Novels.

ASAF SCHURR, *Motti.*

GAIL SCOTT, *My Paris.*

DAMION SEARLS, *What We Were Doing and Where We Were Going.*

JUNE AKERS SEESE, *Is This What Other Women Feel Too?*
What Waiting Really Means.

BERNARD SHARE, *Inish.*
Transit.

VIKTOR SHKLOVSKY, *Bowstring.*
Knight's Move.
A Sentimental Journey: Memoirs 1917–1922.
Energy of Delusion: A Book on Plot.
Literature and Cinematography.
Theory of Prose.
Third Factory.
Zoo, or Letters Not about Love.

PIERRE SINIAC, *The Collaborators.*

KJERSTI A. SKOMSVOLD, *The Faster I Walk, the Smaller I Am.*

JOSEF ŠKVORECKÝ, *The Engineer ofHuman Souls.*

GILBERT SORRENTINO, *Aberration of Starlight.*
Blue Pastoral.
Crystal Vision.
Imaginative Qualities of Actual Things.
Mulligan Stew.
Pack of Lies.
Red the Fiend.
The Sky Changes.
Something Said.
Splendide-Hôtel.
Steelwork.
Under the Shadow.

W. M. SPACKMAN, *The Complete Fiction.*

ANDRZEJ STASIUK, *Dukla.*
Fado.

GERTRUDE STEIN,
The Making of Americans.
A Novel of Thank You.

LARS SVENDSEN, *A Philosophy of Evil.*

PIOTR SZEWC, *Annihilation.*

GONÇALO M. TAVARES, *Jerusalem.*
Joseph Walser's Machine.
Learning to Pray in the Age of Technique.

LUCIAN DAN TEODOROVICI,
Our Circus Presents . . .

NIKANOR TERATOLOGEN,
Assisted Living.

STEFAN THEMERSON, *Hobson's Island.*
The Mystery of the Sardine.
Tom Harris.

TAEKO TOMIOKA, *Building Waves.*

JOHN TOOMEY, *Sleepwalker.*

JEAN-PHILIPPE TOUSSAINT,
The Bathroom.
Camera.
Monsieur.
Reticence.
Running Away.
Self-Portrait Abroad.
Television.
The Truth about Marie.

DUMITRU TSEPENEAG, *Hotel Europa.*
The Necessary Marriage.
Pigeon Post.
Vain Art of the Fugue.

ESTHER TUSQUETS, *Stranded.*

DUBRAVKA UGRESIC,
Lend Me Your Character.
Thank You for Not Reading.

TOR ULVEN, *Replacement.*

MATI UNT, *Brecht at Night.*
Diary of a Blood Donor.
Things in the Night.

ÁLVARO URIBE & OLIVIA SEARS, EDS.,
Best of Contemporary Mexican Fiction.

ELOY URROZ, *Friction.*
The Obstacles.

LUISA VALENZUELA,
Dark Desires and the Others.
He Who Searches.

PAUL VERHAEGHEN, *Omega Minor.*

AGLAJA VETERANYI,
Why the Child Is Cooking in the Polenta.

BORIS VIAN, *Heartsnatcher.*

LLORENÇ VILLALONGA,
The Dolls' Room.

TOOMAS VINT,
An Unending Landscape.

ORNELA VORPSI,
The Country Where No One Ever Dies.

AUSTRYN WAINHOUSE,
Hedyphagetica.

CURTIS WHITE,
America's Magic Mountain.
The Idea of Home.
Memories of My Father Watching TV.
Requiem.

DIANE WILLIAMS,
Excitability: Selected Stories.
Romancer Erector.

DOUGLAS WOOLF, *Wall to Wall.*
Ya! & John-Juan.

JAY WRIGHT, *Polynomials and Pollen.*
The Presentable Art of Reading Absence.

PHILIP WYLIE, *Generation of Vipers.*

MARGUERITE YOUNG,
Angel in the Forest.
Miss MacIntosh, My Darling.

REYOUNG, *Unbabbling.*

VLADO ŽABOT, *The Succubus.*

ZORAN ŽIVKOVIĆ , *Hidden Camera.*

LOUIS ZUKOFSKY, *Collected Fiction.*

VITOMIL ZUPAN, *Minuet for Guitar.*

SCOTT ZWIREN, *God Head.*